CW00525824

The Gravedigger's Tale

By the same author

DARKNESS DEMANDS
STRANGER
IN THIS SKIN
HOTEL MIDNIGHT
THE TOWER
DEATH'S DOMINION
MIDNIGHT BAZAAR
THIS RAGE OF ECHOES
GHOST MONSTER

The Gravedigger's Tale

FABLES OF FEAR

Simon Clark

ROBERT HALE · LONDON

© Simon Clark 2010
First published in Great Britain 2010

ISBN 978-0-7090-9119-6

Robert Hale Limited
Clerkenwell House
Clerkenwell Green
London EC1R 0HT

www.halebooks.com

The right of Simon Clark to be identified as author
of this work has been asserted by him in accordance with the
Copyright, Designs and Patents Act 1988

2 4 6 8 10 9 7 5 3 1

Typeset in 11.25/15.25pt Garamond
Printed in Great Britain by the MPG Books Group,
Bodmin and King's Lynn

DEDICATION

The Argendeli Family: Jim, Cindy and Evangelia

CONTENTS

* Clive Barker is the owner of the copyright of the *Hellbound Heart* and Cenobite mythology, and Simon Clark gratefully acknowledges Mr Barker's permission to draw on this mythology for 'Our Lord of Quarters'. Simon Clark's story originally appeared in *Hellbound Hearts* (Pocket Books, 2009); edited by Paul Kane and Marie O'Regan.

INTRODUCTION

FEARFUL PLACES

TWENTY YEARS AGO, I posed for an important photograph in the back garden of our house.

'Stop smiling,' Janet told me, sternly.

'I'm not smiling.'

'You are.'

'Is this better?' I strove to adopt the expression that many an author adopts for photographs that adorn the backs of their books. Serious, thoughtful and intelligent, but not pompous.

'Now you're grinning,' she said.

'I don't feel as if I'm grinning.'

But I was – and grinning hugely.

My son, Alex, then aged around five, offered to shoot me with his water gun. There was always a chance a dousing with cold water would take that ear-to-ear beam from my face.

Janet gave an understanding sigh. 'We'll have something to eat first, then we'll try again.'

'And I'll have my gun ready, too,' said Alex, ominously aiming it in the direction of my head.

The reason I stood in the garden one sunny evening, two decades ago, is that I'd just had a significant breakthrough as a writer. For years, I'd spent every spare moment penning short stories; some of which had appeared on radio, or in little independent magazines that were highly regarded by aficionados, but only had small circulations. And as for payment? Well, let's just say that the taxman wouldn't lose any of his or her beauty sleep. After all, how do you tax one free copy of the magazine?

Now, back to the reason for that photo-shoot in the garden, with our humble domestic camera that we used at Christmas gatherings, birthday parties and trips to the beach. Just half an hour before, I'd received a surprise telephone call from the editor of *Fear*, an exciting glossy monthly that had recently hit the British newsagents' shelves. Naturally, as soon as I heard about this new publication I'd sent them a story; one entitled 'The Gravedigger's Tale'. Then I did what I always did, I endeavoured to wait patiently, stoically, good-naturedly for a decision. Of course, being a new writer, mostly those decisions were disappointing. Usually, the depressing thump of the manuscript hitting the carpet beneath the letter flap was evidence of its rejection.

Anyway, eternally optimistic, I'd sent my story of uncanny goings-on in a graveyard to *Fear*'s editor. I posted it, I remember, on the Thursday. I got home from my day job on Friday afternoon, little more than twenty-fours hours after consigning the manuscript to the letter box; then the telephone rang. I answered to hear a pleasantly modulated voice say, 'Simon Clark? Oh, it's John Gilbert here. *Fear* magazine. I really did enjoy the *The Gravedigger's Tale*.'

Stunned, I muttered something about only sending it yesterday.

'Yes, and I love it. I want to buy it for the magazine.' He mentioned a fee that he'd pay for the story, which to me seemed so immense I must have misheard. Then he added, 'But we need to move quickly if we're going to get the story in the next issue. What I need from you is a photograph of yourself.'

'A photograph?' I was still in shock.

'Yes, it's our policy to run a photograph of our authors. Can you send me one as soon as possible?'

I promised I would. So, after the phone call, I took a deep, steadying breath, collected the camera and asked Janet to take my picture. And, please, could she make me look moody and interesting? And, if she possibly could manage it, I added (half) jokingly, ensure that the picture would convey that I was a dashingly handsome author, poised on the brink of literary stardom. Her expression suggested she'd just been landed with a tall order. What made her sudden appointment to Author's Official Photographer even more difficult was that I couldn't stop smiling. I'd just made my most important professional short story sale so far. *The Gravedigger's Tale* would be printed in *Fear*, a glossy newsstand magazine distributed throughout the British Isles. And there was a very nice cheque on its way, too (but back then, like most new authors, I'd have let them print the story for the price of a chocolate bar. *Psst, don't tell my editors that, though*).

After the delirious excitement of selling the story, and finally having my photograph taken (with my five year old son sternly pointing the water pistol in the direction of my ear, lest I suddenly grin again), I began to think about the origins of that piece of fiction. What had made me write it in the first place? What events in there had made the editor like it so much? In short, could I gather up all those ingredients again of plot, character and scary incidents to write more stories that editors would be eager to buy?

I don't believe I've ever found a magic formula for writing stories that sell. All I can do is try my very best to write the kind of fiction I hope will entertain the reader. And those are horror stories. Not all are gruesome or bloody. Many involve ordinary men and women who find themselves faced with extraordinary situations. Rather than lashings of out-and-out gore, the characters encounter the strange, the eerie, the ghostly, or a situation where the world has gone off kilter. Sometimes there will be a dash or two of humour, too. Though, it must be said, macabre humour.

So, once more, I'm honoured to present to you my legion of tales – ones intended to chill the blood, to prompt a nervous glance over the shoulder, and be enjoyable, of course. And it occurred to me that I should mention a little about the stories themselves, and their inspiration. After all, most collections of this sort begin with a dry list of where the tales appeared previously, stating in which magazine, and when. Instead of that bone-dry list, I'd prefer to share a few anecdotes about the work that appears in these pages. After all, I feel as if I'm amongst friends here. Because if you read that early work of mine in *Fear* (or the likes of *BBR, Skeleton Crew* and *Beyond*) then we must go back a while.

I won't discuss every one in rigorous detail, but here are a few memories that attach to some of the stories in this volume: -

The Gravedigger's Tale. The first home that Janet and I bought was in Pontefract, a pleasant market-town that's famous for horse-racing and liquorice (on certain days of the week the delicious aroma of liquorice sweetens the town's air – a surprisingly pleasant phenomenon, which still lingers in my memory). The terraced house lay snugly between a former workhouse, a railway embankment and an old cemetery. That's a hell of a location for a horror author. Of course, the shortest way to the town centre shops lay through the cemetery. It was a vast place, with old tombstones that were being slowly sucked underground by subsidence. Because there was little in the way of new burials, the trees had been allowed to grow, so the place began to resemble forest. Local legends abounded about the graveyard. One told of a huge hoard of stolen cash being hidden in one of the graves. A hellhound, by the quaint name of the Pontefract Padfoot, might be glimpsed there (with doom-laden consequences). Nevertheless, it became our route to town, and we got to know those acres of Victorian graves, with their ornate stonework, very well. Bit by bit, as I crossed and re-crossed the cemetery paths in the three years we lived in the area, I began to imagine the life of a gravedigger who'd spent his career amongst those tombs. Maybe it's the trait of a writer, but I began to picture how he'd look, his routine, and the experiences he'd accumulated as he dug those man-sized holes down through the years. One thing that struck me, is that he'd have lots of yarns to tell. And he was certain to embellish them in order to keep his audience spellbound. So, with that in mind, I envisaged my imaginary gravedigger having a visitor one day – a young man who was 'green as he was cabbage-looking', as the saying goes; a gullible individual with whom the bored gravedigger could have some fun. And so the story was born. It appeared in *Fear* in 1989 – thank you, John Gilbert, for choosing it. The excitement didn't stop there: Karl Edward Wagner liked the story so much that he reprinted it in his paperback anthology called *The Year's Best Horror*. Now my story, inspired by a Pontefract graveyard, was appearing in bookshops all over the English-speaking world! I had to pinch myself black and blue to believe it was really happening. For aspiring writers reading this, it shows that a winning story idea can be found on a simple stroll to the supermarket. And that's my tip for the day.

Swallowing a Dirty Seed. As a family, we enjoy holidays in North Wales. The landscape is mysterious and haunting. For me, the lure of those deep valleys, the rushing mountain streams, the seemingly endless forests is irresistible. So, the perfect place to set a piece of atmospheric fiction. But what I needed was, dare I say it, the seed of inspiration? That came from closer to home. One Christmas Eve, our dog Sam and I, headed out in freezing fog for a walk. We found ourselves walking past a rugby field. Alongside it were the usual winter trees, bare of leaves. But there, in the fog, loomed a tall tree that made me look twice. Yes, it was leafless; however, every branch was laden with apples. And they were such strikingly bright yellow apples that it reminded me of a Christmas tree – one almost sagging under the weight of golden baubles. An apple tree full of fruit in the middle of winter? Naturally, I had to investigate. At first I threw the windfalls for Sam to excitedly chase, as if they were balls. Then, call it writer's curiosity, I had to taste one of those apples that decided to hang grimly on to the branches through frost and snow. Cautiously, I bit. And I've never tasted an apple like it. The fruit was flawless and firm. And it tasted strangely scented. Almost a perfume flavour. I walked home through the fog thinking, 'Well, Simon, if you've poisoned yourself with some weird apple, you've only yourself to blame.' Luckily, the family Christmas wasn't spoiled by inflicting bilious attacks on myself, yet I returned home knowing the story I would write would be set in Wales. It would be about a group of hapless campers who venture into a deep, dark Welsh forest in winter. There they find an apple tree – one still bearing a strangely flavoured fruit (although the sharp-eyed will notice I've taken the liberty of changing the colour of the apples in the story). *Swallowing a Dirty Seed* appeared in the anthology *Midnight Never Comes*. Stephen Jones, that resolute guardian of horror and untiring champion of writers, both established and new, liked my story, too. He reprinted it in the *Best New Horror* of 1997.

Is It Still Raining Zombies? It's a funny title and I did intend it to be a funny story. Hopefully, you will, too. It appeared in the British Fantasy Society calendar.

The Image Dissector. Two good friends, John B. Ford and Jeff Hill, decided to publish a volume of tales in tribute to the great writer H.P. Lovecraft. Steve Lines joined the team, too, as co-editor and cover artist. Thereafter, they asked me to contribute a piece to *Cthulhu's Creatures* (which is now keenly sought by collectors). Regarding the story's inspiration, I'd been watching a documentary about the advent of television. In the early days, this device was referred to as an Image Dissector by some. It occurred to me that seventy years ago people might find themselves believing that television might carry so much more than sound and vision ... oh, and a cemetery features, too. Now, you'll be starting to suspect that a theme might be developing for this collection....

My God, My God ... and *Poe, Lovecraft, Jackson* and *Frankenstein, Victor.* These exist because Kealan Patrick Burke invited me to contribute 30,000 words of fiction to *Night Visions 12*. But, believe me, this was no mundane commission job. I was thrilled and honoured to be part of the legendary Night Visions series published by William Schafer of Subterranean Press. Each of these stories runs to near novella length, and I remember being determined to reward the faith placed in me by both the editor and publisher by pulling out all the stops and writing big, powerful stories. Each one is a nod to the great writers that fed my imagination as a teenager. *Poe, Lovecraft, Jackson* enshrines the names of a great literary trio in the title, namely, Edgar Allan Poe, H.P. Lovecraft and Shirley Jackson. It's an admittedly demanding (and deeply strange) account of lucid dreaming. *My God, My God* ... aims to evoke the same kind of atmosphere of solitude and dread that was the province of William Hope Hodgson – a writer who deserves much greater fame than is accorded to him. The son of a clergyman, Hope, as he was known, ran away to sea as a youngster, saved a man from shark-infested seas, and wrote tales of immense vision that continue to influence novels, television and film today. His life was cut short on the battlefield in World War I. *Frankenstein, Victor* imagines what might have happened if Mary Shelley had based her novel on a factual Dr Frankenstein; a scientist who managed to change the world single-handed. It's a theme that fascinated me so much that I returned to it in my novel *Death's Dominion* (Robert Hale, 2006). *Night Visions 12* appeared in 2006. Kealan Patrick Burke, incidentally, is carving out his own career as a gifted author.

One Man Show. Gary Fry was the instigator behind the anthology *Poe's Progeny.* The brief for this one was that each story should capture the essence of what makes certain classic authors of the horror genre special. Bearing in mind what I've just written about William Hope Hodgson, you'd be exactly right if you guessed my chosen classic author was Hodgson. His work was and is an inspiration to me.

Cemetery Wine. A brand new story. My parents took me to the Greek Islands for the summer holidays. When I was twelve we visited Corfu. I especially remember the festival in Corfu Town, where the mummified remains of St Spirodon are carried through the streets on his throne to heal the sick. Unfortunately, the searing heat became too much for me and I had to sit somewhere shady and missed the saint's outing. I'm sure that memory was enough to prompt me to write *Cemetery Wine.* And I'm dedicating this to everyone who enjoys those Greek elixirs, retsina wine and ouzo. Cheers.

Engine of Vengeance. Another new story. Even as a very young child I loved films about rampaging monsters and robots. I wondered why none has ever been set in my native Yorkshire. Well, there is one now.

The Old Man at the Gate. One of the few pieces I've written that had its roots in a dream. It's about childhood, and what turns out to be a very unsettling game of dare.

A Dog's Tale. For me, a relatively light-hearted one. I wrote it for a charity anthology, and sternly told myself it shouldn't be too gruesome.

Our Lord of Quarters. Editors/writers Paul Kane and Marie O'Regan dreamt of compiling a massively ambitious anthology; it would boast a pantheon of stellar authors; and it would be called *Hellbound Hearts.* I'm sure plenty of people said it could never be done. But it was done. And Paul and Marie can enjoy the fact that they've created one of the most talked about anthologies for many a year. *Our Lord of Quarters* is my contribution. Since I don't know when, I've been fascinated by the great city of Constantinople. For a thousand years or so, it was one of the most powerful capitals in the world, as influential as New York, as chic as Paris, as vibrant as Mumbai. This drama unfolds just a few short years before the Ottomans conquered the city, and renamed it Istanbul. A young man arrives from the provinces just as invaders lay siege to this magnificent city that was heir to the Roman empire. Little does the man know that he will play a pivotal role in its fate.

As forewarned, I never intended to set out a detailed bibliography, or had the space, or opportunity to thank everyone connected with the stories' publication. But here's a collective, yet sincere, thank you anyway. All I'd say in closing is this:

Over the page the gravedigger is waiting. And he has a fascinating tale to tell....

Simon Clark
Doncaster,
October, 2009

1

THE GRAVEDIGGER'S TALE

'JESUS!' EXCLAIMED THE electrician, as he levered the back off the hulking great chest freezer. 'What did you have to dig 'em back up for?'

Weathered brown, whip-lean, sixty-plus, half-smoked cigarette behind one ear, the gravedigger grinned, displaying an uneven row of yellow splinters that had once been teeth. He leaned forward, bare wrinkled elbows resting on the freezer lid.

'The new by-pass. It's going to take half the graveyard yonder, so before they lay the new road, we have to lift the blighters and plant 'em in the new municipal ground up on Pontefract Road.'

Pulling a face, the electrician wiped the palms of his hands on his overalls. 'There must have been some sights. Well, they've been dead years.'

'Aye. First one were interred in 1836. So ... most of the coffins were well rotted. Soon as you tried to lift 'em' – he made a wet, crackling sound – 'they just folded – just folded like wet cardboard boxes. And everything – everything spilled out into a heap. Just imagine that.' The gravedigger waited for the young man's reaction.

'Jesus.' He wiped his mouth as if something small and extremely unpleasant had just buzzed into it. 'You must have a strong stomach.'

The gravedigger recognized the inflection in the young man's voice. Disquiet, distaste, unease. He eyed the electrician up and down. The floppy white hat, slack mouth and wide-eyed gormless look signalled, here's a lad who believes everything; every tall story that comes his way he'll swallow; the kind of lad who cropped up on every factory floor, in every shop and office, who when asked would conscientiously hurry to the foreman or stores' manager to ask for the long-wait, or jar of elbow grease, or a pair of sky-hooks. The gravedigger had been steeling himself for a dull afternoon of ten Woodbines, five cups of tea and a solo darts tournament in the cemetery store-cum-restroom. However, a faulty freezer, and Fate at her most obliging, had brought entertainment in the shape of the young electrician in his floppy white hat; someone who was, the gravedigger realized, as green as he was cabbage-looking. 'I'm just brewing up. You'll want a wet when you've done.'

'Oh, ta. Milk and two sugars. Trouble is with this unit, it's been too near the window. Direct sunlight makes them overheat. Shouldn't take long though.' He looked round the untidy, brick-floored room. Spades, shovels, picks, rusting iron bars leaned into dusty corners. Fading grave-yard plans curled away from the corrugated iron walls; at the far end stood a table cluttered with chipped mugs, cigarette boxes, empty milk cartons, and the greasy remains of a Cornish pasty. Overhead, an asbestos ceiling punctuated by dozens of tiny brown corpses – spiders that had died and been mummified by the dry air.

'Are the others out, you know, digging?' the electrician asked conver-sationally.

'Oh, aye.' The old man accurately tossed tea bags into two mugs. 'They're working up the top-side. Look.' He pointed a yellow-brown nicotine-stained finger that boasted a startlingly large black fingernail. Through a grimy, cobwebbed window two men could be seen digging in the graveyard. They hurled spadefuls of soil over their shoulders with cheerful abandon. 'That's where they're going to plant James Hudson, the old mayor. Top-side, you see, is where all your nobs are – doctors, solicitors, aldermen, bank managers. Bottom-side is for your working folk and paupers.'

'And that's where the new road's going through.' The young man returned to work, prising at cables with a screwdriver, while whistling in such a way it would make a saint curse.

'Aye … that's where they have to be dug up.' The gravedigger licked his lips. 'Disinterred. Exhumed. Aye.' Taking the kettle from the solitary electric ring, he limped to the freezer top, which he used as an impromptu table. There, he filled the mugs with boiling water. Then he paused. Dreamily he stared into the rising steam. 'Aye, a bad business this disinterring. You see some things so bad it makes you fair poorly. You know – in some of the older graves? Well, we opened coffins and found ...'

'Found what?'

'We opened the coffins and found that the bodies had ...' Once more his voice trailed away.

The electrician's eyes opened wide.

'Well. They'd moved.'

'Moved? The bodies had moved?'

'You see, sometimes years ago, people got buried alive. Not deliberately of course. 'Spect some poor wretches were in comas so deep they were certified dead. They buried them. 'Course, then they woke up.' He glanced at the electrician to see if he appreciated its full significance. 'Buried alive. Just imagine. No light. No air. They'd be suffocating, trying to fight their way out. But six feet down? Who would ever hear 'em? There, in the grave, they screamed, they fought and clawed at the lid; breathed up all the oxygen and then ... well, you can picture what happened to them, can't you, lad?'

'What did they look like?' Clearly the electrician's imagination wasn't up to conjuring the macabre scene.

'Oh ... terrible, just terrible. You see, in this part of Yorkshire, there are natural salts in the soil. They preserve the bodies buried here. Only turns 'em yellow. Bright yellow like a sunflower. Apart from the colour, they looked the same as the day they died. Like this.' Eyes wide open, his face the distillation of pure terror, the gravedigger hooked his brown fingers into talons and contorted his body as if twisted by unendurable agony. 'Those buried alive, they just froze like that. Like statues. But, dear God in Heaven, the expression on their poor faces.'

'Jesus ... that's awful.'

'Oh, I've seen worse, lad.'

'What-what was the worst you've seen?' The man gulped his tea.

'Ah ... that'd be two days ago. When we disinterred Rose Burswick.

The moment we opened the coffin lid we saw … ah, no … no.' He shook his head gravely, slurped the tea, then scratched his leathery ear. 'No, it's so bad I can't bring myself to … no.'

But he did go on to describe others in lurid, eye-watering detail. 'Old Walter Weltson. My uncle were gravedigger when they planted him – summer of 1946. Weltson was the fattest man in Hemsworth – thirty stone or more. It took so long to build a coffin that the meat-flies got him. Ah … last week, when we opened his coffin up, it were like opening a box of long-grain rice. Couldn't see him. Just this mound of maggots, mummified they were, all hard and white, like dried rice. Then it rained. My God, I'll never eat rice-pudding again. Look.' The gravedigger pointed at something small and white on the brick floor. 'There's one of the maggots. Must've trod it on me boots.' The gravedigger watched with satisfaction as the young man nervously peered at the white morsel.

'Oh, Christ,' he murmured, loosening his shirt collar. 'Awful.'

'Then there was …' The gravedigger had more stories about graves, involving worms, rats, even rabbits – 'you see, the rabbits had tunnelled down and built nests in the coffins, and we found the baby rabbits scampering about inside empty ribcages' – and there were grisly yarns about valuable jewellery lodged in backbones, about pennies on eyes – 'of course when the eyeballs dried they stuck to the pennies, so when you lifted the pennies …' – and then back to maggots, and mole nests in skulls, and … The gravedigger noticed the young man's attention had wandered; he even finished replacing the freezer back plate and swigged off his tea without really taking any notice of what he was being told.

Time to play the ace.

Sighing, the gravedigger lit the butt that had been tucked snug behind his ear. 'You know, I can't get that last one we dug up out of my mind. Aye, Rose Burswick.'

The electrician's eyes focused on the gravedigger. 'You mean that really … awful one?'

'Aye. The worst.' Sombre-faced, yet inwardly gleeful, the gravedigger tragically put his head in his hands. 'The worst ever. And I've seen some terrible things in my time.'

The young man was hooked. 'What happened?'

'Well, promise me you'll tell no one.'

'You can trust me, mister.'

'Remember the old factory down by the river?'

'Yeah, that's the one that got sealed off with those radiation warning signs.'

'That is because during World War One' – the gravedigger jabbed the glowing tab into the air for emphasis – 'that's where they painted luminous faces on watches, ships' instruments and such-like.'

'Uh?'

'Back then, they used radium to make things glow in the dark. And radium is radioactive. They took girls, fourteen, fifteen, sixteen years old, to apply this stuff to watch faces and compasses. 'Course, way back when, nobody knew what radiation did to you. Most of the factory girls were dead before they were twenty – just rotted away as they worked. Rose Burswick was there for five years. She used a little brush to paint the radium on the watch faces. Trouble is it dried quick, so she'd lick the brush every couple of minutes to keep it moist. Each time she did that, she must have swallowed a few flakes of radium.'

'My God. It's a wonder it didn't kill her.'

The gravedigger shrugged. 'It did – at least that's what the doctors said. In 1935 Rose Burswick was buried – she was thirty-six.'

'Bet she was a mess, living that long after.'

'Aye, but that's not the worst of it. Like I said, two days ago we opened the grave.'

'Ugh … what did you find?'

The gravedigger rubbed his eyes as if trying to erase the terrible image. 'Well … we lifted the coffin, it were intact. It was then I noticed something strange … where the lid met the coffin there was like this pale-yellow trim round the edge. Funny, I thought. But reckoned it were just a bit of mould. Anyway, when we came to prise off the lid it – it just flew off. Bang. Like the top popping off a Jack-in-the-Box.'

'Jesus Johnnie!'

'And inside … inside it were full. Ram-jam full to the brim.'

The electrician rubbed the back of his hand across his mouth, as if a bad taste oozed across his tongue. 'Full of what?'

The gravedigger shrugged. 'Rose Burswick.' He pulled on his cigarette, hard. 'They say she weighed six stone when they buried her. But when we opened that coffin it were like opening a carton of ice-cream. There was just this big block – bright yellow. It had grown and grown until the coffin sides had stopped it growing any bigger. But even then, the pressure inside had been so great it were being forced through the crack between the lid and the coffin, making that yellow trim. 'Course, we just thought it were some kind of fungus, so we tipped it out. It came out like a banana jelly from a mould. On the grass was that yellow block – moist, glistening – coffin-shaped.'

'What – what'd happened to Rose Burswick?'

'Oh … that's just it. It *was* Rose Burswick.'

'How?'

'Mue-tay-shun.' The gravedigger rolled the syllables around his mouth like a juicy morsel. 'Mue-tay-shun. You see, the radium'd caused her to mutate in the grave. The coffin had become her – her second womb. Aye, and she like … gestated … she evolved into something that was not human.'

'Did you touch it?'

'Not on your nelly. We ran like hell. But when the Cemetery Board found out, we had to go back to … *it*.' The gravedigger leaned back against the freezer. 'And do you know what we found there?'

The young man shook his head.

'We found it had changed. Just sort of become a soft mound and, aye, it had grown. It had swelled and swollen. Oh, I tell you. That shook us to the core, it did. You see, Tuesday was that sunny day, scorching hot. The heat must have brought it on, and it were growing fast.'

'Jesus. Then what?'

'We tried to lever it into a skip to take it down to the crem. Burn it. But this soft mound of a thing had taken root. Mue-tay-shun caused what were left of the intestine to grow, and to worm its way into the earth. Just like a long yellow snake. It ended up us taking a shovel to it, then cutting through the fleshy tube. She ... *it* screamed. Pain. Real pain! God, it were a living nightmare. Then – there it were – up and moving. Moving like I don't know what. What were left of her arms and legs had turned into swollen, yellow stumps, with back-to-front feet, and hands that had twisted up into hoofs ... oh, I tell you, lad – revolting, utterly revolting.

'It were growing dark,' he continued, 'and we were trying to get this thing into the hut. That's when we noticed the worst part. I held a torch to it and studied it close up. This yellow stuff, almost transparent, like yellow jelly, I – I could see inside of it.'

The young man's eyes bulged. 'What d'ya' see?'

'Terrible. Just under the surface, about four, maybe six inches down through this thick jelly, I could see – clearly see! – Rose Burswick's face. Or what was left of it. Wide, staring eyes coming out of their sockets three inches or more, like red, raw sausages. The tongue ... long, thrusting out the mouth, up through the skin until the top wiggled all pink and wet above the surface. Aye ... and the mouth. Good God. The mouth opening, shutting like this.' Wordlessly, he solemnly slapped his lips together like a goldfish. 'I reckon she was trying to say something. Call for help. A desperate cry for mercy. You know, that expression on her face will stick in my mind forever. Sheer terror. Like a continual state of shock. As if she knew what had happened – mue-tay-shun. That and being buried alive.'

'What happened to it?'

'What happened? Why, it kept growing. So we had to find a way to stop it.'

'And how ...' The electrician trailed off in horror, as if guessing.

'Sub-zero temperatures.' The gravedigger tapped the freezer lid with a nicotine-stained finger. 'Why else do you think that a cemetery store would keep a freezer?' He began to lift the lid. 'Look.'

'No!' The electrician's voice rose to a shriek. Slamming the part-opened lid down, he tightly shut his eyes. 'No!'

Enjoying himself hugely, the gravedigger kept a straight face, but he couldn't keep the mischievous twinkle from his eye. 'Suit yourself.'

'I-I-I've got to go. I'm late.' The electrician snatched his screwdrivers and pliers together, bundled them into his toolkit, then holding on to the limp, white hat ran from the building.

The electrician was starting the van when the gravedigger breathlessly hobbled up.

'Hey … oh, my leg is giving me gyp. Hey, you've forgotten this.' The gravedigger waved a spool of copper wire in the air.

'Oh, ta.' Opening the door, the young man tossed the reel into the back.

The gravedigger fixed him with a look. 'You know, as long the freezer's working,' he said, 'nothing'll happen. Old Rose Burswick is frozen solid – like a block of ice-cream.'

Something occurred to the electrician. 'Wait a minute. How long since the freezer packed in?'

'Ah … let's see … I saw some water on the floor yesterday morning, but Bill said not to bother, it'll only be—'

'Jesus! The freezer's been off more than twenty-four hours? You're lucky it didn't thaw.' He suddenly fixed the gravedigger with a fierce stare. 'Tell me you've switched it back on now? And you've got it on fast-freeze?'

'No. I haven't touched the thing. Thought you did.'

'It's still switched *off*? My God! Just pray we're in time.' He jumped out of the van and hurried back in the direction of the hut, the gravedigger trailing behind and grumbling about his dicky leg.

Too late.

Much too late.

They heard a noise from inside, just like dozens of loose boards being knocked over, a succession of thumps, a crash of mugs hitting the floor, then with a loud crunch the twin doors burst open. And what had once been Rose Burswick, swelled and flowed out on to the path. A mass of quivering yellow, the size of a beached whale, it moved as fast as a man can walk.

The gravedigger hollered a warning to the electrician, turned, then ran. The limp forgotten, he sprinted across the cemetery, leaping over headstones at such a hell of a speed it would have drawn murmurs of approval from any 200 metre hurdles champion.

Luck had deserted the electrician. Stumbling backwards over a mound of soil, he slipped and fell into Mayor Hudson's grave-to-be. Down at the bottom of the pit, the electrician opened his eyes to the darkness. For something had blocked out the daylight. Looking up, he saw that covering the grave, like a lid, was the gelatinous yellow form of Rose Burswick. Briefly, the sun shone through the yellow to reveal shapes suspended in the translucent body; they resembled fruit suspended in a dessert jelly – an arm, a leg, splinters of bone, distended internal organs.

And a head.

The head turned in the jelly ... rotating slowly, and smoothly, and remorselessly, until its face was turned, gradually, to the electrician.

The face. That expression.

On the far side of the cemetery, the gravedigger scrambling over a brick wall, heard the muffled scream. He wanted to go back and help the lad, he really did. But fear drove him from the cemetery as fast as his legs could carry him.

Back in the grave, the electrician's eyes were fixed on that face as Rose Burswick plopped into the hole.

And after more than sixty years of solitude in her cold and lonely grave, Rose Burswick hugged the handsome young man in the floppy, white hat. She hugged him in an embrace that seemed to last forever and ever.

And the expression on her face remained in the electrician's memory, as if burnt there by fire.

She was smiling.

2

SWALLOWING A DIRTY SEED

'COULD YOU SPARE some food?'

'Food?'

'We haven't eaten all day. We were camping up the valley.

'We lost the rucksack with our supplies,' the man added.

It was five in the afternoon. Despite the new electric oven causing the main's fuses to blow every forty minutes, I'd cooked my first proper meal in the cottage. A leg of Welsh lamb in rosemary; to accompany that, fresh vegetables and an apple and walnut stuffing of which I was particularly proud. The oven had behaved itself, on the whole, nothing had burnt, or emerged raw. And I'd poured myself a glass of crisp, white wine, so chilled the glass immediately turned all frosty. That's when I heard the knock on the door. The cottage, tucked away deep in a Welsh valley, was miles from the nearest village and, at first, I thought it must be the man from the garage returning my car a day early.

Instead, there on the doorstep, looking as if they'd just hiked back from the Antarctic, stood a man and woman in their early twenties. Both were exhausted. Dark rings underscored their strangely glittery eyes; the man leaned forward, one elbow against the doorframe to support his weight. He was slightly built with dark curly hair. He wore a pale-brown corduroy jacket and jeans; the girl wore a black suede jacket and matching black trousers. If anything, she looked physically stronger than the man. Statuesque would be a fair description to suit her. She'd tied her long blonde hair back into a pony-tail; her brown eyes fixed on me without a hint of shyness. Both wore trainers. For campers they were pretty poorly equipped. I saw no sign of tents or sleeping bags.

'We can pay,' the girl prompted. She unzipped a pocket on her jacket and pulled out about two pounds in loose change. The man leaned forward, trying not to look too obvious, but I could see he was drawing aromas of roasting lamb through his nostrils, as if he hoped to be nourished on the scents alone.

I smiled. Heck. I could afford to play the good Samaritan now I'd finally managed to sell my apartment in Manchester, and set aside six months' rental on this, my wilderness retreat.

'Come on in,' I said warmly. 'I'm just about to eat anyway. Roast lamb OK? No, put the money back in your pocket. The pair of you look as if you could do with a drink. White wine?'

'God, yes.' The man sounded shocked by my generosity. 'Brilliant. Thanks.'

'Thank you very much, Mr...?' The girl held out her hand.

'Stephen Carter.' I shook her hand.

'I'm Dianne Johnson.'

Her grip was firm, even vigorous. By contrast, the man held my fingers lightly when I shook hands with him. He said his name was Ashley May. I could easily have imagined he was a young Church of England vicar who'd embarked on a camping holiday, only to find the weather, or the girl, or both, were more than he could cope with.

'Pretty lousy weather for camping,' I said, pouring the wine. 'This is the driest day we've had in a week.'

'That's Wales in April.' The girl made polite conversation. 'We thought it might be warmer.'

'I came here for the light,' Ashley said in a small voice. 'Here in April you get good light.'

'Good light?'

The girl explained quickly. 'Ashley's a landscape painter. He's been commissioned by a gallery in Bangor to paint three landscapes. They'll print a limited edition.'

'For the tourists.' Ashley shook his head mournfully and drained the glass of wine in one. 'It would have paid the rent, too.'

Would have paid the rent? He sounded as if some catastrophe had obliterated all hope of life continuing.

'Here, Ashley,' I told him. 'Let me fill your glass. Top up, Dianne?'

'Please … lovely wine.'

They drank as if they needed it. Hell, they gulped it as if they depended on its restorative power. Both were trembling as they raised the glasses to their lips.

They've just had one heck of shock, I realized, surprised by the sudden insight. Yes, they've come through something terrible. But in a quiet Welsh valley, what could have such a devastating effect on their nerves?

Now they were trying to pretend they were tired campers, forcing themselves to make polite conversation, struggling to be nonchalant; yet it seemed to me that at any moment their self-control would shatter and they would run screaming down the hillside all the way to Criccieth.

I served them huge platefuls of lamb and vegetables. They ate every scrap. I offered seconds; they hungrily accepted. In the end, I didn't even have so much as a sip of wine; they drank all that too; then I was happy to give it. In this case, the alcohol had a medicinal affect.

When they had finished, Dianne glanced at Ashley in a way that asked a question. He nodded. Then Dianne turned to me.

'I don't like to ask this,' she began, 'you've been so generous. But would you mind driving us to the nearest town?'

'Normally, I'd be delighted to oblige. But my car's at the garage.'

'Then may we telephone for a taxi?'

'I'm terribly sorry. I'm still waiting to be connected. You see, I've only just moved in. Unfortunately, it's impossible to get a signal on mobile phones, too. It's beautiful here, but remote; that's the trade off, I guess.'

'Is it far to town? Could we walk there before it gets dark?'

'I'm sorry to have to keep being so negative. But there's not a chance, I'm afraid. It would be a two-hour walk. Of course, there are no street-lights out here.'

Ashley glanced out of the window. The expression on his face made me shiver. He looked scared out of his wits.

'God ... it's nearly dark now. *Dianne?*'

'Don't worry, Ashley. You won't be like him. I mean, there's no sign of anything?'

'Nothing's changed outwardly. *But I can feel it.*'

'Ah, sorry to intrude,' I said awkwardly. 'Might I ask, are you in any trouble?'

Dianne glared at me. 'Trouble? We're not on the run from the police, or anything like that.'

'Sorry. I didn't mean to imply that. It's just both of you seem ... unnerved.'

'We're fine,' she insisted firmly.

Ashley shot her a startled look, as if she'd just told the lie of the century.

'We lost our tents, that's all.' Dianne attempted to be matter-of-fact, suggesting they faced a minor glitch in their plans. 'You wouldn't allow us to sleep here tonight?'

'We're so tired,' Ashley whispered. 'The tents went yesterday. Everything did. Food, spare clothes, torches.'

'Went?'

'Stolen.' Dianne shrugged. 'We'd gone for a walk. They had been taken by the time we got back.'

Come on, Stephen, I told myself, you can't turn them out on a day like this. Well ... evening would be a better description now. Darkness fell early as rain clouds avalanched over the Welsh hilltops. Already lights from cottages on distant hillsides twinkled like stars.

I smiled. 'No problem. I've got a single bed in the spare bedroom. Someone will have to make do with the sofa I'm afraid.'

'That's fine.' Ashley yawned. 'I could sleep like a baby on that stone floor. Just as long as I don't have to spend another night outside.'

'I've switched on the immersion heater,' I told them. 'So you can have hot baths.'

'A bath.' Dianne beamed her delight at Ashley. Her face was near child-like. 'Would you be able to manage a hot bath?'

She seemed livelier for eating the meal – the wine and coffee helped, too. I found myself enjoying her company. After losing Anne I promised myself a moratorium on women for a while. But I had begun to wonder lately if I'd start to find myself lonely up here in the cottage – after all, it was slap bang deep in the heart of nowhere.

I finished eating the biscuit then said, 'The water should be hot enough now. I've left out clean towels.'

'You first, Ashley,' she told him.

Meekly, he obeyed.

After he'd gone upstairs, I asked Dianne if she'd like a gin and tonic. She accepted gratefully. Her face bore a pink flush now, and the smile seemed more genuine. I'd just unscrewed the top from the Gordon's and began to pour when, *bang!* The fuse blew again.

Instantly, the cottage lights went out. We were plunged into darkness.

The scream that followed turned my blood to ice. The shock caused me to hold my breath. Dimly, I realized that I was pouring gin over the table top. But that scream. It had been driven out of the man's mouth by sheer terror.

I slotted the ceramic fuse-holder back into the fuse box.

Click.

The lights came on, killing the darkness. The fridge shuddered into life.

I found my hands were still clammy with sweat. Ashley's terrible scream had disturbed me more than I could adequately describe. If a man realized he was about to have his throat cut, he'd probably scream in the same way – a violent outpouring of shock, despair and absolute horror. Ashley must have a clinical phobia of the dark.

Swiftly, I returned to the living room. All the lights had been switched on, as if to compensate for the three minutes or so of darkness earlier. The young man must have found his way downstairs somehow in the dark. Now he sat hunched and scared in the armchair, his fists clenched on his knees.

'Is he all right?'

Dianne looked up at me, her face pale. 'Fine. You'll have the bath now, Ashley?'

His eyes were wide and strangely glittery. 'When the lights went out ... they moved. *Dianne, they moved ...*'

She shot me a glance as if to say, *Please don't listen to what he's saying. It means nothing.*

'In the dark,' Ashley murmured, as if he'd experienced some profound revelation, and now he finally understood a terrible truth. '*In the dark* ... Michael had said those words: "In the dark".'

I stood there. Cold shivers ran from head to foot. There was such a charge in that room. A charge of cold, blue fear.

I was in bed by eleven on that April night. The wind blew down the valley. It moaned around the chimney pots, drawing strange musical notes that sounded like a surreal composition for pan pipes – a song for souls lost in the darkness and achingly alone. The wind carried a flurry of hail to rattle against the windows. It clicked on the patio like so many scurrying insect feet. In the next room slept Dianne Johnson. Ashley May occupied the sofa downstairs. Returning from the bathroom, I'd peeped over the banister down into the living room. All I saw of him beneath the blanket was an expanse of glistening forehead. He was sleeping with the table lamp burning brightly just inches from his face. It's a terrible thing to be afraid of the dark, I told myself. Especially, to the extent of that young man.

Shaking my head, I'd gone to bed, then switched out the light. Burning out of the darkness, the red numerals of the clock radio. They read 11:04.

Disaster struck. I sat up blinking in the darkness; my heart pounded. I didn't know what had woken me. I didn't know what had happened.

But something had. I sensed it: an oppressive feeling of dread bore down on me; a dead weight on my nerves. I checked the clock radio for the time. I saw nothing.

There was only the dark.

Then I sensed movement at the foot of the bed.

Hell. Someone was in here with me. An intruder moved through that all encompassing darkness.

Crash.

That was the chest of drawers at the foot of my bed being struck.

A body thumped across my legs.

I thought: *You're being attacked! Fight back!*

I swung my fist.

Nothing. I'd swiped fresh air. But still that weight stopped me from moving my legs. At any moment, hands would be at my throat.

Next I grabbed, instead of punching into the dark. My fingers closed round long hair.

'Please!'

'Dianne?'

'Please, help me.'

'What's wrong?'

'It's Ashley … the lights went out.'

My eyes snapped back in the direction of the clock radio. *Damn it, Stephen! You forgot to switch off the immersion heater: now it's only gone and blown the fuse again.*

'It's OK,' I told her. 'I've got a torch … there …'

Dianne's face suddenly appeared in the blaze of torchlight. Her hair was wild; a deep, deep dread lanced through her brown eyes. Panting, she said, 'The light went out. Now I can't find Ashley.'

'You can't find him?'

'He's gone. Like Michael.'

'Michael? Who's Michael?'

'He was on the camping trip with us. He went first, but … look, please. Can we just try and find Ashley? I'll tell you everything when I know he's safe.'

My head was spinning. I remembered Ashley's terrified scream when the light went out earlier in the evening. He had a phobia of the dark. At least that's what I surmised. Had that phobia driven him to run wildly from the cottage?

If he had, I might not be able to find him. I still didn't know the area at all well. Beyond the cottage garden and the orchard, there were woods and fields running for miles in the direction of the Lleyn Peninsula. You could hide entire armies out there.

'Dianne, you checked all the rooms?'

'I tried. I found a box of matches. As far as I could see he's not in the cottage. Then the matches ran out; that's when I decided to find you.'

'Damn.'

'God, I'm sorry … I'm sorry.'

'Don't worry. We'll find him. Take this torch: I've a spare in the kitchen.'

First I replaced the blown fuse with the standby ceramic fuse holder. Lights suddenly blazed. The fridge gave that wobbly shudder as the unit fired up again.

I pulled on my boots, and slipped a waxed jacket over my pyjamas. Dianne had already dressed. She followed me outside and we walked across the lawn, calling his name.

'Ashley? *Ashley?*'

Torchlights splashed across grass being blasted into flurries of ripples by the wind. The discordant pan pipe notes shrilled as the wind caught the chimneys – that serenade for lost souls was as dismal as ever.

'*Ashley?*'

We followed the garden wall until it reached the gate.

'Where does that lead?' called Dianne, above the storm winds.

'The orchard,' I said, following her as she hurried through the gate.

Currents of cold air whistled through the branches of the apple trees. I watched as Dianne walked slowly along the lines of fruit trees, carefully shining the torch into the whipping mass of branches. Did she expect to find her friend clinging to a trunk, monkey-like, his face twisted into a mask of terror?

After an hour searching the woodland and surrounding fields, we returned to the orchard. Again, Dianne shone the light into the fruit trees. I followed suit, half-expecting to glimpse Ashley's frightened face peering out from the mass of branches; eyes wide with panic.

Suddenly, she asked, 'In the orchard – how many trees are there?'

That was such a bizarrely inappropriate question in the circumstances that I floundered. 'I … I don't know … actually, it's the first time I've been in—'

She suddenly turned and walked back to the cottage.

Once inside, she quickly slipped off her jacket. 'Stephen, I want to tell you something.' She spoke briskly. 'It's too late for Ashley. We'll never find him.'

'This fear of the dark. Has it happened before?'

'It's nothing to do with being afraid of the dark. Sit down, please.' She sat down and patted the sofa cushion.

I sat beside her, puzzled. Earlier she'd seemed so concerned for her friend; now she appeared to dismiss his present plight from her thoughts.

I said, 'I think it's best if I walk down to the farm and phone for help.'

'No.'

'We should call the police. Ashley might be hurt.'

'No. Please listen to what I have to say first. It's too late for Ashley; it might also be too late for me.'

'For you? Look, just give me half an hour. I can run down to the farm at—'

'Please, Stephen.' She squeezed my hand. 'I want to – no – I *need* to tell you what happened to us.'

The pan pipe notes boomed down the chimney. That mournful song for lost souls … it was becoming increasingly desperate.

'Listen. I was camping with Ashley and our friend Michael. We'd all been to college together. It was still a tradition that we'd go on holiday as a threesome. All entirely platonic. This year, Ashley had been given a commission to paint three landscapes. His first real opportunity to earn money as an artist. And he really was a talented man. I've never seen such delicate brushwork. Anyway, the three of us decided to go camping in North Wales.' She gave a little smile. 'I imagine you noticed we weren't very well equipped – or experienced. So, there we were. Camping miles from anywhere. Ashley painted. Michael and I

34

explored the valley. The weather was awful. Every morning you'd see the cloud come racing across the sky. We had hail, rain, even snow. The wind kept blowing out the stove. The sleeping bags were damp. The bread went all mouldy.' She sighed. 'On the Monday afternoon the three of us went for a walk. And there, deep in the forest, Michael found an apple tree. Just one, growing in the middle of all these huge oak trees. He was really delighted with the find. He picked one of the apples and—'

'Just wait a minute,' I said, puzzled. 'This is April. You wouldn't have fruit on an apple tree at this time of year.'

'This had. Even though the tree didn't have any leaves yet. The apples were red – red as strawberries. If I close my eyes, I can see them now, as they hung from the bare branches like big red globes. Michael picked one. Then he cut slices with his penknife and we all ate a piece.' She frowned as she remembered. 'They were very sweet, but they had a sort of perfumed flavour to them. You know, like the taste of Earl Grey tea. It was only as I was eating that I noticed the apple didn't have a core with pips. Instead, it was simply apple flesh all the way through. Then, do you know what I found?'

I shook my head. I wasn't going to like the outcome of what she was telling me.

She tilted her head to one side, her eyes far away. 'I found the seeds. They were just under the skin of the apple. And they were white and soft; just like tomato seeds.'

'Just under the skin? Then it can't have been an apple.'

She shrugged; one of helpless despair, rather any suggestion of being uncaring at her plight. 'It looked like an apple.'

'These apples. They had something to do with what happened to Michael and Ashley?'

'Yes.' She pushed her long hair back from her face. 'We all swallowed the seeds.' Suddenly, she lifted her sweatshirt to show me her exposed midriff. 'You can feel them under my skin.'

'*Your skin? Feel what under your skin?*' It was as if a series of electric shocks had just tingled across my own skin. 'Dianne, what can you feel?'

'Touch.' She grasped my hand and pressed my fingers against her stomach. 'Hot, isn't it? Michael and Ashley started like that and ...' She gave that despairing shrug again. 'And now you can feel them growing under my skin.'

I stared at her, eyes wide.

'You can feel the roots,' she said.

I could feel nothing but skin and firm stomach muscle beneath.

'Dianne,' I began as calmly as I could, 'don't you think–?'

'And there,' she interrupted, and pointed to a dark growth on her side, just above the hip. 'That's where one of the buds is already forcing its way through. It doesn't hurt. But I'm conscious of them – all those buds – pressing out through my flesh. It makes it very sensitive. All the time, I'm aware of my clothes against my skin. To slow down the growth I should take off my clothes and sit beneath bright lights. That seems the only way to retard it. In the darkness they grow. And then it is at an explosive rate. That's why Ashley was so afraid of the dark. And that's why Ashley disappeared when the lights failed. He would have felt the branches bursting through his skin; the stab of the roots. They'd have been worming outwards through the soles of his feet. He would have felt an overwhelming compulsion to run from the house. A need for deep, fertile earth....'

'Dianne—'

'Tomorrow, if you count the trees in the orchard, you'll find there will be one more than yesterday.'

'Dianne, I really do need to make a phone call. Will you be all right here by yourself?'

She's mentally ill.

The revelation had, perhaps, been too long in coming. But I realized the truth now. She and Ashley had absconded from a hospital some-where. No, probably it wasn't even as dramatic as a midnight scramble through a psychiatric ward window. No, this so-called Care in the Community policy, which places the burden of care for people suffering mental illness on the patients themselves: they're expected to go home and tend to their own psychosis, or neurosis, or whatever malady ails them. Perhaps for some reason, she and Ashley had stopped taking their medication.

'Stephen, why don't you believe me? Look at my stomach. You can see the bud there, breaking through the skin, growing.'

'It's not a tree bud. It's a mole; just a mole. Now—'

'Touch it.'

'No.'

'You're afraid, aren't you, Stephen?'

'No.'

'Press your finger against it.'

'Dianne—'

'Press hard, Stephen.'

'Dianne, please—'

'Press. You can hear the bud casing crack.'

'It's a mole.'

'Just a mole?'

'Yes.'

'Here, watch closely, Stephen.'

'A mole.'

'Watch. As I scratch the top off it.'

'Dianne, don't—'

'When I scratch the top off you'll see a green leaf all curled up tight as a parcel inside.'

'Dianna, stop it!' I gripped her fists in my hands, held them hard. 'Don't hurt yourself – *please.*'

'OK, Stephen.' She gazed up at me, meek as a scolded child. 'I'm sorry. But I just wanted so much that you believe me.'

I met that brown-eyed gaze. One that seemed so calm now. As if she'd accepted a terrible calamity would overtake her. *But it's OK,* she appeared to be thinking, *I'm ready for it now. I won't resist the inevitable.*

'Look,' I said gently. 'You'll be all right here by yourself?'

'You're going to telephone the police, aren't you?'

'Yes ... not because I think you're mad.' It's true, I told that white lie, but my motives were good. 'We need to find Ashley. He'll die of exposure out there on a night like this.'

She gave a sad sigh. 'He doesn't feel the cold now. Neither does Michael.'

'Stay in here. Keep the door locked and the lights on.' I checked the wall clock. 'It's just past three o'clock now. I'll be back by four.'

'Don't worry about me. I'll be all right.' Her voice possessed a whispery quality and, despite my aversion to the comparison, I couldn't help but be reminded of a breeze rustling leaves on a tree. 'I'll sit by the table lamp.'

'Good girl.'

'Stephen.'

'Yes?'

She looked up into my eyes. Lightly she rubbed her bare stomach with one hand. 'Will you do something for me? A special favour?'

'Whatever I can, yes.'

'I'm frightened, so please … will … will you kiss me?'

I ran along the track. The torchlight flashed against tractor ruts, then against the steep banking at either side, illuminating bushes and grass. The wind blew hard. Brambles would whip out horizontally across the track. Sometimes they lashed against my waxed jacket with a crack. By this time, I was panting; the thump of my boots hitting the ground transmitted juddering shocks up into my neck. Briefly, I stopped to zip up the jacket. The gales repeatedly caught it, causing it to balloon around my body.

Then I ran on. Above me, trees creaked and groaned in the storm winds. The skin on my back, rubbed by the heavy winter jacket, began to chafe. I wore nothing but pyjamas beneath it.

What a night, I thought in astonishment. Just think of the e-mail you can send to Big Jim back at the office. Maybe in a few days I'd look back on all this in amusement. But I couldn't now. Although those two strangers had only walked into my life just hours ago, I was deeply worried about them.

I hadn't wanted to leave the girl alone in the cottage, but what options did I have? If I waited until daylight Ashley would surely have died of hypothermia out there in this gale. But would Dianne be all right? Perhaps I should have hidden the knives. Then I would have needed to hide the screwdrivers and aspirin, too. But I didn't have time to do everything. Maybe the girl was only delusional, not suicidal.

Her manner had changed, too. She seemed somehow elated after I left her. That morbid air of resignation had gone.

Perhaps it was the kiss?

She'd asked me to kiss her. Poor kid, at that moment that was all I could give her. Anyway, I'd left her listening to music on the radio; she'd appeared calm enough.

Ahead, I saw the outline of the farmhouse through the darkness. The early-to-rise farmer was already up. I could see him moving about in the kitchen. At least I wouldn't have to stand there hammering at the door. I crossed the yard and knocked.

I arranged to meet the police back at the cottage. So I ran back along the lane. Sweat streamed down my chest. All I wanted was to get out of the sweat-soaked pyjamas and ease my body into a hot, steaming bath.

I took the short cut over the wall, racing through the orchard; the branches of the trees rattled in the wind; then I pushed through the gate into the cottage garden.

I stopped dead.

Damn. My heart sank. *I don't believe it; I don't damn well believe it. It's only gone and done it again!*

The cottage lights were out. The fuse had blown.

Darkness.

I dashed across the lawn. Torchlight illuminated the grass being ripped this way and that by the gale blasting down the valley. The cottage door slammed open-shut-open-shut.

I all but flung myself through the doorway into the cottage. Then I stood there, hauling in lungful after lungful of cold air. Just a second of shining the torch around the room revealed it was deserted. And within a few moments I'd checked every other room in the cottage. All deserted. All silent. For all the world, I could have been in a tomb.

Back downstairs I went, to play the torch over the furniture, the table with the bottle of gin and two empty glasses, the empty sofa with the discarded blankets where Ashley had slept. Storm winds blew the branches of a tree to tap against the room window pane. In here, the only thing to be disturbed was a single chair – tipped on to its back as if someone had rushed by it in a frantic rush to escape the house.

She'd gone.

The emotion took me by surprise, for I felt a sudden loss. I'd really liked Dianne. I remembered the way she'd asked me to kiss her. Her brown eyes, so gentle and trusting. Her hair, the way the wind had mussed it into a light froth that poured around her shoulders. She'd kissed me so passionately. Her hands had gripped my head as she held my mouth to hers.

That kiss.

Suddenly, I shivered. Quickly, I rubbed the back of my hand across my mouth as if to clean dirt from my lips. But it was too late.

Far, far too late.

I shivered again. Points of ice crawled across my stomach. When she kissed me it had felt as if she'd transferred something from her mouth to mine with her tongue. I must have imagined it, surely?

But no. It had felt as small as a seed. When she stopped kissing me and moved her head back I'd felt for the seed with my tongue. There was nothing there. I couldn't have swallowed it, could I? Was that the reason I couldn't find it? Because it had already slipped down my throat into my stomach? That small seed that I had felt slide between my cheek and gum, before it had vanished into my gullet.

Perspiration irritated my skin. Quickly, I unzipped my jacket and rubbed my stomach. God, I needed a bath. A red-hot bath.

The kiss began to trouble me. I shouldn't have agreed to kiss her. Suddenly I wished I could turn back the clock, then when she asked, I'd firmly say, 'No. I won't kiss you.' As simple as that.

But it's too late. Much too late.

My skin felt acutely sensitive. I rubbed my stomach and my chest. The breeze blew the branches to tap against the glass again. Those damn branches ... Tap, tap, tapping....

I grew uneasy.

No, I didn't.

I became frightened.

Because I knew no tree grew so close to the cottage that its branches could touch the glass.

Holding the torch in front of me, I walked outside, swinging the light to my left.

Tap, tap, tap ...

And there, the tree.

Its slender trunk, rooted deeply into the edge of the lawn; its branches swayed to and fro like the limbs of a graceful dancer. And the branches kept tap, tap tapping at the glass.

As if it strived to attract my attention.

There had been no tree there yesterday. I was certain of that. Fear prickled through me. I looked back at the house. No, I wasn't going back there. I couldn't bear to hear those branches at the glass. Tap, tap tapping....

The wind blew; it caught the chimney pots and the pan pipe notes boomed loud and madly discordant.

With a shiver, I zipped up my jacket. There was no alternative. I would have to—

No—

This couldn't be happening.

At that moment the torch died on me. The bulb went from glowing an incandescent white, to yellow, to orange ...

– to red ...

– to dull red ...

– then to nothing ... I slapped the torch into the palm of my hand.

My skin itched. A dreadful prickling that ran over my hips, my stomach, the base of my back. A crawling, burning itching. And all I could hear were those cold gusts, the mad pan pipe music, the rattle of branches against the window pane.

The torch is dead, I told myself as calmly as I could, even though the shiver running through my body had become a deep tremble that would not stop; a tremble that intensified until my teeth clacked together like dry bones being shaken hard in a sack. Savagely, I threw the torch into the grass – the bloody thing had betrayed me.

'It doesn't matter, Stephen,' I panted. 'It doesn't matter one little bit. Because it's going to be light in an hour.'

Better still, the police would be here soon. I'd wait for them in the lane.

I found my way to the wall in the darkness. Then, by sense of touch alone, I reached the gate to the orchard.

Cross the orchard, Stephen; then wait in the lane.

Soon you'll see the lights of the police car as it brings a couple of down-to-earth Welsh coppers up to the cottage. Everything will be all right then. You'll be safe.

The orchard seemed packed tight with trees. There was barely a gap to scramble through. I groped my way forwards with grim determination. Branches snagged my jacket, pricked my face; twigs caught my hair.

Storm winds whipped through the trees with a howl, like they were wild animals, ferociously savaging the branches of a crab-apple tree there, clawing at the grass here, before pawing hungrily at my coat.

Dear God. I wished I could see. The darkness was total. A black fog pressed against my eyes. I didn't even see the branches that gouged my face.

I was growing tired now. I could hardly move. My skin itched. I thought of that kiss. Now I was convinced that Dianne had transferred something into my mouth. I could not stop myself imagining this picture: *There's Dianne – beautiful Dianne – she opens her mouth. It is packed with seeds. Like when you slice open a melon. Seeds! Hundreds of seeds, all neatly packed, all so tightly packed. There, instead of teeth, she has a row of white, gleaming seeds.*

'Stephen. Shut out the picture.' My head spun. A dizzying vertigo tugged at me. 'Shut that picture out.' Then I found myself whispering, 'The seed … I've swallowed it. I'm sure I've swallowed the damned seed.'

Must be nearly at the lane. Nearly there, got to be. The police car will be here any minute. I forged on through the orchard. Fruit trees tugged at me. They were everywhere, blocking my path, scratching my face, pulling my hair, brambles tried to trip me.

Then I was free of them. Away along the lane I could make out the lights of the police car coming up the track – that pulse of blue light illuminated the roadside hedges. I tried to run toward the wall that separated the orchard from the lane. I made it to within five paces.

Then I stopped.

I was too exhausted to move another step. The police car approached. I held up my hands to flag it down.

They drove past, not seeing me.

I tried to lower my arms. I couldn't. For some reason I'd frozen in that position. My face, too, had seized into some kind of fixed mask as I'd shouted. I couldn't move my feet. I could not move at all.

I was rooted to the spot.

'*Mum!*'

'*What' is it? What's wrong?*'

'*Mum, come and look at this!*'

'*Joel, I thought we were making a snowman up on the lawn.*'

'*I wanted to play in the orchard.*'

'*Keep your coat fastened up, it's freezing. And be a good boy or we won't go to the café for lunch.*'

'*But I want to show you this.*'

'*Oh, very well, Joel. What have you found?*'

'*That apple tree over there near the wall. The one by itself. There's a coat stuck up in the tree.*'

'*Ugh, probably belonged to a tramp.*'

'*It's a waxed jacket like Dad's – and someone's pushed the branches through the sleeves like arms.*'

'*Don't touch it, it'll be dirty. Now come back and finish the snowman with me.*'

'*But Mum!*'

'*But Mum what?*'

'*There's still apples on the tree. Can I eat one?*'

'*Certainly not. They'll give you stomach ache. Now, come with me.*'

The two walked back hand-in-hand through the snow. Joel felt in his pocket for the apple he'd picked. He'd eat it later when he was alone in his room. A moment later, mother and son had reached the snowman. Next to it, grew a slender apple tree. The breeze blew. Gently, it tapped a branch against the window pane of the cottage.

As if it were cold and lonely.

And it wanted to come inside.

3

IS IT STILL RAINING ZOMBIES?

'THE WORLD'S GONE topsy-turvy,' she declared, before the zombie dropped on to her and killed her stone dead.

Last year, zombies fell from heaven. The dead rained down on us. They landed in cornfields, in gardens, splashed into ornamental ponds; they flattened cars; one even cannoned through the greenhouse to crush Uncle Barry's tomato plants. Only the dead didn't stay dead. Moments after they crashed to earth, these hideous cadavers twitched, grunted, stood, and walked. Their faces were blank, but their eyes roved as they searched for nourishment. How they hunger for our warm flesh!

Now I hide in a coal mine, far away from the plague of dead-alive men and women tumbling from the blue. For the love of God let me know: IS IT STILL RAINING ZOMBIES? If you go into the street, and cry out your answer as loud as you possibly can, there's a chance – the saints willing – that I will hear.

4

THE IMAGE DISSECTOR

Written in tribute to H.P. Lovecraft (1890–1937)

TERRIBLE THOUGH THE contents of the tomb undoubtedly are, there is nothing to prepare the unhappy discoverer of that which oozes, palpitates and ultimately holds in its dread thrall the kingdom beneath. When you find the wax disk of this recording and hear what I have to relate then you will understand why a surfeit of emotion distorts my voice. Listen carefully! Do you hear that call above the rush of night-wind through the balloon's cables? *They* will soon be here ... and I will be able to speak into this apparatus no more.

The events, which I will describe hereafter, occurred on the evening of the first day of July as my vessel lay suspended 3,000 feet above the city of Providence during the inaugural State Futurity Fair of 1936, when the world's inventors assembled to display their machines. By now you will have surely seen newspaper photographs of my ill-fated vessel *The Brynnwyr*. If not, I hope this sketchy description will at least do my craft some justice. Picture a balloon that is as round as an orange and the same colour. Slung beneath it, amid an intricate webbing of cables, is our gondola. This consists of a cane framework, durable yet light, over which is stretched canvas treated with a clear waterproof lacquer that has the aroma of canned pears. Set in that are large glazed windows, three on each side of the gondola; at one end of the vessel is the open aft-deck, which can be accessed via a doorway. Our gondola cabin is fifteen feet long by six in width. Its interior is completely protected from the elements, and snug within it, we three crew can work, eat and sleep. Herein, are three canvas chairs, a wall-mounted bunk, gasoline stove,

46

lamp, a gramophone recorder into which I now speak. A hatch leads to a tiny bathroom compartment. On the wall behind me are charts together with a shelf for books. And, lo, we have been gifted a cosy cottage in the sky, one that sways gently beneath a cotton envelope containing many thousand cubic feet of helium that has the power to hoist us ever upward into the sky.

Ever upward, that is, if *The Brynnwyr* wasn't tethered to the ground by a ship's sturdy hawser. *The Brynnwyr* was named after a folk hero of the ancient kingdom of Wales. Brynnwyr of Glan Gors had the gift of sight like no other. By day he could peer through mountains; by night, in his dreams, he saw the faces of men not yet born.

We are ... were ... a crew of three. I am the balloon's aeronaut, George Wren. From infancy I knew my destiny lay skyward. My mother would often find me perched in a tree in our garden. There, I pointed up at clouds and sky, as I murmured strange whimsies of sky-dwelling creatures. My two passengers, Lyman L. Pierce and Ivan Kopski operate one of the latest inventions known to man. Pierce was a gaunt man, silver-haired, and wore the white coat of a scientist. Kopski's form was squat, muscular and he possessed the down-turned eyes of the melancholic. Though he regularly shaved the upper parts of his face the underside always bristled with black stubble that extended down his throat into his shirt. Over and over, he'd tug from his jacket pocket a large cross cast in brown bakelite. This holy object he'd gaze at with unhappy eyes, then he'd mouth in silent prayer.

As I've intimated, our purpose wasn't to adorn the sky above Providence, but to be the means to elevate a new electric camera to an altitude of 3,000 feet. This device known as the Pierce Image Dissector sent a living television photograph down a telegraph wire attached to the hawser to the ground below. There it terminated at a television set with a glass screen the size of a table top. This apparatus had been installed in one of Providence's oldest churches. There, during the Futurity Fair, the public could gather around the horizontal screen, peer down into its cathode ray tube (as one peers down into a well) and see contemporaneous images of the houses, offices, chapels and streets.

These were rendered not in colour but in black, grey, silver and a shimmering chrome. I recall, myself, just two days ago, gazing into a small onboard television screen that had been wired to the Image Dissector, which poked its lens through our gondola's window. In astonishment I beheld a pellucid view of the Providence River far below, curving a glittering course through the downtown area of the city. I espied venerable colonial houses, set like jewels in the flanks of Prospect Hill, and the sprawling edifices of Brown University. Beneath us, the waterside warehouses, and over yonder, Swan Point Cemetery with its thousands of tombstones, looking like granite tongues that protruded from the earth to taste the summer air. Hear this fact: seen from aloft, even the most populous city resembles a forest. Trees that aren't noticed at ground level become a verdant green rug that seemingly engulfs the teeming metropolis. I confess that even an experienced aeronaut such as myself became enchanted by the tangle of old streets below me, with mellow roofs of sixteenth-century houses glowing in the sunlight. The superabundance of seldom-glimpsed architectural details from an altogether more exalted age was enchanting: the uncommonly steep roofs, the antique chimney pots amid a tangle of gables, curious urns atop a tower that no earthbound soul can see; Georgian fanlight windows, a quaintly shuttered oculus that held an attic forever in darkness. I gazed on Benefit Street, then the dome of City Hall; after that, my attention turned to a high-flown lane known as College Street, a lofty place for dreamers to gaze out over the city from their garrets, and to conjure mindscapes of lost cities and ancient gods that stalk their blasphemous realms.

Pierce and sad-eyed Kopski were required to lavish their waking hours on the Image Dissector. Variations in temperature required constant re-tuning of the apparatus. Requests from the public, viewing the screen in the church, were relayed by telephone to the gondola. When such a message arrived Pierce directed the instrument in the direction of whatever building or landmark the gentlefolk wished to examine remotely via the television window.

Providence summers are stifling – humid *in extremis*. Food spoils quickly as we discovered when the bread and cheese in the gondola's larder became mouldy overnight, leaving us to exist on canned fare. Worse were the electrical storms that began with thunderous regularity at four o'clock every afternoon. Because we were not earthed, due to ingenious arrangements of fuse wire and India rubber inserts added to the hawser, and so safe from damage if lightning should strike our vessel, I decided we should remain aloft for the duration of our living picture demonstration, which was scheduled to last three days. Happily for us, I saw to it that the hawser had been firmly anchored to a stout tree trunk in the cemetery of the church where the receiving apparatus was displayed.

Just six hours ago I maintained my watch on storm cloud running in from the west. Kopski brewed coffee on the gasoline stove in the cabin. Pierce sat on a canvas chair beside the Image Dissector. It resembled a movie camera, although was little larger than a shoe box; a silver tube that contained the lens pointed out through the window in the direction of the Greek-style edifice of the Westminster Arcade. On top of the Image Dissector five glass valves, of a similar nature to those found in a wireless set, glowed a bright yellow. Pierce held a telephone speaker to his ear as an individual on the ground requested a magnified view of the weather vane on the building currently in view. I saw the image duplicated on the small television set that occupied my chart table.

As the kettle rose to the boil, piping shrilly, Kopski muttered, 'Those storm clouds are worse than yesterday, and that was like sitting inside a kettle drum. We should beg to be winched to the ground.'

I shook my head. 'The balloon is safer at this altitude. There is less wind turbulence up here. Down at ground level the envelope might be torn to pieces.'

'We're not safe.' Kopski stared with mournful eyes at the sky's dark tide that raced toward us. 'The rain. The lightning.'

'I've explained. We are not earthed. Even if the lightning strikes us it can't harm the vessel.'

The melancholic assistant ran his finger across the gondola wall. 'It is nothing but sail canvas stretched over a bamboo cage. We will be at God's mercy.'

'On the contrary ...' Pierce was a sharp-eyed man, who constantly verged on irritation at his assistant's comments that were voiced in the slow, heavy tones of a dullard. 'On the contrary ...' He paused to adjust the focus wheel on the apparatus. 'Rather than God's mercy, we are at the mercy of the electrical industry. If we don't secure a production contract for this machine, I will be ruined, Kopski, and you will be out of a job.'

'I value my life, Mr Pierce.'

'Kopski, when you've finished making coffee, bring me a new copper coil; this one has started to over-heat.'

'But that's in the store outside the cabin, Mr Pierce. I don't like to go out on to the deck. There are no safety rails and we are so far from the ground.'

'This is no time to develop a fear of heights.' Pierce's tones were snappish. 'Obey my orders.'

Distant thunder clumped across the town.

'No matter,' I intervened, 'I'll get it for you. It's in the aft store container?'

'It is, and clearly labelled.' His voice only softened when he spoke to a potential investor on the ground via the telephone, as he did so now. 'You have the weather vane in sight, sir. It is a fine example of gilded metal.' He checked the television screen. 'The camera is now at maximum magnification. You can clearly make out the feathers on the eagle's wings. Magnificent, aren't they?'

Soon, the storm had struck. Lightning raged. Thunder pounded with the mad beat of drums – the same dread rhythms that cannibal tribes might employ to call their warriors to the feast. Electricity? One smelt ozone inside our cabin; its molecules scintillated the nerve. It crackled through our hair. The static charge made our very teeth tingle. Sheets of silver raced through hell-black cloud. When Kopski went to secure the brass window-catch blue sparks discharged into his fingers, making him jerk back.

'Tell them to haul us down,' he howled. 'The lightning will burn us alive!'

'We are not earthed,' I countered. 'This is the same effect experienced by ships at sea during a thunderstorm. Static charges, St Elmo's fire – all harmless phenomena.'

Rain began to lash the canvas walls and roof. Thunder boomed loud enough to crack a window pane. The concentration of electrically charged atoms in the air caused objects within the gondola to glow with eerie ghost-lights.

'You've murdered us,' Kopski shrieked. 'Look, the hawser is on fire!'

'It's not.' I gripped his arm. 'It's merely a static charge. There is no heat; all that you are seeing is a luminous glow.'

'Lord,' he cried, his ugly face wet with tears, 'we're burning. We're burning to cinders!'

I cuffed the fool aside. Immediately he scrambled into the bunk where he hid his head under the pillow. At this time I noticed that Pierce hadn't scolded his assistant, as was his wont. Instead, he stared with a strange rigidity at the television screen.

Lightning sent forks of fire to sear the air around our craft.

'We are earthed,' I stated, as if this phrase had become my personal chorus by virtue of repetition, 'but the static might harm your apparatus. Switch off the power.'

'I have,' Pierce breathed, and not for a moment did he avert his eyes from the television that sat upon the chart table. 'The battery wire is disconnected, too.'

'You must be mistaken. I see images on the television set.'

'Remarkable, aren't they?'

'But if the camera has been switched off ...'

'You see them? You see what's on the screen?'

'Phantom signals—'

'No! What you are seeing are images that are being transmitted *up* the wire from the ground.'

'Impossible. The camera is up here – three thousand feet *above* the earth.'

'Nevertheless. You have the evidence of your own eyes.'

'But what are they – what are those shapes? They're in ceaseless motion ... palpitating ... *alive*.'

Storm-winds struck the balloon. It raged against its tether. Pierce and I had to grip the cane framework of the gondola to prevent us from being hurled about its interior. Beneath the pillow Kopski prayed volubly to his protecting saint. I saw him sneak his hand into his pocket for the solace of the Bakelite cross that was as brown as wet dirt.

My eyes returned to the apparatus despite the violent pitching. 'But what's manifesting itself on the screen? What is it showing us?'

'An effect of the lightning. A redistribution of electrical forces. No battery power; the television now draws its energy from nature.' Pierce's once stern face blazed with wonder. 'Images are being transmitted up the telegraph wire from the earth to this television screen. And where does the wire make ground fall, my good sir?' His laughter came in a manic burst.

'The graveyard. The graveyard of the church!'

'Exactly. What you are seeing are images from beneath the surface of the earth. See these forked limbs, and this tangle of filaments.' He pointed at the glass screen. 'These are tree roots. And these elongated geometric shapes are—'

'Tombs. Good Lord, man! We are looking *into* the cemetery; the soil has become as clear as glass.'

It was as if the coffins that were buried six feet beneath the sod floated in a thin mist. Those boxes of death drifted above a viscous lake – yet a lake that was alive and squirming in a most horrendous manner. My eyes fixed on the television glass as living objects extruded themselves from the lake, yet they did not part from it absolutely, for they were connected by fleshy strands that resembled the human intestine. The living objects, those swollen orbs of nightmare flesh, venous and quivering, swam up through transparent soil; they were monstrosities suggestive of power, speed and a malevolent intent.

Up, up, up they swam … eager in their ascent. They flowed round subterranean boulders with fish-like grace. Yet when they reached the ancient tombs, those oblong cadaver-boxes, the creatures paused as if in delectable anticipation of the feast to come; this echoed the wine connoisseur inhaling the aroma of a fine claret before plunging their lips into the blood-red liquor. Then the balls of flesh swam *into* the coffins. Somehow they agitated their own forms to agitate, in turn, the bones of Providence's ancient dead. Picture vegetables suspended in jars of vinegar – then imagine violently shaking the glass jar and you will have something of that hideous sight. Skulls bounced inside the caskets; ribs and thigh bones performed a *danse macabre*. But a second later those hell-born creatures with all the allure of verminous-corpses raced upward once more.

'*They're coming to the surface.*' Pierce could hardly contain his glee. 'See how they rush through the tree roots, yet notice how they are still connected by a line of flesh to the living mass beneath the graveyard!'

'Pierce.' I gripped his elbow. 'Those creatures are heading for the tree – our tree! – the one that secures the balloon's hawser!'

'I must see what happens next.'

'Pierce! They've sensed us. They know we're up here!'

Most nerve-shattering of all shocks is that of the unexpected, and that which evidences the destruction of Natural Law. Nothing I had hitherto experienced as an aeronautical adventurer – a most hazardous profession in its own right – could compare in soul-riven terror to what I now witnessed. Those evil sights, which I will now describe, all reached my horrified eyes through the viewing glass of the television perched on the chart table.

Suddenly, the television screen revealed what was seen through the eyes of the monstrosities … or whatever passed for sight organs, for there were no discernible eyeballs embedded in those veined orbs. By what eerie power I know not, yet we watched from their point of view as the beasts surfaced through the grainy mist of soil, Then we – *they!* – saw the rough and riven bark of the venerable yew. A moment later, a clear sight of the hawser wrapped round and around the thick wood of the trunk. After that, one of the creatures raced up the hawser. The woven hemp ran upwards in front of the hell-born thing; that rope – that accursed rope! – a bridge between muddy clay and our vessel floating in the storm-blasted sky.

We saw through the creature's eyes as it fixed its predatory senses on the orange sphere of the balloon. Constantly, lightning flashed, rain tore from clouds that turned day into night. Thunder screamed its rage at man. And now ... and now ... I gasped in horror. For when I tore my eyes from the television apparatus and looked through the gondola window I saw the shining pinkness of the subterranean demon gliding up the hawser. It moved like a snake up a rope. Yet with such speed that it stripped rainwater from the cable in a silver plume. When I glanced at the television I saw through the demon's eyes once more. And I saw what the hideous entity wanted most in the world.

Me.

It fixed its senses on my face. I was to be its prey. That bladder of toxic fluid would savour my blood, it would taste me: sinew and bone; my life essence would nourish its unholy appetites. I nearly fainted to the floor as that dread realization roared through my brain.

'Nearly here,' Pierce breathed. 'Soon it will board our vessel. Oh, what wonders we will encounter....'

I reeled backwards. 'If it reaches us, we'll be doomed!' I raced across the cabin to where a leather satchel hung from a peg. A second later, I pulled out my revolver then scrambled wildly to the doorway.

'No, no, no, you mustn't ... think of the scientific discovery we can give to the world.' Pierce babbled in this vein as he tried to hold me back. In no time at all, however, I'd exited the hatch to the little aft-deck, which was just six feet by four square. On gaining the exterior of the gondola the rain stung my face. Howling winds tugged at my clothes, my jacket flapped with so much violence that for a moment I feared I'd be carried away into oblivion.

And through a thousand yards of swirling water droplets I saw the lights of Providence beneath us. Yet emerging from the evil fog came the gleaming hawser. Swimming up that with the speed of a shark, the living orb of flesh. Its skin had flushed pink; veins formed purple branches in its flesh. Slender spines emerged from the turgid body, dark and porcupine-like, they were open at the ends as if to emit, or to receive, liquid.

I aimed my pistol at the loathsome hump of flesh that threatened like a bunched fist.

Pierce howled like a lunatic. 'Wren, do not fire … Let it live!'

I squeezed the trigger. Before the weapon discharged, however, the inventor felled me with a blow. The gun dropped from my nerveless fingers. In an instant it vanished into the vortex of rain. Pierce wrenched me from the edge of the deck so he could welcome that vile thing, which he saw as the epitome of beauty.

'I won't hurt you,' he called down, as it scaled the hawser toward the gondola. 'No harm will come. Enter as a friend.'

I watched in a daze, still stunned from Pierce's blow to my head. He extended his hand. The creature thrust out its spines.

The man screamed as he was drawn into the body. The creature simply gulped him into itself through the forest of spikes, erupting from that nightmare form. Yet he did not vanish inside the monstrous demon. As I sat there, too stunned to either help myself, nor Pierce, nor even flee back inside, I watched the man descend the hawser *inside* a membranous sheath. Like a rabbit passing through the slender length of a python snake, Pierce's bulging torso, head and limbs deformed the intestine that stretched from the demon up here at the balloon all the way down back to the evil essence that dwelt beneath the graveyard.

I sagged forward, dizzy from the sight of the horror, and weak from concussion. Rain smote my face. Thunder roared in my ears. The balloon twisted like a wild cat tethered to a leash.

At that moment I could not move. All I could do was passively wait for the demon's noxious embrace. A skin as cold as corpse flesh touched my out-flung hand. The flesh orb of the body rose level with my eyes. Its spines extended to prick the skin of my face – a sensation both vile and strangely titillating. It explored my features. I sensed it calculated the possibilities contained within my body. Another spine touched my lips, pressed, then entered my mouth. I tasted earth, I tasted the decay of the tomb, I tasted a sugar-sweet quintessence. Penetration by the pointed quills shot me through with waves of emotion. Revulsion and heart-pounding excitement vibrated back and forth. My soul melted into the hungry muscularity of the demon. Its pulsing veins seemed to whisper the promise of not only unspeakable torment but an undying bliss. A teasing promise of an old, old mystery soon to be revealed in all its shining glory.

As I fell into a sighing faint I dimly glimpsed a figure blunder over me. It dropped to its knees at the very stern of the vessel.

In a vague, half-conscious state I witnessed Kopksi wrestle with the steel linkage that secured the hawser to the gondola. A moment later he hefted the lever. Dumbly, I watched the cable float down toward the town far below.

'We're free,' Kopski shouted above the storm. Thunder applauded his act of pure insanity. 'I've saved us!'

Indeed, the bulbous demon fell. Dragged down by the hawser, it vanished into the turbulent sheets of rain, amid splashes of searing lightning. However, *The Brynnwyr* no longer boasted an anchor to the earth. Screaming gales caught it and bore it away into storm clouds, snapping the telegraph wire in the process.

Lying flat to the deck, as I was, I could hold on to the boards. Without such handholds the pitching deck flung Kopski out into the darkness. He vanished in an instant. Yet I heard his death scream between bursts of thunder. In ten seconds he would be lying smashed on the ground.

Rainwater spattering my face roused me. With an aching head I re-entered the gondola where I fell in a dead faint upon the bunk.

Hours later I awoke. Now, in the dead of night, the vessel's ropes creak; air currents fill the gondola with ghostly sighs. There is an all-encompassing sense of peace.

And here I sit before the microphone. The spinning disk of black wax nears its end. There are no lights in *The Brynnwyr* as it drifts free and unfettered on the night breeze some three miles above our planet Earth. The sole illumination emanates from the television screen – flickers of silver, grey, onyx and spectral white. Although Pierce's Image Dissector is switched off, the screen still reveals strange pictures.

Images of the monstrous subterranean entity? No … not at all. Now the screen reveals altogether more ethereal beings at play. My chest is tight. Blood skitters through my brain – one as light as a bird's feather floating on a summer zephyr. My recording disk nears its end. I gaze at the screen. It reveals airborne night-gaunts that flit around my vessel on vast membranous wings. We are above the clouds. There are stars; a comet draws its golden signature through the sky. When the disk ends I will stop the mechanism, rest the needle-arm back on its cradle.

Then I will emerge from the gondola to watch the night-gaunts cavorting upon the breeze. The creatures possess horned heads. Their sharp, triangular faces have no eyes. Their black, lustrous bodies resemble those of Man, yet from the base of their spine flicks a barbed tail with the speed of a whip. And when I have mustered my nerve I will step off the deck. I, too, will fly with those cosmic beings. We will rocket into star-bejewelled skies where, in sight of the Eternal, we will soar through gleaming cloisters wrought from moon-fire. And so: with my new companions we will rise higher and higher above the green Earth until, at last, there comes a time when I look back and realize that my home world is lost to the universe. That I can see it no more.

5

MY GOD, MY GOD ...

*'Many fishermen still fear pagan gods. For this reason it is considered
unlucky, even dangerous, to discuss Christian beliefs at sea ...'*

The Seaman's Lore by Penny Hedge (Bramblewick Books 1988)

December 3: Sunrise! My God, what an amazing sunrise! If you live in
a city, you just don't witness dawns like this one now bursting over the
horizon. This is what I'm seeing from my tower window: on the cobbled
yard stands a black swan, gazing out across the marsh toward the sea. It
seems as awed as I am. The sun is swimming up through the fog bank;
a vast ball that's the colour of blood. Light cascades through layers of
mist, turning swamp water pools into little lakes of fire. Apart from the
spars of all those derelict boats lying out there, poking up from the mud
like so many bony fingers, it's perfectly flat. Now the sun is turning
gold, the swan stretches its wings as if in worship. It's gone, flapping
away into this sea of fire that the mist has become. I know I'm repeating
myself but **My God** what a breathtaking sight. What an absolutely
breathtaking sight!

I moved here to write TV scripts for the *Fable & Legend* series (yeah,
that one: with the laughable budget of $15,000 per episode – I hope
you're reading this, Tony Tosspot Greereson, head of television production at So Tru Flix). But now I know full well that this little slice of
countryside is going to be as distracting as hell.

I sat down to write this diary, which (when it's cleaned up and libellous
statements excised) is going to be posted here at mandrake-madness.com.
I planned it would tell the whole process of shooting the TV series. From
its genesis, with my co-creator, Keith Vitterrai, over fried eggs and hot

chocolate in the Asda café, to months of pre-production, pitch writing, networking and downright pleading, to its eventual shooting and broadcast. What a cool idea, I thought. There's a genuine public interest in the nuts 'n bolts of TV production, why not cater for it with a website diary? I've rigged up a webcam here to shoot out images world-wide of the 'genius at work' (me), fingers rattling the keyboard, cigar clenched between my teeth, endless cups of coffee, countless profanities, especially when Keith e-mails to say, 'Hi, James *<that's me, folks!>* Bad news: the budget won't allow for the hire of a steady-cam, never mind those sweeping helicopter shots of surf pounding against majestic cliffs . . .' – fifteen thousand lousy bucks an episode – call that a budget, Tosspot Greereson? I'm even renting this place out of my own pocket in the hope against hope that the book of the series is going to recoup costs.

But there are very visual compensations. I've got this beautiful sunrise. Ten thousand acres of evocative marshland, plus the rotting cadavers of a dozen old sailing boats, are mine for the next three months as I sit here writing. I've got invigorating sea breezes, open skies, and freedom to work whenever and however I want – even stark bollock naked, if the whim takes me (go to the side bar, people, click on 'Web-cam Archive' to find out if I actually do write *sans* trousers – if you've strong enough stomachs!).

And, yes, I know full well this scenery is going to distract the be-Jesus out of me. Of course I've gone and broken the first rule of writing: **WRITE FACING A BLANK WALL, NOT THE DAMN WINDOW.** I'm guilty as hell, so help me. Right in front of me is the big window that overlooks the marsh. What's more, it's a view that draws your eyes to it. See, I'm typing looking at the screen here, but already I can feel the pull of that vista, my eyeballs swivel up and over the top of the computer monitor: there are the blackened bones of ships – the nearest lies just beyond the yard wall. There are the little streams, pools of water, quicksand and tussocks of grass; there are wading birds, dipping beaks into the water, hunting shrimp and catching eels that look like wriggling bootlaces.

The letting agent told me that if I'd come here a hundred years ago I'd have been sitting here at the edge of open ocean. Fishermen would bring their boats right up on to the beach that lies just beyond that wall, which, no doubt, would be picturesquely festooned with drying nets. My neighbours would have been fisher folk and boat builders. All that's gone now. The sea enjoyed one of its capricious whims. Within the space of a couple of decades the whole estuary silted up. Open sea in the bay became marshland. Now there's more than a mile of oozing silt and that rough, wiry grass between me and the ocean.

Right, I'm turning the web-cam to get some shots of the sunrise. Be sure to click on 'Web-cam Archive' to the left of this page to see them.

Just as I promise myself to make a start on the first script, I found myself gazing out across the marsh once again. This is addictive! The mist is golden. Blobs of fire that are the water pools roll away into the distance; I'm struggling to find an elegant comparison here, but imagine gold coins scattered on a carpet of dark green and you're getting close. And above that hangs the sun as a red-gold ball. A beautiful and alluring sight without doubt. But something also has caught my attention this time.

It's probably even more difficult to describe than this vast marsh-scape. What I am seeing is perhaps a denser bank of fog within the mist, but it appears as a dark shape. It's huge. In my field of vision it glides from right to left, then back again, at a pace that can be described as stately. The shape and movement is suggestive of something long and tapered that swims through the ocean. OK, so it's a trick of the light but it's an eerie spectacle. Eerie enough to splash a cold shiver or two down my spine. And it sends a big reminder that I'm alone out here on the marsh. The nearest inhabited house is two miles inland from here. Hell, just the thought of that has sent a great cascade of goosebumps through me.

Still that dark shape swims out there in the mist, just a few feet above the marshland. It comes close enough to announce its presence to me. But not close enough to reveal its true nature.

See, that's the kind of place this is. Strange thoughts intrude; boy, do they take some shifting. I'm going to pour myself another coffee. Maybe by the time I get back it will have decided to haunt some other joint. Well, that was intended to be a joke ... sort of ... But I've got those chills running their spiky legs up and down my back and, blast them, they just won't quit.

December 4: Work is the exorcism king. Seeing that shadow looming through the mist yesterday unsettled me more than I can adequately express. But after two coffees straight, followed by eight hours of solid work that saw one whole script on its way to Keith I was one happy honcho again. Last night I treated *moi* to a few whiskies, a little music played **LOUD** and permitted myself to rationalize like crazy. The Shadow Of The Marsh was nothing but a trick of the light as the sun burned through the mist. I'm a city guy, born and bred; what else do you expect if you stick me out here in a house that's as weird as Eldritch-ville in the middle of nowhere? Alone. In winter. With no neighbours for miles. If I didn't start imagining ghost pirates and big wicked beasties the Society of Authors would revoke my membership like yesterday. A writer without imagination is like a bus driver without his bus, a gravedigger without his spade, a vampire without fangs (enough of the horror imagery already!) ... so I should only start to worry if I don't see phantoms ... right?

This afternoon I took a break from sitting hunched at the computer and enjoyed a leg-stretching, joint-cracking walk. For the first time, I headed into the marsh, taking care to follow the white posts that mark the footpath. One foot wrong and glug, glug, gone. There, I got a different perspective on the house. Built by a fisherman a couple of hundred years ago, it's basically a long, one-storey cottage with a three-storey tower at one end. The tower stands about thirty feet and consists of one room piled on top of the other. The letting agent told me the tower wasn't just the builder's quirk: it meant the structure could be seen way out at sea: local fishermen used it to navigate by. What's more, to use the writer's imagination again, I could picture generations of anxious wives setting lanterns at the top of the tower to guide husbands home on stormy nights.

The path zigged and zagged away through the marsh, skirting those pools that had all the appeal of congealing blood. Here and there, remains of long dead boats jutted through the mud. Planks had rotted clean away to leave those noxious spars that reminded me of bones, which, you'll allow, sort of complement the notion of ponds of congealing blood. Here, the smell of the swamp wasn't shy about getting up your nose. Decay, stagnant water odours, all mixed with the not overly pleasant aroma of fish entrails left by gulls.

The carcass of a particularly large boat, perhaps some old sailing schooner, lay hard against the path. The spars came up higher than my head, while the remains of two masts lay crossed on the ground to form a huge X. I'd intended this to mark the furthest point of my walk; dusk and the mist were racing neck and neck across the marsh. I wanted to be back indoors with a glass of lovely single malt in my hand before it was fully dark.

But the lure of the boat's skeleton was something I couldn't resist. The ground alongside the path looked firm enough. I took a tentative step on to the marsh grass. It sagged a little with an attendant squelching sound, but it held. I figured the grass had woven a tough surface membrane between me and the goo beneath. And seeing it was holding I decided to have a little looksee before the daylight quit this bit of God's earth completely.

I followed the ship's keel that formed a spine of black wood to the pointed end, which was, I told myself, remembering my smattering of nautical jargon, the prow. To my surprise, there a head jutted up from the silt with swathes of curling hair. In turn, the hair framed a face that was the picture of sheer rage. I moved forward of it looking down to where it glared at my knees, its nostrils flared, mouth partly open as if to snarl a threat.

My God. A ship's figurehead. I'd have thought it would have been valuable enough to be removed when the vessel was scrapped. This carving should be in a museum, even if it was a god-awful monstrosity. Whoever had chiselled it had managed to distil enough venom and rage into the figure to chill the blood. Now the evil-looking woman lay rotting up to her shoulders in mud. I reached down, put my hand on the cold head and gave it an experimental push on the off chance it was loose. No, not a prayer of moving that; the mud had glued it tight, even if it had come away from the prow timbers.

I'd been so absorbed by the carving I'd not noticed how dark it had become. Or how the mist had thickened. That cold air bit right through my coat, chilling me bone deep. I looked round. The marsh had all but disappeared into gloomsville. My house had vanished, too. So I lost no time in walking back through the spars toward the path.

I took a couple of paces away from the boat, looking to my right for the white posts that marked the line of the path. Mud gurgled under the membrane of grass beneath my feet. I stopped. Suddenly the ground didn't seem overly firm.

What's more, I couldn't for the life of me see any of those blasted white sticks.

Damnation. They had to be here somewhere. White sticks that came about waist high: they ran at intervals of around twenty paces, marking a route on firm ground through the marsh. I took another step. The 'ground' sagged beneath my weight. The pressure caused a build up of methane gas to vent, bubbling, through a pool to my left.

Idiot, I told myself. You've left the ship at the wrong side. The path's on the other flank of the wreck, not this one. Retracing my way, I walked between the upright spars, over the keel, and back to the other side. This time I didn't notice the white sticks because something else caught my attention.

Gliding from left to right, perhaps a hundred paces away in the thickening mist was a shadow – a gargantuan shadow at that. I caught my breath, and my heart began to hammer against my chest.

Damn ... that shadow I saw yesterday. It had come sliding back through the fog, a long streamlined shape, ominous looking. This time I was close enough to hear noises. Immediately it reminded me of the time I'd been walking in the countryside. I'd passed a farm in the distance. I'd pulled up short when I heard the strangest sounds coming from the place. A mixture of screaming and bellowing. I couldn't decide whether I was hearing sounds of excitement or terror. Just when I'd decided mass murder was being wrought I saw a herd of pigs pour from an outbuilding into a fenced enclosure. The swine were responsible for the cacophony. Now I heard something similar. Although so faint it appeared to echo from a cave, I heard – or thought I heard – the sound of pigs coming from the shadow out there in the mist.

Maybe a herd of swine did roam out here? Maybe they moved together closely? So they appeared as that vast, yet indistinct shape? No, that just didn't seem possible. The shadow was too regular – too stream-lined to be a herd of animals. Come to that, the pigs would sink into the marsh and drown, wouldn't they? I must be hearing animals from a farm way off inland. No doubt such sounds could carry miles on this motionless air.

Shivering, I watched the shadow slip into reverse, then glide seaward again.

I walked, still staring back across my shoulder in the direction of the shadow, half-anticipating it would suddenly dash in my direction, which would surely—

Hell. A sharp point dug into the pit of my stomach.

I recoiled, half expecting to see the snout of a pig thrusting at my midriff. But, damnation, no … I'd found one of the white sticks simply by walking into one.

Right, I told myself. *Home.* And quickly. My walk through a night-time marsh now seemed like sheer, bloody lunacy. If I hadn't found this path again it would have taken a flip of a coin to decide whether I died of exposure out here, or if I wandered into quicksand never to be seen again.

With my painful rediscovery of the white markers it took just moments to retrace my way back home. I found myself rushing through the front door, eager to get that solid timber between me and the outside world – and that pig-laden shadow, I told myself, at a deeper, more personal level. With the door locked, I buzzed round, turning on lights in every room, lighting the gas fire, hitting the 'play' button on the CD to fill the house with a window-rattling Hendrix track. It wasn't long, I can tell you, before I'd got a tumbler of whisky in my hand.

Dear God, maybe this place is playing tricks on me. The marsh, the solitude, every shadow and distant sound … they're sending my brain into a high-revving frenzy. To try and deflect my runaway imagination from what roams or it imagines roams, outside, I've just spent an hour sending e-mails, checking out websites; then, with the music blasting and lights blazing like the whole house had turned incandescent, I read through the script notes I'd written a month ago. After that, I began to wonder if what I'd written had sown seeds that now sprouted so wildly inside my imagination.

I'd spent a day or so researching maritime folklore. Almost straight away I came across a page relating to ships' figureheads: '*The fate of the ship was inextricably bound with that of its figurehead. Equally, sailors believed that each ship possessed a soul, and that the figurehead was the embodiment of the ship's soul.*' Hell, what kind of soul would that ship out on the marsh possess, with such a ferocious-looking figurehead? Taking a slug of whisky, I shuffled the notes. The mythology of the sea was considerable. Fishermen and sailors had a whole arsenal of protective magic against the sometimes sinister forces of the ocean. Ships were built with a gold coin hidden on board for magical protection; ships were female, a tradition harking back to when ships were dedicated to pagan goddesses. Fishermen threw a coin into the sea when they sailed to pay for safe passage. There was a whole bunch of taboo words that couldn't be uttered when at sea. Salt, salmon, knives, cats, foxes, rabbits – none of these must ever be referred to by name. Salt was obliquely referred to as 'that white stuff'. A fisherman called salmon 'the gentleman' or 'the red fish'. Strangely, the most ill-omened animal that sailors feared to carry, or even name, were pigs. By tradition, pigs cannot only see the wind but they also have the power to call it up at hurricane force. With their cloven hoofs they are also associated with the Devil. Seafarers would never call a pig a pig; instead they had their own code. A pig would become a 'grumphie,' a 'curly tail,' or 'the Grecian'.

That's as far as I'm taking the diary tonight. I can as good as hear that malt whisky calling my name. Besides, I start reading about pigs and I start imagining I can hear the damn swine screaming out there on the marsh. It's probably only a night bird or two calling their mate, or whatever night birds call, and my hair-trigger imagination has done the rest.

Now for that whisky, that nerve-soothing, beautiful whisky. Good night.

December 5: A day full of writing and minor glitches. Keith e-mailed that the original choice of narrator for the series is demanding more money now he has 'starred' in a series of mobile phone ads. Blast his eyes. We're now on the trail of a new 'voice' for the show. A bit of good news: our oh-so meagre budget may be topped up a little with sponsorship from a mobile phone manufacturer – irony spotters please take note! Script two nearly complete. I've earned my glass of Scotch.

With the breeze springing up this afternoon, I enjoyed a stroll along the seaward path. Everywhere you walk the earth groans around you. The ground must be full of marsh gas. Even my 150 pounds is enough to displace gas pockets under the turf. Mental note: don't smoke cigars out on marsh in presence of highly inflammable methane. I took another gander at the shipwreck with the figurehead. Poking round in the turf with a stick, maybe hoping for a gold doubloon or two (at least enough for the steady-cam hire, Goddamnitt), I saw that the marsh grass had matted together a mass of bones. 'My God, the remains of the crew,' I gasped, with a juicy side-order of morbid glee. When I pulled out a few leg bones, however, I saw they were short (maybe ten inches in length) and thick as baseball bats. If human, the ship would have been crewed by unfeasibly stocky dwarves. Then I turned up a skull.

Pig. No doubt about it. They were all pig bones. Hundreds of them. A ship carrying a cargo of swine had foundered, I surmised. And here was the animals' grave.

Gales swept across the marsh nearly knocking me flat. After steadying myself with the upright spars, I took some photographs of Miss Nasty Drawers, the figurehead. (Click 'Archive' on the left of this page to view her evil physog; there's also a pic of the pig-bone tangle embedded in the bottom of the wreck.)

Just in. Another e-mail from Keith. Sponsorship from the phone company will run at $500 per episode. I get my steady-cam!

December 5. Long past midnight. Woke for something. What? I don't know. Noises like people screaming. Animals screaming? God knows. Mouth tastes like I've gargled with mule piss. You wake like that all hot, sweating, scared ... yeah, scared. Wondering if you've heard an intruder overturning stuff in the room downstairs. So, you run through the house yelling, '*I know you're here! I'm armed. I'll blow your head off!*' Yeah, I was armed all right. I'd armed myself with the first thing I got my hands on. An empty coffee cup.

And yeah, yeah, yeah ... all I found were the usual suspects: a blind tapping in a draught; airlocks knocking the heating pipes ... otherwise the house was empty. The winds had gone. The screaming had stopped. Back had come the fog, rolling right up to the windows to caress them with feathery fingers and wispy tentacles. Eat your heart out, Mr Lovecraft. The knees of the gods are exceedingly bony.

Now I'm wide awake. I can no more sleep than fly round the moon naked.

So, I sit and stare out of the window, here in my tower. The mist plays weird tricks. Thickening, changing shape. For a few seconds I saw what looked like the upper part of a ship's mast moving above a lake of fog. I could make out the crucifix shape of timbers gliding with just the eeriness you'd expect for a god-forsaken place like this.

Uh, God help me. There it goes again. I'm cold as dead bones – I sit here in shorts and T-shirt. I wish Sonia would come. I wish the sun were shining. I wish I could sleep. But I know wishes are worth squat. Here I am: a cold and lonely writer, looking out at what appears to be a ghost mast that glides toward me. The rest of the ghost ship is invisible, hidden by fog. Here come the ghost pirates (so says my imagination); here come ghost pirates to cut off my ears and make me dance the plank. But wait ... now ... here's a neat thing. Suppose I'm dreaming all this? I'm really asleep in bed. This is a dream. My God, it certainly *seems* unreal. If I wake up tomorrow, switch on the computer, open the file and find this text *isn't* here, then I'll exclaim, Wow. It really *was* a dream! Wasn't that weird?

But what if I open the diary file and find this entry? Me, talking about a weird cross-shaped mast that cuts through the mist.

What then?

December 6. I switch on. I open the file. It's here. A record (albeit slightly garbled) of what I saw last night. I re-read it. My verdict? I'm a city boy. This solitude is starting to tinker with my mind. I'm going to knuckle down to writing those scripts. Work exorcizes demons.

December 13. Pig Christ. Swine Christ. Porcine Saves. Honk your horn for Pig Jesus. Make way for the Pork Messiah. Hallelujah! Let Pig Jesus save your bacon. Damn it, I've burnt away half my hair. No eyebrows either. All that happened to me, and you know, I don't feel a thing!

December 15. It all happened on December 12 – my mind was pretty scrambled when I wrote the entry for the 13th. And, believe me; it took time, too, to get the computer working – those property repairs will have to wait. Anyway. Picture me sitting here at the computer on the 12th. The white mist returned as the sun set. Soon, out there in the dark, was a noise. A dirty great noise that didn't make sense. I pushed my snout (yeah, snout: nice one) – pushed my dirty, great snout to the glass, looked out into the mist, in the dirty, great darkness – apologies for repetition; my mind is still scrambled. All I could see was the wall that surrounds the yard. This sound comes *scrawww … scrawww … scrawww.* Imagine tree trunks being dragged across the ground and you've got the juice of it. *Scrawww….scrawww …*

I had to see what this was. Down I went to the kitchen, pulled on my boots and coat. Went outside. Cold – bitter, bitter cold went slicing through the coat into my bones. Frost dusted the ground. Slowly … tentatively as a sniper entering no man's land … I moved into the yard, with the light from the kitchen shining on me, making my shadow grow all big and orang-utan like in front of me on the wall.

Scrawww ... Scrawww ... scrawww. That scraping loud came louder ... louder. Was someone dragging a heavy object across the marsh? Because that's the mental image that went through my brain. Heavy blocks of stone dragged across grass. Maybe people were hauling away the old ship's timbers for firewood. But at this time? In thick mist? They could wander into quicksand to gloop-gloop out of sight forever.

I reached the gate in the wall. There lay my immediate neighbour the shipwreck – all broken spars and hauntingly evocative. Beyond, I could just make out the first couple of white posts marking the path. At either side of that, pools of muddy water. A skin of ice was beginning to form around the edges.

Now the *scrawww ... scrawww* came, to my ears anyway, like the aspiration of some huge creature.

Scrawww ... inhale.

Scrawwwwwww ... exhale.

I listened between the breaths, or whatever they were. Once more came the sound of pigs ... like they were squealing in high excitement in some sty far, far away.

Fascinated. Fatally fascinated. Like a moth homing in on searing flame, I stepped out of the yard into the marsh, telling myself I'd just take a looksee out there. I remembered the figurehead in the old ship a few hundred paces away. That thing must be bloody valuable. Maybe what I heard were rogues trying to pry the carving out of the mud? I took more steps into the freezing mist. My feet squelched on the rough sod. Bubbles of methane displaced by my body weight came fizzing up in the pools.

Scrawwww ... Scrawwwww....

And again, between that rasping, the squeal of pigs. It didn't add up. My dislike of being in the marsh at night played tug of war with curiosity. I took another ten paces in the direction of where the wreck with the figurehead lay. I could see nothing but grass and mud and mist. Not much of that, either. It probably wouldn't have helped a deal if I'd brought a flashlight, seeing as the murky vapour was so thick. I stood up straight to strain my eyes forward. No result. I couldn't even see the spars of the ship from here. And yet …

And yet the mist seemed to thin just a few feet above the ground. And maybe the sky above was clear allowing the moon to spread a little pale illumination on the upper layers of vapour. Because then I realized I could see the masts of the wreck. Or at least the upper part forming a cross shape.

No … that didn't make sense. I remembered the last time I saw the ship's masts they were lying flat on the ground. What were they doing upright again?

The sound of squealing pigs grew louder. Then something happened that stopped me dead. The mast moved. I watched as the upper timbers cut like a blade through the mist.

Ghost ship. The thought barrelled through my skull. But the timber looked solid, three-dimensional. Not phantom-like at all. Remains of ropes swung down from the cross member. Even in this paltry light I noticed that one side of the mast wore a black coating where it had once rested in the mud.

Someone has picked the mast out of the marsh. Now they are carrying it upright.

Sure. That was my logical deduction. But why would anyone want to do that? *How could they do that?* Those timbers'd weigh a ton or more.

Scrawwww …

Cutting like a blade, the timbers glided through the mist toward me. Frozen there, like a rabbit caught in headlights, I watched. My eyes going wide … wider, wider.

Because I now saw what carried the ship's mast. I stared, scalp prickling, blood running like ice water, my heartbeat hammering into overdrive, my breath detonating in airbursts of white vapour. I saw its coming. There, out in the marsh, shouldering the mast like it was a gigantic cross, a massive figure laboured to reach me. Its two pain-filled eyes locked on to mine.

You'd recognize the image. Anyone would. Christ on the Via

Dolorosa. Being whipped and degraded on His way to Golgotha, crucifixion, and luminous immortality. The images of Christ carrying the Cross haunt us from childhood. We've seen them thousands of times, from children's Bible stories, to paintings, to stained-glass windows, to films. Christ shouldering the huge wooden cross that is brutally heavy. Those soulful eyes full of pain. That upturned face, suffering yet noble.

This is what walked toward me. Only this figure was fully thirty feet tall. The mast from the shipwreck formed the cross. Old ropes from the rigging swung down to flick against the naked torso. I looked as each foot – a foot that must have been larger than me – crunched down into the mire. Mud rose in gouts between the toes. The ground sagged beneath the weight. Water filled the footprints to form new pools.

Scrawwww ... Scrawww....

The base of the mast scraped across marsh grass; its sheer weight cut a dark glistening furrow that soon, too, filled as water haemorrhaged through the membrane of mud. So that was the sound I'd heard. The scrape of the timber dragged by this monster that aped Christ.

Encased in a shell of super-tense muscle I could not move. I was a statue – one with living eyes that watched the figure approach. My stomach churned. My emotions flashed from awe, to revulsion and back to awe again.

The huge eyes held mine. The mouth was a huge open **O**. For whatever carried the cross was nothing more than a vessel of suffering. The naked skin flamed a vivid, living pink. I watched that pinkness flicker, brighten, change hue from delicate rose tints to blood red.

Closer. Closer. It toiled across the swamp toward me. It had a message. It needed my help. It *needed!* I sensed that. And I sensed it needed that *something* from me. Only me.

The Christ figure drew nearer. With a titanic effort it lifted one foot after another, as if exhausted. One foot after another crunched down into the swamp. Its sheer weight forced marsh gas to discharge from the earth all around it. Mud fountained around its ankles, spraying the pink flesh. That pink flesh in turn flickered as if lights played on it. Then I saw. The skin shifted. Twitched. Torso, chest and throat writhed. Arms and legs rippled, pulsed, squirmed.

I forced myself to stare harder through the gloom and the mist. Because at that moment I began to realize what it really was.

The hide of the Christ-shaped thing was hideous. What I was seeing was a compressed mass of pigs. Snouts, cloven hoofs, ears, tiny, hard pig eyes, porcine backs – they formed the body of something that resembled a giant man. A fat sow lying in its mouth, complete with suckling young, was its tongue. A jelly of swine foetuses formed this behemoth's glistening eyes.

The tragic face changed. An expression of vicious glee contorted the mouth into a snarl. Hefting the cross up on to its shoulder it began to run. The ground shook. The gigantic feet blurred as it raced toward me.

Spinning round, arms whirling out, I turned to run back to the house. A cry erupted from my throat. My eyes must have been wide, staring things that blazed pure, pure terror.

Straight away, I fell forward on to my outstretched hands. My legs wouldn't work. I tried to stand but shock had exploded my co-ordination. Again and again, I tried to get to my feet, but my limbs slithered uselessly away from me. In the end I had to move on all fours. All the time I heard the *scrawwww*! of the timber slicing through earth behind me.

Freezing mud squirted between my fingers as I crawled. Ahead were the lights of the house – blurry blocks of light. Panting, sobbing, I scrambled on, expecting to feel at any second a crushing blow on my back, as one of those huge feet mashed me into the dirt.

My God, my God, my God, the prayer blurted through my lips with gobs of spit. *My God, my God ... oh my God*!

The blow came. Not as I expected in my back, but to the top of my head. Dazed, I cried out knowing I'd die there and then on the marsh. I looked up ... I was no longer in the marsh. That blow was my head hitting the house door. I'd reached home in a wild, mindless fugue state. The collision shook me awake. I opened the door, crawled inside, then bolted it behind me.

Scrawwww ...

Still that sound. And then it changed. The cross wasn't being dragged across soft marsh but hard stone.

'The yard ... the yard... it's here....'

I wormed across the kitchen floor on my chest, hoping that if I stayed low it wouldn't see me. I'd barely reached the door to the hallway when I heard the crash. I turned to the blizzard of flying glass and saw the end of the cross come thrusting through the window. The timber slid through the shattered frame deep into the kitchen, knocking over the table, before slamming hard into the dresser, shattering plates. A second later the baulk of timber swung sideward at me. I hurled myself through the door into the hallway as it crashed hard against the doorframe bringing down plaster in a snowstorm.

I knew what it was doing. I knew it perfectly. Like a rat-catcher ramming a stick into a hole to dislodge the rodent, it was using the massive timbers to catch me.

With a burst of energy I raced upstairs to the top of the tower. There, in this very room, I could look out of the window directly into the pig monster's face that produced a counterfeit image of Christ. Now I could see the compressed animals that formed the flesh; squirming and calling in excited grunts and squeals. The tiny pig eyes were freckles in its face. A thousand open swine mouths, the monster's pores. Those eyes burned with murderous ferocity.

It still attacked the lower floors, driving the timber mast through window after window to find me. Stealthy now, I backed through the door. This much I knew: if I did nothing, if I tried to hide, it would find me. When it found me it would kill me.

As the creature continued its assault on the house, I scrambled downstairs to the hallway again. The force of the timber shaft being rammed through windows caused doors to burst open; paint flakes swirled down from ceilings; the house reverberated with crashes loud as thunder.

I remember two words beating to the rhythm of my racing heart: 'My God, my God, my God ...' I must have said it a hundred times, as I half fell down the steps into the basement, where I ransacked cupboards with the manic energy of a burglar on speed. What was I looking for? A weapon. Of sorts. But what, exactly, I didn't know. A shotgun, a harpoon, hand grenades ... yeah, as if. All I found were cobwebs, old crockery, paint cans, paintbrushes, newspapers, folded dustsheets, empty bottles. Nothing you could exactly call a weapon.

Meanwhile, I heard the excited squeals of the pig monster as it systematically destroyed the house with its titanic cross. Electric lights flickered. If I didn't act soon the power supply would be knocked out from a short as the swinging boom shattered light-fittings upstairs. Then what would be left for me? To sit weeping in the dark? Waiting for the thing to rip up the floors, and find me here?

No way. I pulled open drawers. Nothing but rusty hammers and screwdrivers. I reached the end of the drawers and started on the cupboards again. More paint cans. Bottles.

My eyes went back to the bottles. There, gleaming through the mist of paint dust streaming from the ceiling, I saw a bottle of brush cleaner. It was neat spirit in a delicate shade of blue. My mind seemed to orbit it like a satellite, gazing down on a planet of infinite promise. Yes ... that might do.

I lunged back for the dustsheets. Grabbing one, I tore strips from it, even using my teeth to get the tear going, then gagging on its accumulation of dust.

'Fire ... bring me fire!' I panted half-delirious with terror and adrenaline rush.

Unscrewing the top of the bottle, I worked a strip of the cotton fabric inside. Then I tied more strips round the neck. Gently ... or as gently as I could ... my hands were shaking like crazy ... I tipped the bottle up. With the fabric blocking the neck none of the blue spirit poured out, but it seeped into the strips of material. The smell of neat alcohol went spiking into my nostrils making me sneeze.

Bottle in hand, I ran upstairs, praying I wouldn't drop it. For it to go spinning out of my hands to smash on the floor would spell disaster. Utter disaster.

Lights flickered madly. High above me, the crunch of the timber cross smashed through doors. The pig monster grunted with a dark ferocity. It wanted me.

In the hallway hung my coat. I went through the pockets until – *eureka!* I pulled out my cigar lighter.

But now what? I had my makeshift incendiary bomb, the means to light it. But how to deliver it to its target? That monster was out there. It could crush me like a worm. I paused, listening to sounds of destruction. It appeared to be attacking the far side of the house now. If I exited by the kitchen door that would take me into the yard. It seemed so fixated on ramming that damn timber through the windows, trying to pin me with the thing, that it wouldn't notice me creeping round behind it.

But would my firebomb work? It had to! I reasoned like fury. Although man-shaped that thing consisted of pigs. Pigs were animals. Animals feared fire. Even if my bomb didn't kill it, it might drive it off in terror. That single thought drove me out the house and into the night once more. I paused in the yard. Still the destruction sounded like thunder. I heard the nerve-jangling squeal of swine in frenzy. Mist coiled around me. Out in the marsh, a dense wall of fog. Panting so hard my chest felt raw, I edged through the gate and on to the marsh path. Now I could look back to where the giant thrust the mast through my bedroom window. Again, I thought of the rat-catcher trying to dislodge his prey from a hole. What it planned to do if it found me God alone knew. The hundreds of pigs that formed its flesh writhed, so it looked as if its skin boiled. Breath spurting from their snouts formed a misty halo around the head and torso.

Now. The voice sang out inside my head. *Do it now before it sees you.*

I pulled the lighter from my pocket, spun the milled wheel. It flamed first time. I touched the little tongue of yellow to the spirit moistened rag. And it blazed brilliantly. Heat tingled my face. I looked from my firebomb to the pig monster. It had seen the fire suddenly spring from the darkness.

The lights of the house – those that still shone – revealed the monster head as it moved. I watched as that snout-face turned down toward me. I saw the eyes swimming with pig foetuses fix on me. They glared in cold fury.

It withdrew the cross from the window and raised it above its head in both hands. Now it had become a club to smash me to nothing.

My arm went back with the bottle and I hurled it. Or at least tried to.

The rush of spirit in the bottle must have dislodged the burning fabric. The cotton bung fell to the ground followed by a gush of spirit that burst into flame on contact. A wave of fire exploded up at me. I twisted away from it, feeling my face sting with the sudden heat. Now the bottle slipped from my hand to fall somewhere in the darkness.

The flames revealed me – weaponless – standing there as if in a spotlight. The pig monster leered; the great sow that was its tongue, slithered out between its lips to wetly slide from side-to-side. The thing was licking its lips. Hungry. Greedy.

Run. Where to? Running was useless. It could catch me in three giant strides.

It took one step toward me. Its foot that was larger than a man came down with crushing force fifteen paces from me. I found myself staring at the foot. Knowing it would descend on me next. I saw mud squirt between the toes. The weight of the creature ruptured the membrane of the swamp. Marsh gas bubbled around the foot. I even saw the stream of escaping gas zither through the coarse porcine hairs on its legs.

Marsh gas.

Methane.

Burn.

The words crunched in my skull. In one movement I'd scooped up the knot of still burning rags with my bare hand and hurled it at the gigantic foot.

The fiery cloth never touched the foot. It didn't need to. Inflammable methane gas greeted hungry flame.

I staggered backwards as the blast struck me. But still I watched, not taking my eyes away. No siree, not looking away for an instant, even though the tower of fire seared my eyes and melted my hair.

I watched as the pig monster stood in what resembled a Bunsen burner flame – a fifty foot jet of dazzling blue fire – tall, slender – tapering to a point at its very summit. The creature screamed with pain-driven fury; it raised the giant cross in one hand as if to smite me. That, too, now blazed. Flames rolled upward from it, driving away the fog.

The monster tried to step out of the inferno, but every movement of its hugely heavy body forced more marsh gas to vent from the ground. Gas that constantly fed the flame. Now it retreated back into the swamp, seemingly taking with it a column of fire, so it walked within its own aura of incandescence; one that melted its flesh into dripping gobs of hog fat. As it walked it left behind deep footprints in the earth that still burned with methane. I followed the fiery footprints, skirting pools of the burning gas. And all the time I heard the screams of the giant. Pain, frustration, anger. All these things and perhaps more seamlessly welded into an ear-stabbing sound.

In moments, it had reached the wreck of the ship where I'd found the figurehead. Still burning blue and yellow, it stood within the spars of the ship, then in one massive fist, it lifted the cross of burning timbers heavenward.

Then the pig monster screamed – a great bellowing roar that rolled into the distance. And just for a second I believed it roared in fury at its own dark god. An inattentive god that had turned away when the creature needed it most.

The roar came again. This time it sounded hollow. The cross disintegrated in a shower of embers. Moments later, the pig monster that so blasphemously aped Christ, joined it. Like a figure of burning straw, it fell in on itself with a loud hiss. There appeared to be nothing solid now. Merely a deluge of sparks that cascaded into what remained of the ship's hold.

Later ... as the flames died down ... a shadow poured from the ship. At first I thought it would be the same streamlined shadow I'd seen earlier. I was mistaken. This one was irregular in shape; it moved in a series of feeble jerks; its structure wobbled as if unstable. Then, like a mortally wounded beast, the shadow lurched seaward to vanish into the fog. Now I believe the shadow I'd seen in the days before, and the pig monster, were one and the same in a way I don't understand. But I do understand one thing: *I've beaten it. I've won. And I believe to the depths of my heart that the creature is never coming back – at least not in my life-time anyway. And that's good enough for me. As for ham salads, or roast pork dinners, or bacon sandwiches? Never ever again will so much as a morsel of pork ever pass my lips – not until Hell freezes over – so help me God!*

6

ONE MAN SHOW

A tribute to William Hope Hodgson (1877–1918),
and to his classic story *A Voice in the Night*

Faceless bureaucrats, draconian politicians, relentless dumbing down.
You've got to ask yourself:
'Where will it all end?'

IT WAS A dark, starless night …

Jay Cee and Dillon were annotating the script in the living-room when Connor heard the strange voice. He leaned across the sink to open the window. Here, they were on the first floor of a converted gatehouse deep in the heart of rural Kent. Connor had to push his head forward through the window opening before he could look down on to the roadway.

'Hello …' The voice came only faintly through the thick fog that shrouded the surrounding countryside. 'Hello, sir.'

'Hello yourself. Who's there?' Connor deliberately gave his voice a snappish quality – an indication of lurking short temper. The voice probably belonged to a kid who intended to hurl a vulgar comment. When the stranger didn't respond Connor added a brittle, 'What do you want?'

'I wonder if you could spare some food?'

'There's a supermarket down the road.' Again Connor tried to see the owner of the voice. He leaned so far forward the mixer tap dug into his chest.

'I can't go to the shop. It's not possible. If you could please spare something?'

'It's not my house. It's not up to me to—'

'Connor. We're leaving the TV sketches until we get signed contracts from the BBC. Jay Cee wants us to work on the opening of his stand-up. I thought he could start by talking about why he's touring with a One Man Show. We could even play around with the title. So, this is what I've got so far: Jay Cee nips on to the stage, he's doing that thing with his arms; he says, "My name's Jay Cee. Welcome to my One Man Show. I was going to theme it around indecent exposure. Instead of calling it a One Man Show you'd be sat there watching Man Show One." What do you think? Connor? What are you doing hanging out of the bloody window?'

'There's this guy.'

'At this time of night?'

'He wants food.'

'Is he drunk?'

'I don't know.'

'For God's sake, Connor, don't encourage him. Get your head back in here; we've got to finesse this intro.'

Jay Cee walked into the kitchen. He had a mass of frizzy hair that could only be described as a blond Afro. Despite not being a day over thirty he constantly smoked a pipe while he was at home. True to form, he sucked on the stem as he ambled in. He said, 'What do you reckon, Connor? One Man Show: pervert it to Man Show One?'

Connor leaned out as he stared into the fog-smeared darkness. Jay Cee was bemused.

'Why's Connor got his nut out the window ? Is he throwing up?'

Dillon shook his head. 'He says there's some nutter out there demanding supper.'

Connor drew his head back into the kitchen. 'I didn't say he was a nutter. It's a guy asking for food.'

Jay Cee puffed on his pipe. 'Who is he?'

'I don't know. I can't see him.'

'Ah, Mr Invisible.'

'What should I do?'

'Do?'

'It's your house, Jay Cee.'

'Take Mr Invisible some food out, I suppose.' Jay Cee pressed the embers in his pipe with his thumb as he added vaguely, 'Put stuff in a carrier bag; bread, pies, whatnot.'

Connor glanced back at his employer. On stage Jay Cee was a bundle of comic energy. He constantly changed voices, persona and gestured wildly. Off stage he was as reserved as an ageing university don.

Jay Cee squinted through the tobacco smoke to read the clock on the microwave. 'Show Biz is on at ten-thirty. I want to catch it; s'posed to be a mention of Split Your Sides with yours truly as host. So, go feed Mr Invisible, then we'll watch it.'

'If he's still there,' Dillon said. 'It's cold enough outside to freeze your cods off.'

Connor called down into the darkness. 'Hello? You still there?'

'It'd be a bit weird if he *wasn't* and he *still* answered you,' Dillon quipped.

The voice came back through the wall of pale vapour, 'If you could spare some food we'd be very grateful.'

'We?'

Jay Cee pointed vaguely with his pipe. 'Oh, it'll be that lot. There's some asylum seekers living in the woods. Hurry up, Connor. I'm on the box in ten momentoes.'

Connor leaned out into the cold air. 'OK,' he called to their night visitor. 'I'll bring it down. Come to the side door.'

'No ... please. I can't do that.'

'Just how am I going to give you the food, then?'

Dillon tugged the sleeve of Connor's fleece. 'What's he saying?'

'He can't come to the door.'

'Why ever not?'

'How should I know?'

'On in five,' Jay Cee reminded. 'I wonder if I should record it?'

The voice sailed out of the mist again. 'We do have a great need for the food. Only I can't come to the door. If you could be so gracious as to leave it by the side of the road?'

'Oh, all right.' Connor began to reckon it was a wind up after all, but with Jay Cee eyeballing the seconds scrolling by on the microwave clock he decided to grab the food then leave it at that. Quickly, he filled a carrier-bag with cold meat, cheese and a tub of prawn cocktail from the refrigerator, then added cans of meat, fish and fruit from the larder.

'How many is Mr Invisible feeding?' Dillon made a point of suggesting Connor was being over generous with their employer's food.

Jay Cee's mind was elsewhere. 'I could come on stage with the inflatable pig. That always gets a laugh.'

'I'll be right back,' Connor told them.

'We'll keep your seat warm. Chop, chop, laddie.' Dillon had turned sulky because Jay Cee hadn't picked up on the cue to criticize Connor over the large quantity of food. Then again, Dillon had been writing Jay Cee's scripts single-handed for three years. The guy hadn't been wildly enthusiastic when the comic hired a second writer to, 'you know, broaden my range', was how Jay Cee justified it.

Connor ran down the steps to the ground floor. With it being a converted gatehouse to a manor that no longer existed, the building was really a glorified archway. Its living quarters were on the first floor in the span above an arch, built in the heroic style of the Arc de Triomphe. Down here, the stairs led only to an entrance vestibule that was occupied by a pair of big green wellies. It occurred to Connor this might be a ploy by the Invisible out there in the fog to either hurl eggs at him, or, more soberingly, to whack him with a dirty great stick. Connor kept the security chain on the door when he opened it a couple of inches. When he was satisfied no one lurked nearby, eager to brain him, he slipped off the chain. The road ran immediately outside the gatehouse so it was simple enough to lean out through the doorway then set the yellow Netto carrier-bag down at the edge of that seemingly deserted byway. That done, he quickly closed then locked the door before nipping back upstairs. He discovered both Jay Cee and Dillon leaning out of the kitchen window by the dishwasher.

'We're waiting for Mr Invisible to show himself,' Jay Cee explained.

Dillon added, 'Jay Cee figures it might be the former host of Split Your Sides who's fallen on hard times.'

'Aye, aye, here he comes.' Jay Cee poked his blond head out of the window with his pipe clenched between his teeth. 'He can't be that potless, he's riding a push iron.'

Connor leaned over the sink so he could get a view of the road. Wraiths of mist drifted from the fields to blur the figure that approached. It pedalled an ancient bike so slowly it was as if the thing had almost rusted to a standstill.

'Is it just me,' Jay Cee asked, 'or is there something odd about him?'

The cyclist cranked the bike along at walking pace. Connor saw the shadow emerge from the mist. A pair of wheels supported a shapeless mound on the bicycle frame. A misshaped nodule where the head should be nodded to the rhythm of its legs that pumped the pedals. Connor had the impression of a pulpy, blobby fungus that, somehow, in a fit of random genius had learnt to ride a bike. With aching slowness it reached the gatehouse. When it was alongside the bag of groceries, the blob's shape deformed as a hand grasped the bag, picked it up, then the pulpy mass pedalled on down the road. The rounded lump began to nod slowly once more as it matched the rhythm of the pedalling feet.

A faint voice came from the nodding mass. 'Thank you, sir. You don't know how much I appreciate your gift. God bless you, sir.'

'Am I dreaming,' Dillon asked, 'or is that guy really riding a bike with a bed quilt cover over his entire body?'

Before the man disappeared into the mist Connor found himself committing the strange sight to memory. The man rode an old bike with flat tyres. Covering his head and his body, was a quilt cover from a child's bed. It was a bright blue one with a pink cartoon pony standing on a rainbow in the centre. Magic sparkles haloed the smiling animal as it pointed one dainty hoof.

'Bloody hell.' Dillon shook his head.

'And where did he get that bike?' Jay Cee asked. 'Have you ever seen a bike as old as that? It's unequivocally antediluvian.' He chuckled. 'Even Noah wouldn't be seen dead riding that.'

Dillon followed his boss's jokey cue, 'Hey, Connor? I hope you gave the guy food with a long sell-by date. It's going to take Duvet Cover Man at least a month to pedal home on that pile of crap.'

'*That* bike,' Jay Cee marvelled. 'Can you believe *that* bike?'

Connor shut the window. 'Jay Cee, it's nearly half past ten.'

Jay Cee glanced back at the clock. 'We better not have missed it. Connor, matey, grab some beers before you come through.'

Connor brought three bottles of San Miguel into the living-room. Dillon had taken his place at the right hand side of his boss on the sofa. After handing out the beers, Connor chose a rocking chair near the television. On the walls were masses of framed posters that declaimed Jay Cee would be performing in such-and-such a theatre. On the coffee table in front of the sofa pages of script had been marshalled into a running order.

Dillon talked in a soft voice to Jay Cee. What he was telling his boss Connor could only guess. Probably some of Connor's ideas that Dillon passed off as his own flashes of genius. The thing is, Jay Cee didn't pay any attention. His eyes were locked on the screen. He didn't want to miss a moment of himself.

However, the news anchorman and his co-newsreader were filling in before the next item. 'Bill, I don't know about you,' the anchorman was saying pleasantly, 'but when I started work on the news you had to apply a face powder. The lights back then were so bright that they'd flare right off your nose. These days you don't need powder anymore. A little tan goes a long way, though.'

A newsflash interrupted the discussion for a moment. 'Sorry to bring a change of mood here,' a female voice arrived by audio link. 'We have breaking news. We're getting reports that a hostel is ablaze in the Birmingham area. The building, used by asylum seekers, is reported to be extensively damaged. Police sources are stating that there has been heavy loss of life. I'll bring you more when I have it. Back to you at the studio, Kevin.'

'Thank you, Anna.' The anchorman turned to the man beside him.

'Bill, you know, one thing we learnt for those Monday morning shows, when you're still in weekend mode, and you're having a devil of a time waking up, is to pinch your cheeks. It gives you that rosy wide-awake look. How many newsreaders use face powder these days? Gosh, I don't know – I'm talking about the men here. Of course, the ladies have to—'

'Jesus Christ.' Jay Cee looked outraged. 'Just listen to these guys prattle on. Can you believe it? Show Biz should have started at ten-thirty. It's now almost twenty to.'

Dillon started to say something, but the long-awaited entertainment segment burst on screen with animated searchlights probing the sky over a glittering title: *SHOW BIZ EXTRA*. Jay Cee sighed with pleasure as he saw his face appear in close up.

The man kept his eyes on the television as he said, 'They're showing the old Comic Relief clip. Not bad. It still holds up well.'

'Do you remember,' Dillon laughed, 'I spent all day writing the script then my computer crashed? I had to redo the whole thing in long hand.'

Jay Cee chuckled. 'Just after this sketch they wanted me and the guy dressed as Hitler to fall into the vat of baked beans. Wait … watch this. It's great. I pretended to fall in, but I pushed Hitler into the poop-adoop instead. Oh … they're not showing that. The bastards. It's the funniest bit.'

The item continued describing Jay Cee's career, then speculated about his potential in Split Your Sides when it returned in the New Year. When *Show Biz Extra* moved on to interview the winner of a reality game show Jay Cee showed no inclination to return to work on the script. Instead, he reminisced with Dillon on their shenanigans in the Comic Relief green room.

With them chuckling between themselves Connor knew he was excluded from their conversation – after all, he wasn't at the after show party, which, by Dillon's account, was the best thing since God Almighty created the heavens and the earth; he sidled into the kitchen to make coffee. Work on the script might continue late into the night.

As he filled the kettle at the kitchen sink a voice ghosted through the night air. 'Sir? Sir? They've asked me to thank you for the food. You don't know how much it means to them.'

Connor realized the cyclist, who draped himself in the child's duvet quilt cover, must be able to see him when he'd returned to the kitchen.

'We are grateful, sir. We're going to remember you in our prayers tonight.'

Connor pushed open the window. The fog was as thick as ever. He couldn't see the man. Come to that, visibility was so poor he could barely see the road.

'Hello? Can you hear me?' He called out through the window. It sounded muted by the veils of mist that swarmed in from the dark countryside.

'I hear you, sir.'

'Was there enough food for you all?'

'We'll have a good meal tonight, thank you, sir.'

'What about tomorrow?'

'I'll go out, and God willing, I'll find something to eat.'

'Why don't you show yourself?'

'I can't do that.'

'Why?'

'There's no need to trouble you with that, sir. Thank you for the food. We were desperate.'

'Wait a minute. I'll bring some more of the canned meat down. There's plenty here.'

'No, you mustn't, sir.'

'Why not?'

'I've been out for too long. I must return to the others.'

'No, wait.'

'We are grateful sir. Good night, and bless you.'

Once more the figure approached on the bicycle. A nodding pulpy shape that pedalled laboriously along the road. The bed linen covered the man from head to knee. Connor saw the cartoon animal on the man's back; it playfully tossed its head, the sparkly mane flowing in make-believe breeze.

Connor called down, 'I'll fetch you more food for tomorrow.'

The figure didn't reply. It merely pedalled the ancient machine along the road. The mist began to wrap around it.

'Wait!'

The swathed cyclist didn't stop. Connor ran to the drawer, dragged out another of the bright yellow carrier-bags then stuffed it with cans of Irish Stew from the larder. When he'd done, he darted downstairs to the door. This time he didn't faff around with the security chain. After he opened door with another shout of 'Wait. I've got you some more cans,' he tugged on the green Wellington boots; the carrier-bag full of cans clanked as he did so. A moment later he ran out into the misty night. The cyclist was slow. Connor recalled the man's direction. It would be easy to follow. Connor loped along the road into the misty night; his breath gusted white in the cold air; the cans jiggled in the bag. Behind him the gatehouse, with its windows glaring a diffuse yellow, blurred into invisibility.

'Wait … just wait a minute,' he called.

The figure had disappeared into the fog. Connor followed resolutely. For some reason he knew he had to see what kind of man concealed his identity beneath a cartoon cover.

Connor jogged after the cyclist. It should have only taken moments to catch up; the man had been pedalling the ancient machine so slowly. Connor, however, wasn't familiar with the landscape around Jay Cee's rural retreat. Soon he found the road began to run down an incline. Although Connor did glimpse the mystery cyclist, he found he wasn't gaining on him. The indistinct blob that was the man's head beneath the fabric still nodded, but clearly he was moving much faster than before.

Cans of stew clunked in Connor's carrier-bag but not loud enough to catch the man's attention. Come to that, he didn't appear to be aware that Connor was following him at all. Just as Connor decided to call out he told himself, *No, why don't you just follow? See these refugees for your-self. Find out how they live.* Maybe it was his old journalistic experience reasserting itself? He sniffed a news story here: TWENTY-FIRST CENTURY

CASTAWAYS MAROONED IN ENGLAND'S GREEN AND PLEASANT LAND. That was good enough for starters. He could fine-tune the title when he had his copy. There should be good, hard cash to be earned here. He followed the cyclist more discreetly now. Carefully, he hugged the bag of cans to his chest so they wouldn't rattle and give him away. *OK, Connor, what if these asylum seekers turn nasty? Come on, that's hardly likely, is it? I've given them food. Now I'm bringing more. So they're hardly likely to rip me to pieces, are they?*

Connor pushed on along the narrow country lane. Even though darkness and fog rendered the surrounding countryside nigh-on invisible, he could just make out the dark barrier of the hedges flanking the road. Every so often, he'd pass a tree that emerged from the mist to loom over him with giant limbs outstretched as if to prevent him continuing. When an especially formidable tree materialized from the darkness to reach out, with a pair of branches that resembled massive arms, he recalled a verse from Virgil: -

> *Who are you*
> *In dark armour, haunting our rivers?*
> *Speak from where you are! Stop there! Say why you come!*
> *This is the region of Shades, of Phantoms, and Sleep,*
> *And drowsy, eternal night.*

For a second, Connor imagined the gigantic man-shaped growth of timber lunging at him with those titanic limbs. Alone, apart from the plod-plod of his rubber-booted feet, he couldn't see any other houses or vehicles. For all the world, it seemed as if he'd wandered into some desolate borderland between the world of humanity and the world of night and fog. Jay Cee and Dillon would be wondering where he'd vanished. Dillon would add a snide comment to suggest his fellow writer was work-shy. Oddly, Connor didn't give a fig about that. All that mattered now was to follow the cyclist back to his camp.

Connor nearly missed it. He'd already jogged by the end of a track with his cargo of canned stew when he realized that the man must have turned off the road. Quickly, he returned to the junction of the dirt track. Fifty paces away, the man still managed to pedal along the ruts. He'd pulled back the duvet cover that had formed his hood. The darkness and the mist, however, still made it impossible to see much apart from an indistinct head-shape.

Must be nearly here, Connor told himself. Panting hard now, he jogged determinedly along the track. From what he could glimpse it crossed a ploughed field to a copse. 'Coming ready or not,' he murmured. The cyclist pedalled into the midst of the trees where a camp-fire revealed itself as a smudge of yellow. *Dear God, how can people live out here in November? It's freezing. Even if they've enough to eat they must be half dead from exposure. This isn't camping, it's murder.*

Connor found twenty or so men, women and children huddled around the fire in the clearing. They wore sacks draped across their shoulders in an attempt to keep out the cold. A pot simmered on the fire. With the scent of woodsmoke was the savoury aroma of gravy.

The moment he stepped through the bushes into the firelight he knew that there was something wrong with their faces. The instant the group saw Connor a howl of panic burst from the camp. A number of them scrambled away into the shadows. Others dragged their makeshift shawls of sackcloth from their shoulders to hood it over their heads so that faces were hidden. Connor saw the man with the pony duvet cover do the same, so his head, face and entire upper half of his body were swathed in blue cotton.

Connor stopped dead. The firelight had revealed enough detail to turn his stomach. Even though every single head was now covered, the details of the faces had seared themselves into his memory. Fronts of heads weren't flat but protruded like snouts. Prominent noses ended in cavernous nostrils. The mouths possessed thick, muscular lips that were somehow nauseatingly mobile – prehensile lips that would allow their owners to grip food if they chose not to use their hands. Jaws were heavy; they had straps of strong muscle running beneath the skin, while the eyes of the people – *ha, people!* – were unusually large. Even when he closed his own eyes for a moment, the image returned to him of the cluster of faces around the fire, staring back at him in shock; their huge almond-shaped eyes glistening darkly in the firelight. Dear God, there was a beast-like quality to those faces. Large circular nostrils, prominent noses, the big teeth, those mouths drawn forward so they produced a jaw that thrust out from the skull.

The man under the duvet cover cried out as if in pain. 'I asked you not to come close to me! I tried to keep my distance from you! Now you've followed me here!'

'Did he see us?' A woman's voice filtered through the piece of sacking she held over her face. 'Did he get a proper look?'

'Yes, I did,' Connor replied. His heart thumped hard with shock. 'I didn't mean to distress you. I followed your friend because I wanted to help.'

'Help us?' echoed the woman in astonishment. 'But we came here to help *you.*'

'Pardon?' Connor echoed. 'Help me?'

'Help all of you,' the cyclist added. 'We believed it was the godly thing to do, but you can see what's happened to us. We're forced to survive out here in this wood.'

Connor shook his head in confusion. 'Survive out here? You make it sound as if you've been marooned? Shipwrecked?'

'As good as. For a while we stayed in one of the refugee hostels in London, but we soon learnt that the hostels are burnt before long. Many lives were lost. Some of us, who managed to escape, talked about fire exits being nailed shut.'

'Surely, you're not suggesting—'

'Murder?' He took a deep breath. 'Sir, now you are here I should explain the situation. Come closer to the fire. Please sit down ... but, I beg, don't attempt to pull away the veils.'

'You have my word.' Connor realized his voice was faint with surprise at this strange encounter. When he moved forward those nearest to him shuffled swiftly away. By the time he sat in front of the fire he was alone at one side of it, the refugees kept safely at the other. Some of their number who had fled when he'd blundered through the bushes returned, although two or three hung back in the shadows, reluctant to brave his proximity. Connor mentally replayed some of the sentences they'd spoken. Clearly, they were too frightened to remain in the refugee hostels because they believed (surely wrongly?) that the buildings were little more than execution chambers. Now they'd found themselves scratching an existence here in the wood deep in the middle of nowhere. In their eyes (and what strange shaped eyes!) they saw themselves as castaways. OK, he could get his head round that. But what was it the woman said? ... *we came here to help you.* What did she mean by that? Surely, it couldn't be the result of a poor grasp of English. They appeared to speak it perfectly with only a slight lilt to colour it. Possibly Asian accents? He wasn't so sure. But their faces ... what had happened to them? Hell, it was a catastrophic transformation for sure.

The cyclist had composed his thoughts. In a calm, understated way he began to speak from beneath his vivid cowl. 'Six months ago we travelled to England from the East. Reports had been reaching us that were of concern. When we saw the photographs and the films, we realized that you in the West were in serious trouble.'

'The West's always in trouble for something,' Connor said bemused. 'What kind of trouble?'

'You have changed.'

Connor grinned. 'You mean, we don't remember to send a card on your birthday? Or take you out to dinner on your anniversary?'

'You've identified one of the problems. For one, you people don't take the rest of the world seriously anymore. No matter how profound our question, it will be greeted with a flippant response. Grievous events outside Western nations receive scant attention; your news reports relating to great disaster are presented in such a shallow way that they trivialize calamity. Invariably, earthquakes and famines become little more than vehicles for your newsreaders' vanity.'

'Well, that's told us. But what are you going to do about it?'

'We did what we could.' The calm voice continued from beneath the cowl. The man spoke like a doctor taking care to describe a patient's malady. 'We are a deputation sent to explain what has befallen you.'

'How can you do this from the middle of a wood?'

'We underestimated the severity of your condition. First, we were refused visas to visit your country. So we made our way here secretly. We crept by border crossings, then, when we reached the English Channel, we gave a driver all our valuables to smuggle us through Customs in the back of his truck. When we tried to visit your Prime Minister in order to voice our concerns we were sent to a hostel.'

'You're not telling me a pork pie here?' Connor began to see through the man's argument.

'Pardon? Sir, I don't understand the meaning of—'

'Pork pie. Lie. You're not telling me a lie?'

'No, that would be ungodly. We never lie.'

The people, gathered around the fire, stirred beneath their sacks at Connor's question. They were clearly shocked by his implication they weren't telling the truth.

'Let me get this straight,' Connor said. 'You've come thousands of miles to help us. But I find it strange you'd bring your children, too, if this really is a mission of mercy. It all smacks of you arriving in the hope of being given a nice council maisonette and cash handouts.'

'We brought our children because they are part of our evidence that all is not right with you in the West.'

'So it's not down to the two hundred quid a week income support and free school dinners?'

'We are saddened that you accuse us of being parasites.'

Connor pulled a branch from a pile of wood then dropped it on to the fire. Sparks gushed into the night sky. 'OK, let's cut to the chase here, guys. You talk of evidence that something untoward has happened to all us good folk in the West: exactly what is your evidence?'

'This.' His hands came up to grip the fabric of the child's duvet cover. He plucked it from his face. Connor flinched. Hell's bells, so it wasn't a trick of the light. The cyclist did possess a snout. In the firelight, huge almond eyes held his. Then Connor noticed movement. He glanced round as others sitting near the fire raised the sacking from their faces. Men, women, children – they all had the same kind of exaggerated features. Everywhere, muscular lips curled back to reveal over-large teeth that made Connor think of knife blades. All those dark, almond-shaped eyes fixed on him ... He shuddered.

'In God's name,' he breathed, 'what happened to you?'

'That's just it,' the cyclist told him. 'Nothing happened to us. *It* happened to you.'

'What the hell do you mean?'

'We've noticed over the last few years that the faces of Western people have been undergoing a transformation.'

'You believe that? *Really, genuinely believe that?*' Despite the stomach-churning appearance of the faces, Connor laughed.

'See for yourself. Study photographs of your great grandparents. Put them alongside photographs of yourself now. Compare them.'

'That's just crazy.'

'Really. How do you see us?'

'Well ... I don't want to be rude, guys, but you're not going to win any beauty pageants.'

A wounded expression flickered across the grotesque visage of a woman sitting closest to him. As her eyes glistened she shook her head. 'You've not noticed what's become of your own faces because slowly, year by year, they have changed.'

'Look.' Connor stood up. The heat from the blazing logs made him giddy. Probably that and being in the presence of this assembly of monsters. 'You're well meaning. I even think you genuinely believe what you've just told me: that you're here to help us in the West see what we've become. But let me tell you the truth. It's you that are ... facially challenged ... uhm, a more sensitive description might be that you have all developed distinctive features. Only you've been isolated for so long that you perceive how you look is normal – the prominent sn— noses. The heavy jaws and large – very generously proportioned eyes. It's like the pygmies in Africa; they consider themselves to have a normal stature, while everyone else is a freakish giant. There's a tribe of Inuit Indians who believe they're the only bona fide human beings in the world; the rest of humanity, they claim, aren't the real McCoy; they're a kind of subspecies plonked on Earth to make the numbers up. You follow me?'

'We are listening to what you are telling us, sir.'

'Then you understand that, while you believe you are normal in the physog department. Heck, to each other you're beautiful. I applaud that. Good for you. But do you want to know the truth? You'd be judged to be freaks in the West.' He gestured at the surrounding trees. 'That's why you're stranded out here in the middle of nowhere. You understand what I'm saying?'

'We do,' replied the cyclist. 'We're not the only victims of your media's relentless dumbing down.' He nodded to an old man sat beside him who opened a leather satchel. 'We are uncontaminated by the vision of yourselves promulgated by your television.' With a nod of thanks he took an antique book from the old man. 'Maybe these images will change your mind.'

'What's this? An album of the local beauty pageant?'

'Your humour is flippant, sir. That is your defence against accepting the truth. It is the same device employed by your newsreaders, isn't that so?'

'OK, show me the book, but it's late. I'm going home soon.' Cold, damp, a camp-fire tended by the freak troupe? *I want out.*

'Of course, but come closer to the fire so you can see the photographs.'

Connor crouched beside the cyclist. Woodsmoke masked what Connor suspected would be an interesting whiffy body odour. Thank heaven for small mercies. In the golden light that flickered across the pages of the open book Connor saw photographs of men and women. And, ye Gods, there was the same parade of snouts, big eyes, heavy jaws, prominent eye ridges and fleshy ears.

Connor sighed, 'And your point is?'

'The point is, sir, where do you think these people in the photographs come from?'

Connor grinned. 'On the face of it, from your neck of the woods. It's as plain as the nose on your face.'

'Your flippant response is indeed your blindfold.'

'You don't say.'

'These are photographs of travellers from your country. They span a period from the late nineteenth century to the early twentieth. Sir, do you see now?'

'You mean my ancestors looked like that? *Like you*! And it's us here in the West who've changed?'

'Yes.'

'Jesus H. Christ, man. Don't you think we would have noticed?'

'It's been a gradual change.'

'Even if that's the case, *which it is not*, what caused the change?'

'Surely I don't have to tell you?'

'So, why don't we look like you lot anymore?' Connor's voice rose. 'Is it radiation from mobile phones? Artificial preservatives in our microwave curries? Pollution in our air?'

'It's the thoughts in your heads.'

'Pardon me?'

'Your artists portray oafs with a vacant, wide-eyed expression. Thugs have brutish faces. So if minds habitually trivialize important events in societies beyond their own....'

'So, you're saying our minds have mangled our faces? That our dumbing-down has given the old bow-brace a re-model?'

'We came to your country to warn you. God willing, it's not too late.'

'Late? Late! It's after midnight. Christ, that's how *late* it is, you bunch of idiots.' Connor stood up. 'It's time I was getting home. Just don't go cracking any good mirrors, hey, guys?'

Some of the group were insulted. Annoyed voices rippled along the line of seated men and women. However, the cyclist held up his hand. 'Don't be angry with our guest. He's frightened.'

'Frightened? You've got to be joking. Hell, you people fell out of the ugly tree, you hit every branch on the way down, then climbed back up for more.'

'Sir—'

'No, don't get up. I'll see myself out of your lovely home.'

'It is late, sir. And I apologize if we have distressed you.'

'Forget it. I know I will.' Connor walked away. He seethed with anger. '*Ciao*, my dears!' As he passed a tree he noticed the old bicycle propped up against the trunk. 'Hey, I don't care for the walk back. Mind if I borrow the old push iron? Cheers!' Without waiting for consent he gripped the handlebars and began wheeling it through the fallen leaves.

The man called out in that gentle voice. 'Thank you for the food, sir. We appreciate your kindness.'

Muttering to himself, angry at having his time wasted by the bunch of oddball refugees, Connor shoved the bike as far as the dirt track then he climbed on the seat. As he pedalled along, he realized the fog had cleared. Above him, a brilliant full moon shone down to light his way. For the first time he noticed that the bike possessed a mirror. It was attached to the handlebars by a slender metal stalk. As he rode, he saw his face reflected in the mirror. Moonlight bathed his skin.

Of course, it's all a question of comparison. Connor recalled the assembly of freakish faces with their snouts, heavy jaws and huge eyes. Even so, as he searched his own face in the reflection, an alarm bell sounded in the back of his head. Was his face really so bland and featureless? Were his eyes really that small? A pair of tiny blue beads, each one set in a shallow dimple in his skin. Why hadn't he noticed the way his jaw receded so much? Now it appeared so weak. His mouth resembled a pair of soft pink rose petals, his teeth were tiny slivers of mother-of-pearl. While his nose swelled from his otherwise wide, flat face like a pimple. Was it really the case that the entire visage was as characterless as a near-blank canvas?

As he pedalled along the road, with the moonlight piercing the last of the mist like a searchlight, he suddenly saw himself as the others around the fire saw him. There he was, a figure pumping slowly at the pedals. He saw his head as an almost featureless balloon set on a pair of shoulders. The head that would be completely faceless in a decade or two – the fate in store for the rest of his kind – lifted up and down, to the measured rhythm of his pumping feet, as he went nodding into the night.

7

POE, LOVECRAFT, JACKSON

Exercises for the apprentice dreamer. Prior to bed: from your imagination construct a house. Furnish it. Occupy it with people you know, or know of. Now, sleep....

WHY THE HOUSE was so dark soon became obvious. When I opened the door I saw that the building had sunk underground. Immediately beyond the door, a wall of brown dirt. Crisscrossing it, tree roots. These were the colour of milk. A tad disturbingly they resembled octopus tentacles. I closed the door. The view from the kitchen windows revealed the same 'non' view of soil pressing against the glass. The house lay as deeply buried as a freshly planted coffin in a cemetery.

I went to find the house's occupants. I found Poe in a book-lined study. He wore a velvet coat in dull bottle-green. Both lapels and front part of it were stained, while loose thread dangled from the cuffs. A three-cornered tear picturesquely marked out an elbow where the coat's tragic owner had fallen, perhaps, or been damaged during an assault by thugs. By candlelight, he wrote on loose leaves of paper with explosive speed. His eyes would narrow, then bulge wide-open. I don't know if his eyesight was so bad he was struggling to focus, or whether it was a mad passion that gripped him. He wrote with a quill pen that scraped across the page. Raven claws scratching at the door of the tomb. A pleasing detail.

'Mr Poe?' I said.

His eyes bulged as he stared at his script with its jagged peaks of text.

'Mr Edgar Allan Poe.'

Furiously he drove the nib across the paper. I noticed his fingernails had been gnawed until they'd bled. Then he began to read what he'd written, his voice rapid, breathless sounding. 'For the most wild yet most homely narrative which I am about to pen, I neither expect nor solicit belief. Mad indeed would I be to expect it ... Yet, mad am I not – and surely do I not dream.' He stopped reading with a twitchy, 'Yes?'

He'd noticed me?

'Mr Poe?' I saw that there was incredible tension in his body. His shoulders were hunched. His hands quivered. He didn't turn to look at me but locked eyes on the paper instead. 'Yes. What is it?'

'I'm sorry to interrupt.' I smiled, pleased by my success. 'But I thought you should know: I am dreaming.'

'Oh?'

'More importantly, I know I am dreaming. I have intentionally dreamt about you in this house. Although for some reason my unconscious has insisted on burying the house underground.'

'You dream about me, sir?'

'Yes. But don't let me stop you writing.'

'Then what I am writing is dream nonsense. There is no point.' He spoke so forcefully saliva sprayed from beneath his thick moustache. 'Then I will not be able to sell this to my publisher.' Violently, he balled his fist before pounding it down on the desk. His face turned a fierce crimson; his eyes bulged even further. 'This I can not sell, so I will have neither money for food or rent.'

'If you are in my dream then there's no need to worry about money. Food and rent are immaterial.'

'I wish I were in your dream, sir. Truly, I wish it so.' From somewhere at his side his shaking hand found a brown bottle. Wine? Whisky? Gin? Laudanum? My dream lacked the precise detail. Moreover, I lacked a sense of smell for the moment. Nevertheless, my dream Poe tugged out the cork then drank ... a hard slug that had the Adam's apple bobbing above the tightly knotted cravat. A mighty shudder ran through his frail body as the liquid splashed into his stomach.

He didn't look at me now. When he spoke he seemed to be talking to himself. 'If I was but a dream, I would not be compelled to drink this poison. For when I don't drink my hands shake, my brain is on fire. I weep and I don't know why. Now I drink and talk to my own imaginings when I should be writing.'

'Mr Poe. I am not your ... "imagining". I am the one who is dreaming you.'

The man in his green velvet coat, with its worn elbows and stained lapels, made a sound that he tried hard to catch in the back of his throat. If I wasn't mistaken he was near to breaking down. Closing his eyes tight, he took a deep breath, then he opened them, and without looking in my direction, started writing again with the quill. The nib flew across the paper with a desperate urgency.

'If only I could dream you up a bag of gold.' Even in my dream the expression of misery on my literary hero's face tugged my heart. He heard my words. I know he did, his thin, undernourished body flinched as I said the word 'gold'. I thought of adding a few complimentary words about his work, only the grief writ large on his face decided me against it. Silently, I backed out of the room.

I knew the layout of my dream house. From an elegant hallway adorned with a bust of Pallas (of course!), complemented by a painting of a raven above it, I climbed a curving sweep of stairs to the next floor. The walls here bore murals of sea creatures that were some mutant mix of naked men and women with gills. The beasts' lower halves subdivided into masses of moistly pink tentacles. That was the instant that I gained my sense of smell. For those images were powerfully reinforced with a distinct odour of raw fish. Nicely Eldritch. The next door I slipped through boasted book-covered walls. On one table stood African juju dolls, carved wooden primitives with white painted staring eyes. Looming above them, a statue of the multi-armed Kali. A ruddy light shone from a tinted lantern set on an antique bureau in the corner.

The tall, thin man with the oddly erect stance gazed out of the window – a window that revealed the press of soil – my dream house remained staunchly subterranean. As I imagined, he was in his early thirties with short black hair that had been oiled down flat to his head.

He wore a deep crimson smoking jacket of quilted silk, clearly to make himself appear Victorian, but plainly he was not.

'Mr Lovecraft?'

He turned from the window. 'At last! I've been expecting you.' There was a moment of hesitation I attributed to shyness, then he crossed the floor, his hand outstretched, long quivering fingers slightly splayed. Good fingernails, I told myself. He takes care of them,

'Delighted to meet you, Mr...?'

'Bennett.'

'Mr Bennett. Please come closer to the window... but not too close. As you know from my letters, extraordinary events have been unfolding here.'

'Your letters?'

'Yes, for a while I didn't think they were reaching you as I received no reply. After all, I didn't know your name. I had to rely on simply addressing them to the Professor of Palaeontology, Miskatonic University. But thank heavens you've come now.'

'Ah. Perhaps there's something you should know about that.'

A nervous energy fuelled Lovecraft's long limbs. He paced the room, explaining why he'd *sent* for me. 'I rented this house on the cliff-top to work in peace. I am in the process of composing a vast work that incorporates a mythology – mythos, I term it – that I have invented. Hence this lonely house that is fully one hour's walk to the nearest village. But this is perfect for my needs. Solitude. Inspiring walks on the cliff-top where I can gaze upon one hundred-ton waves dashing themselves to pieces on the rocks. At sunset, gulls glide out from this strange headland with its tangle of bushes and ugly trees. And the birds fly across the sea toward the setting sun that rests like a majestic dome of fire on the horizon. Yet for all the world that hemisphere of the sun looks like a golden city there. The gulls migrate toward it as if that – *not this!* – is their true home.' His eyes locked on me. 'How ill-mannered I am. You must be tired after your journey here. Aren't those twisting lanes infernal things? More like the tracks through a madman's mind.' His laugh was shrill. 'Sit down, please. I have milk and cake. I have to confess I consume nothing else, so I can not offer you liquor.'

'No, thank you. Besides, there isn't enough time.'

'No time? How right you are. How right you are!' His eyes grew large. 'Don't you sense it? Pressing ever closer. You feel it, don't you? Pressing so forcefully at the membrane that separates our world from its own domain. Soon it will break through ... then death itself will be the only true escape for anyone unfortunate to inhabit this godforsaken wilderness.'

'Mr Lovecraft, your letters ...'

'Yes?'

'Uhm, you ...' My dream didn't contain any letters. That's the beautiful unpredictable nature of dreaming. So – letters? I hazarded a guess. 'You described an invasive force from another dimension.'

'Yes! Don't you see for yourself? Look to the window, man ... *the window.*'

I moved toward the window. There was an aspect about the darkness beyond the glass that made me uneasy now. I had taken the featureless mass to be the soil I'd seen before, now there was a shifting quality to it. A swirling. A suggestion of mass in motion.

Lovecraft stared out through the glass, his face mingling awe with horror. 'It started within days of my arrival. I noticed that the tides rose higher each day. Yesterday, waves broke over the lip of the cliff. This morning I awoke to find the house submerged ... I know, I know. Impossible. But, Mr Bennett, see for yourself.'

I looked out into the swirling mass of water that was black as the deepest shadow. My unconscious had generated a fabulous dream. So real. I could feel the cold of the ocean through the glass panes. My breath even misted it when I drew close.

'Mr Bennett, there are forces at work here beyond comprehension. Why has the tide risen so far? Why doesn't the ocean break through? Why aren't we drowned? And' – he pointed – 'what, exactly, is *that* on the other side of the glass?'

I looked out to see a shape swimming toward us. It was pale, undulating, drawing closer and closer, as if it were a man coming to peer through the sides of an aquarium at two little creatures standing there. A face began to emerge from the darkness; two huge eyes, an open mouth. Ice surged through my blood. My heart hammered. I froze, dreading the moment the underwater face resolved itself.

'Don't stand too close to the window,' Lovecraft warned. 'When I saw it this morning ... I can't begin to describe the horror ... I thought I'd go mad. It was beyond words. Awful ... awful.'

Panic crashed my senses. Seeing smell. Hearing colours. Tasting sound. Something inside my head grew until it was bigger than the world. Impossible. Mad. Nightmarish. I know, but that's the only way I can describe this agonizing sensation of my mind and body being invaded by a veritable beast of an emotion that had the power to scramble my thoughts so.

The door loomed at me. I grabbed the handle, dragged it open.

Lovecraft called out to me from the room. 'Please, Professor, we must face this together!'

Then the door slammed shut behind me. I stood on the landing. I had to fight for breath. Perspiration soaked my neck until my collar prickled so uncomfortably that I had to rip it open. I glanced at the door to Lovecraft's room. It remained closed. There was no sound now. For five minutes – five dream minutes, at least, I stayed perfectly still, catching my breath, waiting for my heart to stop its furious hammering. When, at last, I felt better I climbed the next set of stairs. This led to an oak-panelled landing with a dark-brown door. An aspidistra shot green, leathery leaves from a bright pink pot. I opened the door.

A woman sat at a typewriter. She wore large glasses – the same kind that make you think of wise old owls. She wore a woollen skirt and jacket in a dog tooth pattern. Her fingers hit the keys with a powerful *clack-clack-clackety-clack*. The elegant room was simply furnished with straight-backed chairs lining the four walls. A polished rosewood table, bearing the typewriter, stood in the room's centre. The woman sat on one of the straight-backed chairs that she'd moved from the far wall. A grey light from the window illuminated the room in a way that left the place lacking colour, almost monochrome.

'Mrs Shirley Jackson.'

'Hmmm … yes?' Dreamily, she paused typing, her eyes magnified by the lenses. 'Have you come to take me to the dentist?'

'Dentist?' What a curious detail. Ah, the power of dreams. 'No, I've simply come to chat with you.'

'Then do come in.' She peered back at the sheet of paper in the typewriter for a second. She hit another key with a forceful *clack*! 'Period.'

'A new novel, Mrs Jackson?'

'Short story. I don't want to start a new novel in case I'm called away to see the dentist. But then he has kept me waiting rather a while.' She glanced across at me. 'Do sit down, dear, otherwise you'll give me a stiff neck peering up at such a tall young man.' She touched the neatly stacked manuscript on the desk beside the typewriter. 'A story of a woman of average age, average height, average life. She has boarded a bus for a journey to her childhood home. She travels alone. A dreadful headache nags at her. The sun is bright, so very bright. Her sunglasses aren't in her purse, so she sits with her eyes closed on her journey. "I know this route well", the woman tells herself. "I'll keep my eyes shut and count the stops. After the ninth stop, when the bus slows for the tenth, I know that will be the stop to open my eyes and alight". It's a game the woman played often as a girl. She counts the first stop, the second, right through to nine. But the bus never does stop for the tenth. So, with her eyes closed, she rides the bus for evermore. Now, young man. Do you have any suggestions for a title?'

'*The Last Bus.*'

'I like the first part, *The*. I do love a title that begins with *The*. *The Lottery. The Sundial.*'

'*The Haunting of Hill House.*'

'Absolutely. Perhaps I should call it simply, *The Bus.*' She jotted the title on a pad. 'Now, is the dentist ready to see me now?'

'The dentist?'

'Ah, yes!' She smiled a smile of breathtaking warmth. '*The Dentist.*

Perfect title for a story. Dentists always strike me as being so sinister, don't they you? But it is strange, you know.' Her face clouded. 'Some time ago I developed a toothache. Terrible nagging thing it is. Like an electric bell ringing in the side of my jaw. So I came here to see my dentist. I've been told to remain in this waiting-room. Only that was the last time I saw anyone. And it's been such a long time. Fortunately, there was this typewriter here so I've been able to while away my time writing.' She sighed. 'The view from the window isn't what you'd describe as especially pretty. A very overgrown garden. A path runs out across the lawn then doubles back on itself to return to the front door. The light is always grey – very grey. I wish I could see the dentist now. I'm really starting to become anxious.'

'Mrs Jackson. This is a dream. *My* dream.'

'Well thank goodness for that.'

'You don't mind?'

'No, why should I?'

'I thought you might be upset.'

'On the contrary. A dream explains everything.'

'I guess I've gone and interrupted your work now.'

'I suppose so. Say …' She rolled the paper out of the typewriter. 'It's no good to me now. But could you use my story? *The Bus*? It's almost finished.'

A new story by Shirley Jackson? Even a dream-generated Shirley Jackson story, albeit unfinished, is too good to be true. And too good to be true it was. As I reached out to grasp the manuscript I woke with the hem of the bed sheet clutched in my hand.

Ruth sat on the edge of the bed, stretching with that feline grace of hers. 'Tom, what on earth were you dreaming about last night?'

'Uh …' I grunted, then yawned. 'All sorts.'

'Well, lay off the cheese before you come to bed. You were shouting so loud you nearly woke the neighbours.'

'What neighbours? We live next door to a cemetery.'

'Exactly.' She tweaked my nose between her finger and thumb. 'Come on. You'll be late for your meeting.'

*

The meeting was at the Federal Gallery of Internet Art. The curator had just received a grant to stage a virtual exhibition of three ground-breaking writers of supernatural literature and their relationship to the visual arts. *Poe, Lovecraft, Jackson.* I had won the contract to provide the promotional artwork. The curator was a clear-eyed woman dressed in a sharp business suit with a mind to match.

'Tom, why can't you just use your imagination like any other website designer?'

'Because this will be different, Josella. Imagination is something you control. Dreams you *don't* control. When you dream it feels like real life – a total reality where fabulous images are generated.'

'But you told me that this … lucid dreaming is different. You decide what you're going to dream about before you go to sleep.'

'I try. What I do is picture a house as I brush my teeth, then as I turn out the light, I imagine the people who are in the house. I tell myself that in the dream I will visit them. Talk to them. Interact with them.'

'And that works?'

'It does for me.'

'I see that it would furnish plenty of weirdness – men sipping tea in deep sea diving suits, purple dogs playing basketball, that kind of thing, but where will you find the image for the exhibition homepage? Visitors will expect to see something that reflects the title of the exhibition, *Poe, Lovecraft, Jackson.*'

'I'm getting close.'

'How close? I need to present a draft of the artwork to my committee on Friday.'

'I'll have it,' I told her. 'I'm confident I'm close to a real break-through.'

That night, as I brushed my teeth, I pictured the house. The first floor was underground. The second floor was underwater. The third floor looked out on to a grey-lit lawn where a path U-turned on itself. A path to nowhere. I climbed into bed beside Ruth who murmured a good-night. She was half-asleep so I kissed her lightly on the cheek.

Now for the occupants of the house. Poe. Lovecraft. Jackson.

I switched off the light. A second later I lay flat on my back. Light played across the ceiling from cars passing along the street.

Something's now got to happen to the three occupants of the house, I told myself. *This is where the phantom glides through the door. Or the night-mare thing in the water breaks through the window and* – I shuddered. Just for a moment a thousand cold insect feet marched over my skin. No. I'm having no water monster. Why? To my surprise I nearly asked the question aloud. But some defence mechanism had the quick answer. Josella, the exhibition's curator, would never accept anything as lurid and in your face as a ferocious beast with fangs and claws. She'd stressed 'subtlety' in the brief. So, definitely no water monster.

Do you ever pinpoint the exact second you fall asleep? All I knew was that the words: 'So, definitely no water monster' trickled through my mind as I walked up to the door of Poe's room.

Oh, righty, I told myself pleased. *Back in dreamland*!

Tapping lightly on Poe's door, I opened it. Damn … my dream generator had neglected to insert Mr Edgar Allan Poe into my dream set. Candles burned in empty wine bottles on the table, only there was no sign of the tragic writer who had haunted my imagination since I was nine years old. I crossed the bare boards to the table where I'd seen him writing. There, a quill with its matted feathers; he'd sucked at it as he'd wrestled with nightmarish plots. On a sheet of paper one word was written in stark gothic capitals: *NEVERMORE.*

Then I noticed scraps of rag on the floor. I picked one up. As quickly, I dropped it. It was soaked with blood.

This wasn't supposed to be how the dream unfolded. I'd practised lucid dreaming techniques for months. This, however, was becoming a rogue dream that threw in incidents I hadn't intended. But then, isn't a modicum of the unexpected acceptable within the parameters of lucid dreaming? That's the whole point: to push back the barriers of creativity. Marry the expected to the unexpected, then take a good gander at their progeny. Since I'd lost my dream Edgar Allan Poe I decided to find the remaining pair of my cast. Quitting Poe's room, I ran upstairs to the next floor with its artwork depicting those Eldritch monsters – men and woman sprouting a mass of tentacles beneath hip level. Only standing there on the landing with her back to me was Shirley Jackson – or at least the Shirley Jackson my dreaming self had produced. Slowly, she turned … her eyes glared at me. But it was the huge wound in her forehead that held my eyes. A bleeding, oozing, sticky valley of a wound that sank in a deep V shape into the top of her skull. Her spectacle lenses were speckled with yet more blood.

She hissed through blood-smeared lips, 'What have you damned us with?'

I stared, my mouth dry, as if I'd dipped my tongue in dust. 'What's happened?'

'*You* are what has happened. *You* brought us here. *You* inflicted torture on us.'

'I didn't intend to. I—'

'Didn't intend? You might not have intended damage. Any more than an idiot throwing dynamite into a classroom, but look at this.' She inserted her fingers into the head wound to touch her exposed brain that bled rivers of blood down her face. 'This is your responsibility.'

'Where are the others?'

She inclined her ruined head back at the door. 'In there. Fighting for their lives. I'm only here to make sure you didn't avoid your responsibility by running away or … by waking.'

'You know that I am dreaming,' I told her. 'That all this is created by my unconscious mind?'

'But you intended to bring the three of us together. You breathed life into us.'

'You are not real. You can not feel pain.'

'Mr Bennett, I feel agony. My two brothers in damnation feel it, too. That and terror and despair.'

'Mrs Jackson, it is a dream.'

'Then make everything all right. Stop us suffering.'

'Of course.' I nodded. 'Trust me.'

'Trust,' she echoed with contempt. 'So prove it.' She nodded her bloody head at the door to Lovecraft's submarine quarters. 'They're in there.'

I hadn't intended to enter his room again. Even in a dream the weight of all that water pressing against the glass made me profoundly uneasy. But I'd uttered the word 'trust'. I couldn't retreat.

Besides ... what had I to be apprehensive about? *This is a dream*, I told myself. *If it gets too disturbing all I have to do is wake up.*

In a rush I hurled the door open to chaos. Papers whirled around the room. I smelt brine. The air was bitingly cold. Books had been flung from shelves, the Native African artworks had been knocked from the table. Poe stopped himself from collapsing on the floor by leaning back against a table. More dishevelled than last time I met him, he was panting. He clasped a piece of torn sheet against his neck. A rich, dark stain seeped through it from a wound beneath. I recalled the bloody scraps of cloth in his room. He must have dressed his wounds there. Lovecraft stood by the window as if on guard. His thin shoulders heaved as he gasped for breath. His face carried a mottling of grazes, while one sleeve had been torn from his smoking jacket.

'Come to gloat over your woeful creations, Mr Bennett?' This was Poe, his voice a rasp. 'When we are done, will you resort to pulling wings from flies?'

Jackson stepped into the room. 'It's gone?'

'Just moments ago, madam,' Lovecraft told her, still panting from the exertion. 'We battled with it to prevent it from entering ... but it must have heard *his* voice.' He nodded at me. 'It departed.'

'Tell me ...' I looked at the two battle-weary men. 'What have you been fighting?'

Lovecraft wiped blood from his mouth. 'You tell us, sir. You dreamt it.'

'It was after you left, Mr Bennett,' Poe grunted, clearly in pain. 'Then the beast attacked. It tried to gain entry into this room. The lady and I came to this gentleman's assistance when we heard the tumult.'

'I'm sorry,' I said. 'Genuinely, I didn't mean this to happen.'

Lovecraft shot glances at the window as if expecting the creature's return. Beyond the glass, the dark, liquid body of the ocean swirled, carrying strands of kelp that drifted by on the submarine current. When he appeared satisfied that whatever had attacked wasn't returning ... yet ... he spoke to me. 'Both Mrs Jackson and Mr Poe tell me that you're not really a professor at Miskatonic University. Moreover, you claim that you are, in fact, dreaming this scenario, with we three as your phantom players.'

'I am dreaming this,' I agreed. 'But not with the intention of tormenting you.'

'But don't you see?' He pointed to the wounded neck of Poe and the head wound of Jackson's. 'We are suffering. We hurt. We bleed.'

'That is not possible. Or, at least, you should feel no pain.'

'If only you could walk but an hour in our shoes, Mr Bennett,' Poe breathed, the blood seeping through his makeshift dressing. 'You have condemned us to a living hell.'

I had an idea. 'Wait. This is my dream. If I wish you well I'm sure I can ...' I concentrated, while hissing the refrain. 'Be well, be well...' I looked up. 'There. Mrs Jackson, didn't I ask you to trust me?'

The dream mechanism now effected the healing. Within seconds, the cleft in Jackson's head closed up. The wound in Poe's neck was sealed. Even the mottling of grazes on Lovecraft's face vanished to be replaced by a healthy, if pale skin.

Jackson touched her head, exploring the instant repair with her fingertips. 'Congratulations. You've fixed us. But are you able to rid this household of its monster?'

'I won't permit it to hurt you again,' I told them with feeling. 'It has been created by my unconscious.' I smiled. 'Now I can *un*create.'

Poe touched his neck where the wound had been. Clearly, he was relieved that the pain had stopped. 'Yes, better, much better. But, Mr Bennett, what manner of creature did you create?'

'I don't know. Although this is my dream I haven't yet seen it.'

Jackson looked at me, her eyes narrowing behind those formidable glasses. 'Why are you perspiring, Mr Bennett?'

'It's getting warm in here.'

'I must say I find it rather chill,' Lovecraft confessed.

Poe rubbed his hands with a sudden relish. 'The icy miasma of the tomb.'

'And yet you perspire, young man.' Jackson's magnified eyes were shrewd. 'This monster that you have created, yet have not seen, troubles you greatly, does it not?'

'No.'

'Then dig deep into your memory. Search for it there.'

'I can't.'

'Why not? The creature is a denizen of your skull.'

'And extraordinarily vicious,' Poe added.

'If I'm not all together mistaken,' Lovecraft breathed, as he stared through a windowpane, 'something's out there.'

'Now's your opportunity. Mr Bennett. Look for yourself ... Mr Bennett?'

Uneasy now, my legs quivering, I faced the window. There was still that turbulent darkness with slivery particles swinging past the window. The same shreds of weed; the feathery ribbons of kelp. Then, beyond that, an all engulfing blackness of ocean depths.

Lovecraft's eyes locked on some distant object I could not see. 'It's out there. I did see it. Come closer, Mr Bennett. Help me look.'

I shook my head. A desperate phrase rang inside my head: *Wake up ... wake up, wake up*!

'Don't leave us now,' Jackson gripped my hand to draw me closer to the window. 'Stay sleeping. Help us confront this thing.'

'No.'

'You asked us to trust you. You can defeat this.'

I shook my head. 'I'm not sure if I can.'

Lovecraft turned sharply. 'I see it. It's coming closer!'

Poe clenched his fists. 'Be ready to fight! If it tries to enter push it back.'

'How can it come in here?' I asked, my heart thudding. 'It won't be able to get through the walls.'

'You tell us, sir, it's your dream!'

Jackson drew me closer to the window. I moved zombie-like now. My entire body had stiffened. I wanted to run but couldn't. Then what was it I so desperately longed to run from?

'It's getting closer,' Lovecraft warned. 'Be ready.'

'From out of Stygian depths,' breathed Poe. 'It comes ... it comes ...'

With terror pealing through me – a great, dark emotion with all the morbid power of a funeral bell – I stared into the body of the ocean. Through the suspended particles I saw a pale mass. Too distant to see clearly, I sensed it writhed as it approached. A massive body that pulsated; a body that was pulpy, somehow billowing, and inside it – *inside*! – condensed to unimaginable degree, a distillation of the darkest of all human emotions. Just to gaze on it was to be filled with despair.

'It's going to attack again,' Lovecraft warned.

Jackson whispered in my ear. 'Only you can stop it, Mr Bennett.'

'No.' Dread flowed over me in cold waves.

'Look at its face. Identify it. Tell us what it means to you.'

'No. I can't ... please, don't make me look at it.' My heart hammered.

'Look,' Lovecraft hissed. 'It's turning. By God, it has a face! Bennett! Look at it. See its face ... oh God, its—'

Then it struck. I'd kept my eyes down, so I wouldn't see the face as its billowing body turned, something like a white bed sheet blowing in a storm. Now there was a tremendous concussion as this apparently flimsily thing struck the house with tremendous force. Ceiling lamps swung. More books cascaded from the shelves. The three had to grab hold of furniture to prevent them from being hurled to the floor; the house quaked under the assault.

'Bennett, you must stop this!' Jackson fought to stay on her feet as the beast slammed into the house wall again. Bubbles turned the water into a turbulent blizzard of white. 'For heaven's sake, man. Look through the window. Once you see what it really is you can stop this happening.'

Then the walls between the windows dimpled as if breaking out into some ugly rash. Even the windowpanes formed puckering crystal spots.

'It's coming through!' Lovecraft ran to press his hands at where the glass deformed. Only he couldn't clamp his hands over them all. 'Help me!'

Jackson and Poe scrambled forward to press their hands at the dimple patterns as they rose into sickening-looking blisters. A second later, it happened.

Wall and window blisters burst. From them streamed white tentacles. Squid? Octopus? I don't know ... they did resemble the creatures' tentacles, yet instead of suckers they possessed softly bulging eyes that glistened weirdly. Each of those thousands of tentacle eyes stared at me. I knew that. They were examining me. Identifying me. Step by step, I moved backward. Through the storm of bubbles I saw the thrashing form of the white creature. I saw the mass of tentacles that were now perhaps a dozen feet in length, bursting through the walls – long, tapering tumours. I saw Poe, Lovecraft, Jackson battle with them. Either trying to force them back into the wall, or snap the pulpy shafts with their hands. In the cold white flesh of the tentacles blinked those lines of eyes ... lines that were as straight as punctuation marks on paper ...
... staring at me....

But what of the face that loomed through the cloud of bubbles just beyond the glass? Why didn't the brine gush in through holes punched in walls and windows by the tentacles? Gusts of dread blew through me with a cold I'd never experienced before.

And then, a terrible realization. *I've forgotten something*, I thought, panicked by the battle raging in the room in front of me. *What is it that I've forgotten?*

Lovecraft struggled to turn to me; tentacles coiled round his chest. Blood streamed from a cut above one eye. Desperately, he cried out, 'Help us, man. You've got to stop this.'

Elsewhere in the room, tentacles entangled Jackson and Poe. They were losing the battle. And all the time I kept my gaze away from the billowing shape of the creature beyond glass. I must never see its face. Never.

And just what is it I'm supposed to remember? I wondered about this as those sinuous limbs, studded with dark eyes, snaked through the air toward me. *What is that vital fact I must remember?*

The tip of the first tentacle was just a foot from my face. I was frozen. I could not recoil from that loathsome, dripping tip of white skin. *A fact eludes me. I cannot remember it. But I should remember. If I can, everything will be well.*

Poe, Lovecraft, Jackson cried at me to help them.

Then I remembered.

Out loud I spoke the words: 'This is a dream.'

The tentacle reached out to touch my face.

A flurry of white. I flung my arms out. The bed sheet flicked away from my head. Perspiration formed a sopping patch in the crook of my neck. My lips were dry. My mouth tasted … awful … bitter … For a second my eyes darted wildly about the bedroom. Then, when the normality of it all – TV on the drawers, curtains closed, landscape painting on the wall – when all that registered with me, I sank back on to the bed with a sigh. Ruth still dozed beside me.

Stretching my stiff arms, I swung out my legs to sit at the edge of the bed.

So what did you do wrong, Tom? I asked myself. *Answer: you made the fundamental mistake of the lucid dreamer. You forgot you were dreaming. You believed the dream was real. And it grew teeth and it bit you. Or in this case tentacles….*

I shuddered to the roots of my bones, just at the recollection of them.

It was still early, but right now I could use a drink of ice-cold orange juice from the refrigerator – pure, liquid balm to ease the burning in my dry throat. Just the thought of it was a beautiful, lovely thing. Carefully, so as not to wake Ruth, I eased myself off the bed, then went downstairs to the kitchen. Switched on the light. As I moved toward the refrigerator, something made me pause. A sound. Probably the refrigerator's motor kicking in with that gentle shivery sound. My eyes settled on the featureless white door of that monolith, standing there with its back to the wall. A box full of chill air almost the same size and shape as a coffin standing upright.

Strange thoughts ... strange early morning, half-awake thoughts, I told myself with a yawn. I took a step toward the refrigerator then as quickly stopped. Dimples deformed the smooth white surface of the door.

I knew before it happened. *I knew.*

With a hiss, tentacles sprang out from the refrigerator door. Like a nest of rattlesnakes striking out at their victim. Turning, half-stumbling, I ran across the kitchen, knowing that those sinuous white things followed. Ahead lay the door to the back yard. There was no other way but *OUT.* I raced out into the yard. Those things came after me. All I knew then was that I must keep running. I scrambled over the fence into the cemetery that ran alongside our property. Through early morning mist, and a deeply oppressive gloom, I ran between headstones.

Keep running ... keep running....

The words pumped through my head.

Keep running ... keep running ... keep running....

Whatever happened, I knew I couldn't let those tentacles coil round me. Once they did that I would be lost forever.

After racing through the half-darkness, I dashed out through the cemetery gates. Now I followed a dirt track uphill. My chest ached like rocks had been piled on it. I could hardly breathe.

Not once did I look back. But I knew with a cold-hearted certainty that those moist, white tentacles would be following. Ahead, I saw the track led up through barren-looking pasture to a house standing alone on a hill. There was something familiar about it. Something disconcerting, too. Unsettling. Creepy. I didn't want to run toward it but there was nowhere else to go. I couldn't go back. The tentacles would surely be sliding through the grass toward me. Fleshy ribbons of white. More dangerous than any venomous snake.

So, no alternative. Run forward.

The house loomed larger as I approached. A strange, old house of odd angles, and a shape that lacked rational geometry. The three storeys were of dull, red brick. The lower part of it seemed to have sunk into the ground somehow. Window lintels of the first floor were level with the earth.

I glanced to my side. Tips of tentacles hovered level with my head. They could coil round me in a second. I had to get away. The house. It was a place of safety. If I could only get inside.

Charging at it, I found myself approaching huge picture windows, with panes of glass that were as high as the interior ceiling. Movement … I saw movement. Without hesitation now, as tentacles appeared to float all round me, I raced at the window, then pounded furiously on the glass. Inside, three figures recoiled in horror. Their faces turned to mine. I saw fear and panic in their eyes.

My fists pounded the glass. 'Let me in! Let me in!'

Early morning mist swirled over me, for all the world engulfing me like the tide of some vast ocean of deadly cold brine. They had to let me in. They must!

With a huge effort, I pushed my hands at the glass. A sense of yielding. Then my arms slipped through the windowpanes. Only there was something different about my limbs now. They were long, sinuous, white … and what were those marks speckling the surface … something like black dots?

I cried out to the three to let me in. Because the tentacles writhed all about me now. I cried louder when I saw a pale billowing shape reflected in the glass. Close by must be the monster of my nightmare. Don't look back, I thought, frantic. Never look back. Keep trying to reach the three people in the room. They can help you … Can't they?

I tried to concentrate on the faces of the woman and the two men beyond the window. But I saw the billowing shape of the sea creature in the reflection, too. *I see its face.* The shock confused me, because the face it possessed was the same as mine when I was nine years old. The same age I discovered the work of my three favourite authors. And something else, too. Only my mind still suppressed the truth.

With an effort, I struggled to push myself through the barrier of glass to reach the three individuals within the room. *They can save me from the monster that torments me,* I tell myself. *They can help. If I can only reach them.* However, my arms had become the tentacles that attacked them in my dream.

My voice had gone, but with my mind I called to them: *Poe. Lovecraft. Jackson.*

And here I waited, a man poised in those uncertain borderlands between safety and total destruction.

Poe. Lovecraft. Jackson. Can you hear me?

It's been some time now. I am still waiting for their reply.

8

CEMETERY WINE

Wine pressed from grapes found growing in a cemetery would have to be the darkest and sweetest of all. Wouldn't it? Is there another liquor that could be more intoxicating? More invigorating? More of a restorative?

Yes, yes, yes – a thousand times yes.

But then what is your attitude to alcohol… or do you call it booze, or brew, or the demon drink? Our relationship with alcohol has become as coarsened as our relationship with God. We misunderstand its real purpose in our lives. 'Demon alcohol' is considered by many to be merely a bolthole from this perplexing state of affairs we call reality. But, in truth, intoxicating drink was once revered as the elixir of life. The properties of gin were highly regarded in the sickroom. Whisky derives from the Celtic words 'Uisge beatha' meaning literally 'the water of life.' And there is another drink, my friends, that is altogether more intoxicating and infinitely more powerful. This is the liquor known here on the Greek island of Valkidas as Cemetery Wine. It is a powerful spirit blended with angelica root, fennel, coriander, marjoram, anise and wormwood. What is so vital for this infusion to be effective is that its ingredients are gathered in ancient cemeteries on this rocky island in the Ionian Sea. Imagine the roots of those herbs! Visualize them! How deeply the filaments of milky white root dive through the soil to those coffins that lie deep in the earth. Picture root tendrils of wormwood penetrating casket lids to feed on such moist parcels of nutrient. Moreover, consider this arid land so devoid of rainfall. For the wormwood to survive, it must draw every drop of moisture from what lies in the grave in its putrescent, liquefied state. Appreciate the potency of such nourishment for the plant. Consider what qualities its leaves might impart when steeped for a dozen years or more in neat alcohol.

Can you picture such a liquor's colour? Its aroma? Can you imagine its taste when this distillate floods across your tongue?

What is most remarkable about this drink, is the legend that attaches to it on the Isle of Valkidas: **Cemetery Wine has the power to restore life to the dead.**

Those words are mine. Written in the spring of this year when I first arrived on Valkidas after a two hour ferry crossing from Zante. I came here to write an article for a travel book. Having a lump the size of a pomegranate sliced from my lung eighteen months ago made me acutely aware of my mortality, so when I uncovered the legend surrounding Cemetery Wine I became – and there is no other word to describe it – obsessed. **OBSESSED** in big, glaring letters. A big mistake?

Nope. I wouldn't have changed the last six months for the world.

'You have the time at your wrist?'

'Pardon?'

'You have the time at your wrist?'

'Oh, my watch? It's just after eight.'

'The sea's a bitch. You know that? She doesn't give me fish, like my bitch wife doesn't let me make love to her. I can't afford ouzo no more.'

The man who'd limped up to my table at the pavement café had the kind of skin that rivalled that of ancient Egyptian mummies, so withered and taut across his skull. A savage sun had burnt the old Greek man black, too, something that made his pale grey eyes glitter strangely in his face.

'You like ouzo?' the man continued. I felt a sigh building inside. This quiet evening drink by the harbour was going to be anything but. I allowed my eyes a regretful scan of the waterfront houses and harbour filled with brightly painted fishing boats beneath a deepening blue sky. I was going to compose prose poems about the place. Now that pleasure would be delayed a while.

The man peered at me with bared teeth … or chips of yellow enamel that passed for teeth. 'It's not bad for boys and tourists. But ouzo's not a real drink. Once you've tasted Cemetery Wine then you realize for the first time in your life you have tasted the drink of men.'

'Cemetery Wine? No, I've never come across it.'

'No, you're not likely to. The bastards don't let us poor, honest working men have it. People like him keep it for themselves.' He managed to weave a spitting noise that combined hatred and disgust into the Greek dialect he was speaking. 'Not that they dare drink it themselves. They are too weak and cowardly. No, they steep their cocks in it.' He glared at me. 'So you're never likely to taste Cemetery Wine. Not ever. Not if you were a millionaire a dozen times over. No, the only bottle is under *his* lock and key.'

The sight of the Greek Orthodox priest, who was the target of this old man's venom, walking along the road in formal black robes, stirred up even more ferocity in the guy. 'He keeps it to wash his dick with. It kills the urge for women.'

Even though the priest wouldn't have heard what the old man was raving about, at least not clearly, he noticed that I was being harangued by what must be the town drunk. The priest's eyes had an unnerving sharpness to them. This was a man who could detect a sinful act through walls six feet thick. Now he fixed the laser stare on the old man and strode across to the taverna. Maybe it was because the robes he wore resembled a lady's long skirt that prompted him to over-compensate: the priest blazed masculinity, and an aggression that seemed only barely under control.

'Dimitri,' the priest whispered. Incongruous, because I could have sworn he was going to yell. 'Dimitri, I've asked you before not to bother people. Especially not tourists.'

'He's not a tourist, Father.'

One hell of a deduction by the old guy. I must have looked like a just-arrived, just-sunburned tourist.

'Dimitri, you've been warned by the police, also.'

'This stranger is not a tourist. He's a writer. He's come to write about this wasteland. A dirty rock that's only tolerable to me when I've a bottle of ouzo in my belly. If only I could afford one glass. But the sea is a bitch.'

Ah. Revelation time. I pulled banknotes from my pocket.

'No, please don't give him money,' the priest told me. 'It only encourages him to beg from tourists.'

'He's not a tourist. The stranger's a writer.'

'Dimitri ...' The priest locked eyes on the old alcoholic then slid his eyes right, which in any language clearly meant: *You've been warned. Now go.*

Dimitri went singing an ah-ah-ah sound, which I guess signalled his sense of injustice at being deprived of a ten euro note.

'I'm sorry about that,' the priest said, as Dimitri wove away into the dusk. 'He's not well and can't fish anymore.'

'Don't worry about it.' I smiled. 'He was giving me a colourful description of a local speciality.'

'Oh?'

'Something called Cemetery Wine?'

The priest laughed. 'The drink of the gods. Yes indeed, Dimitri has been known to wax lyrical about that.'

'It exists?'

'Yes, but these days it's what you might call moonshine. It was banned a hundred years ago. I've heard that it tasted worse than kerosene and was guaranteed to leave you blind.' The priest smiled as he talked, his eyes twinkling with a sudden good humour. I realized he was probably only in his thirties. It was the big patriarchal beard that jutted from his chin that made him look older. He swished his priestly robes every so often with his hand, so they flapped like the wings of a huge raven. Dear God, the man was impressive, I'll give him that.

'So you're going to write about the island?' The priest fixed me with that laser-beam glare. 'All of it will be favourable, I hope? With the decline in fish stocks we don't have much in the way of income except through tourism. Without that, nearly every bar and store would close on Valkidas. In the winter, unemployment runs at thirty per cent. That statistic would apply the year through if foreigners stopped coming.' Maybe this formidable priest was going to suggest that he dictate the article to me, just in case I got any unChristian ideas about saying how crap his island was? And that it was only fit as a dumping ground for toxic waste. No, I liked this sun-baked stone in the Ionian Sea. I wasn't here to assassinate the place.

'The caves are worth a visit,' the priest said, mindful to point out beauty spots. 'There are sandy beaches on the south and east sides. Scuba diving can be booked at the harbour office. That's the building. The one with the pink walls.'

'Ah, no … I'm more interested in the folklore and legends relating to the island.'

'You're not a travel writer?'

'No … and yes, if that doesn't sound too stupid. There are so many guidebooks advising visitors where to eat the best lobster or catch the best breeze for sailing … the company I work for specialize in catering for specific interests. Mainly, they publish tour guides that focus on the culinary aspects of destinations. They even published a guide devoted to Swiss chocolate: its manufacture and where to find the best chocolate stores.'

'Innovative.'

'Now they're moving into other speciality niches. I'm contributing an article to a book entitled *Greek Island Mythology: Ancient & Modern.*'

'I see.' He lowered the scalpel-sharp gaze to the ground, thinking. 'Odysseus reputedly landed here when a storm blew him off course on the way to Ithaca.'

'I'm sorry,' I said, sensing a fund of material. 'Please excuse my manners. Won't you sit down and join me?'

'Well …' He made a show of flicking back the robe sleeve to check his watch. This was a busy priest with people to meet, communions to plan, sermons to write, souls to wrest from Satan … But I sensed his understanding of the more secular aspects of island life. He wanted to keep tourists flowing in to ensure his flock was solvent.

'Please,' I coaxed, 'if you can spare the time. A drink?'

'A small ouzo, thank you.'

Beaming, the priest sat down. A chance meeting that would yield miraculous events. And do I regret asking him to join me? Nope. I wouldn't have changed it for the world.

The waiter brought the priest his ouzo, accompanied by a tiny brown jug of water, and a glass of retsina wine for me. I watched the priest add water to the potent spirit, instantly turning it white as milk. The retsina had ample strength for me. Besides, my doctor had warned me to avoid spirits ever since my lung carving session eighteen months ago.

'Ah, thank you. Your good health, Mr—?'

'Shay. But call me Thomas, please. Cheers.'

'Thomas, then.' He nodded then took a swallow of the ouzo, savouring what must have been a powerful blast of aniseed across his tongue. 'And please call me Dimitri.'

'Dimitri?' I thought of the washed-up fisherman. Wasn't he called Dimitri? I found my eyes drawn to the name of the taverna. *Dimitri's.* The priest noticed and smiled.

'Nearly every male on the island is called Dimitri. Newcomers find it confusing when they learn how many here answer to that name. It's because our patron saint is St Demetrious; we name our sons so in his honour. You'll find something similar in Corfu where males are named Spiro after their St Spirodon.'

'I see.' I mentally filed the information. It would add local colour to my article. 'The mummified remains of St Spirodon are displayed in Corfu's cathedral. I saw them a few years ago.' I was aiming to lead the priest along a particular conversational track. Mummies are good copy.

Father Dimitri smiled. 'Ah, here St Demetrious resides in the church tower.' He uncurled one of the fingers that held the glass so he could point at an ancient whitewashed church on the cliff-top overlooking both town and sea. Its tower was astonishingly tall. 'See the window set high in the tower? St Demetrious sits there, so he can keep watch over the town.'

I laughed politely, interpreting this as an example of ecclesiastical humour. But I saw Father Dimitri's face expression was completely serious.

'I do beg your pardon. I thought you were joking.' Ooops. That's what they call a *faux pas* on my part.

'No, don't be embarrassed, Thomas. Just as the Virgin Birth and the Resurrection of Christ are the warp and weft of my faith, so part of that fabric is my belief in St Demetrious's immortality. Ah, you look uncomfortable now. It's me who has embarrassed you, Thomas. Here let's have another drink.' He called to the waiter. 'Dimitri, another wine for our guest.' The good-humoured twinkle returned to his eye. 'See? Another Dimitri. We are legion. Ah … now for St Demetrious. You'll find he has counterparts on many an island round here. Corfu, as you know, has St Spirodon. His mummified remains sit on a throne. Those who are unwell visit him and kiss his feet in order to be cured. On Kefalonia, the body of their saint, St Denys, lies in a golden casket. Every year he rises from his tomb to walk round the island to leave gifts for the poor and heal the sick.'

'And St Demetrious stands guard?'

He shot me one of those sharp looks, satisfying himself I wasn't mocking him, but read swiftly enough that I was interested. Equally quickly, he realized that if I featured the island's patron saint in my article it would bring more tourists, which in turn would boost island income.

The waiter brought the drinks. 'Thank you, Dimitri. Here's to your health, Thomas.'

I noticed that the waiter didn't add the drinks to the tab – he'd also automatically brought the priest his ouzo. I guess the good father here didn't need to spend much money. Father Dimitri took a deep swallow of the spirit with the relish of a connoisseur, then he stroked that formidable beard as he gathered his thoughts.

'Saint Demetrious was born in 1643, to a woman who believed she was barren. When St Demetrious was simply Dimitri Barbouris he was a crippled boy. He could only walk with the aid of a stick. And then only slowly. They say he had to hop on one foot from the steps at the top of the cliff down into town. He had to make the same painful journey twice a day, because his employment was limited by his disability to that of grub catcher. That is, he would stay in the fields all day picking insects from the crops before they could damage them. Sun, rain, tempest – he never missed a day's work. The farmers were concerned for the young Dimitri. Believing the daily journeys were too arduous for the crippled boy, they built him a small house of drift wood where the church stands now. At that time, these seas were under the control of a pirate called Gestades, a Turk, who delighted in having the hands of his captives sewn to certain parts of their body. I think you don't require me to elaborate further than that?'

'No.' I smiled. 'I get the picture. Unfortunately.'

'Well. Gestades was furious with Valkidas and its neighbouring islands, because they had failed to pay him tribute … his extortion money, yes? So he sailed his ships from one island to another. Burning towns, murdering their inhabitants, violating churches, abducting women. Everyone on Valkidas knew that the pirate Gestades would one day reach here. Only its people decided that this time they would not submit to piracy. Of course, they realized this would be suicide, as they did not possess an army or fighting weapons. But they all swore that death was preferable to tyranny.'

Around us, the day settled deeper into dusk. Boats sat out on placid waters. Overhead the moon shone bright as a new silver coin in the sky.

The priest continued in deep, even tones. 'Gestades arrived by night, bringing his ships tied nose to stern, as if they were the linked carriages of a train. This is an old pirate trick, to keep the ships so close that the fighting men could step from one ship to another, then on to dry land as soon as the first ship beached. This would make for a speedier deployment of Gestades's men. They'd take the town by surprise. That night, however, Dimitri saw the ships approach. You can imagine them tied together, end to end, to form a strange snake in the moonlight, with the Turks dipping their oars as silent as can be into the ocean. Then God whispered into Dimitri's ear, telling him he must protect his people from the evil Turk. High in his driftwood house Dimitri saw the men-of-war approach, hugging the deep water at the bottom of the cliffs, the oarsmen driving the vessels toward the harbour so quietly not even an owl could hear them. But Dimitri saw. He watched and he waited. Then all of a sudden he knew what to do: he scooped burning coals from his hearth and hurled them on to his bed. Immediately his house caught fire. With no thought for his own safety now, he seized two burning timbers with his bare hands. The flames burnt his skin and set fire to his clothes but he did not cry out or drop the burning wood. Instead, he ran as hard as he could for the cliff edge. God had given such power to his legs that now he ran faster than any man alive. Dimitri ran and ran, and when he reached the cliff, where it falls five hundred feet to the sea, the young man leapt as far as he could. There he fell like a shooting star, burning and blazing so bright, that the pirates were forced to shield their eyes against the glare. Some force beyond gravity guided Dimitri's descent. Holding the burning staves in the shape of the Cross, he plunged into the lead ship. Flames spread from the fiery Cross to the ship itself. Decks caught alight, the gunpowder brought on decks for the coming battle ignited. In moments the ship was engulfed in flame. But it didn't stop there. Fire ran along the tarred connecting rope to the next ship in line, then the next and the next, detonating gunpowder stores. Within minutes, every single pirate ship was ablaze. In the morning, the islanders found the wreckage of the ships on the beach along with the burnt bodies of pirates, including Gestades – he'd been pierced through the heart by a scorched timber from Dimitri's house.' The priest sipped his ouzo. 'When the islanders searched amongst the wreckage they found Dimitri. There wasn't a mark on his body, except for burn marks in the shape of a cross on each palm. His clothes weren't even marked by fire or smoke. Thinking he was dead, they called for sailcloth on which to carry him back to town. But at that moment he climbed to his feet. Then he told them all what had happened to him, and that they mustn't fear invasion again, because he would keep watch from the cliff-top. If the island were ever threatened in the future, he would destroy the enemy. The townspeople were amazed when they watched the cripple boy walk back to the harbour without so much as a limp. At the priest's house Dimitri stopped and bade the father to bring him a flagon of Cemetery Wine, then he asked the holy man to bless it. After the

sacred rite Dimitri proclaimed, 'This wine is the blood of our fore-
fathers. It will sustain me for eternity and give me strength to watch over
you and protect you.' And after drinking from the flagon he handed it
back to the priest. Then, still with no limp, he returned to the cliff top
where he sat on a large rock overlooking both the town and ocean.
That's where he remained until the Patriarch ordered a church be built
with a watchtower to house St Demetrious.'

'That's some legend,' I said, impressed, while looking up at the white
church on the cliff with its soaring tower.

Father Dimitri shrugged. 'A question of perspective. Legend for you:
historical fact for us.'

I stared at the window in the distant church tower. 'And St
Demetrious is still there? In the tower?'

'Yes, of course.'

'The body was mummified like St Spirodon's?'

'I can't have made myself clear, Thomas. St Dimitri is like you and I:
he is alive.'

Dusk continued its customary glide down into night. Bats emerged to
whirl round streetlights. The sea captured the moon's reflection. Stars
appeared. A meteor threw a silver dart through Orion's belt. In the
taverna kitchen I could hear the sound of cooks baking moussaka and
pizza for tourists taking their seats under the night sky. Spicy aromas
filled the air. My eyes, however, were all but locked on to the church
tower. Even a little tug of the imagination produced the image of an
ancient face gazing back at me. As legends went (or historical event, as
Father Dimitri would claim), it was pretty good. I could see it finding
its way into the article I planned to write for the book. I needed a little
more, however. Including photographs. Greek priests, stern gentlemen
at the best of time, are protective of churches and holy relics in their
care: they eject disrespectful tourists from sacred places in two shakes of
a lamb's tail. But I realized I had leverage. Father Dimitri was pragmatic
enough to understand that the island depended on tourism. I could ask,
tactfully, for the equivalent of an access-all-areas pass. After all, the more

I thought of it, I'd got a hell of story. You've got to agree, a title singing out: *Four-hundred-year-old man alive and well in church tower* is a real attention grabber.

'So,' I said, careful not to rush things, 'it was this drink … this Cemetery Wine that made St Demetrious immortal?'

'Yes, although specifically it was the flagon of Cemetery Wine blessed by the priest.'

'Then that flagon would become a holy relic in its own right?'

'Indeed so. The flagon was sealed and placed with St Demetrious in the church tower.'

'You've been into the tower and seen St Demetrious?' *Ooops.* Too much, too soon. I saw that look again, assessing me, checking for any sign of mockery.

'Thomas, I'm a priest of the Greek Orthodox Church. I don't need to witness Christ raising Lazarus, or touch the face of God in order to believe what the Bible tells us.'

'It's just that – well …'

'Go on.'

'The room in the tower might be empty.'

I anticipated annoyance to flare in the man's eyes, instead he laughed, amused by my implication.

'No. I've never been into the tower room. And, no, it isn't empty.'

'You're certain St Demetrious is still there?'

'Yes, of course.'

'How? I mean what makes you so certain?'

'Faith. And …' He beckoned with his finger, so I'd lean closer. Then he whispered, 'If you stand outside the door you can hear the sound of him breathing.'

I returned to my taverna room with promises of help for my article. Yes, I could take as many photographs as I wanted of the church, of Father Dimitri, of examples of pre-prohibition bottles that once contained Cemetery Wine. Made available to me would be a cache of paintings by eighteenth-century local artist Dimitri (yes, Dimitri again) Mantaki, depicting scenes from the life of St Demetrious, including his fiery dive into the pirate boat. As for access to the tower room where the immortal saint resided? Father Dimitri was perfectly polite and friendly, but, no. I'd have as much chance selling the island to the Turks as gaining access to that tower room. You know, there's a legal phrase: habeas corpus – Latin for 'give up the body'. It applies to journalism as well. If you're going to write about a legendary mummy, the editor's first question is going to be, 'Where's the body photograph?' This time there wouldn't be one. That meant the value of my article had just plunged from megabuck syndication to a bargain basement three cents a word.

Still, as the man said, 'It's early days.' Born optimist that I am, I began to wonder if I could coax Father Dimitri round to my way of thinking. Just imagine: install a discreet viewing window in the tower door, then 'Roll up, roll up! Come see the 400-year-old man! Made immortal by one sip of liquor!' OK, the Orthodox Church wouldn't hop on the exploitation wagon so quickly, but if they handled this with sensitivity and pragmatism Father Dimitri could anticipate a flood of big spending tourists. After all, the authorities aren't so shy on Corfu. If you want to see the green skinned mummy that is St Spirodon you only need stroll into the town's cathedral, passing many a souvenir store as you go.

So, I adopted the stealthy approach. I didn't again mention photographing St Demetrious who, I guessed would be composed of some decidedly decomposed bones in a box, and nothing more. Instead, I accepted the priest's invitation to his house where I photographed paintings of St Demetrious flying with pious grace toward the pirate ship, while holding aloft two spectacularly blazing timbers in the shape of a cross. I copied excerpts from local histories, along with a letter from an Athenian doctor who, ten years after the miraculous intervention, examined St Demetrious (from a respectful distance, and before the church was built) and pronounced the man in perfect health, with no sign of a lame leg. He noted that such was the saint's piety and devotion to keeping watch over his people that he'd not moved from the rock, and that vines grew in profusion over his legs and torso to mingle tendrils with his beard, and that bunches of grapes hung from his body. If anything, that indicated to me a blending of pagan images of Bacchus with Christian icon. In a touching postscript, the doctor added that he'd personally witnessed doves hovering close to fan the saint's face with cooling air when the heat of the summer's day became searing.

I guess, in reality, if you could grab a glimpse back in time, what you would have seen there on the cliff top would have been a rotting corpse propped up on a rock. Like beauty being in the eye of the beholder, absolute faith allows the true believer to view ugly realities through the rosy glow of their chosen mythology. And there were yet more documents. Letters from the Patriarch announcing deification. Building plans prepared by ecclesiastical architects for the church with its special 100-foot high tower. These blueprints were drawn in ink on creamy-hued sheepskin, not paper, and were so tough they were nigh impossible to tear. A nineteenth-century daguerreotype photograph of the flagon that contained the life-giving Cemetery Wine, *ergo*, it had been brought out of the tower room on at least one occasion. A monograph by a French academic on Cemetery Wine stating that 'Every nation within Europe has produced its own variant of the potent alcoholic beverage flavoured with aniseed and wormwood. It is known by various names – anis, anisette, ouzo. In France we recognize it as absinthe. On the Greek island of Valkidas it is blessed with the marvellously picturesque epithet, Cemetery Wine.'

And so the days passed. While tourists relaxed on beaches, inhaling the scent of wild wormwood that grew in profusion in the graveyards, or swam in the warm ocean, I sat in a back office of the priest's house and fed words into my laptop. I thought I'd merely been too focused on work to bother eating. I simply didn't notice any lack of appetite. When my chest became tight, and a niggling little cough developed, I put it down to all those dusty books I was pulling off shelves. My neck grew stiff and an area in my left armpit became too sore to touch. Well, I attributed that to straining muscles when hefting all those bundles of heavy files. See? I did a neat job of ignoring the telltale symptoms.

It was only when I sat up in bed in the middle of the night, coughing loud enough to wake the dead that I thought to myself, *Wait, this can't be right, can it?* The answer came in the form of what I coughed into my hand. There, glistening in my palm like Stevenson's Black Spot was a lump. When I switched on the light I saw that it was a red object, the colour and texture of a thumbnail-sized scrap of raw meat from a butcher's block.

On leaving home I somehow left behind my fear that the tumour would return. Now, when I looked at that lump of crimson in my hand, I realized I'd unwittingly carried a stowaway.

The next day I ate a breakfast of fresh fruit washed down by shuddering mouthfuls of that sticky black Greek coffee from tiny cups. Then I went back to work at the priest's house. In the small office with whitewashed walls, that were otherwise plain apart from the painted icon of St Demetrious himself who gazed down at me, I fed more words into my laptop.

Father Dimitri appeared in his fabulous black robes. 'Good morning, Thomas. How's the article progressing?'

'Good morning, Dimitri. I think I've material for a whole book, never mind an article.'

'Excellent. You don't mind my interrupting?'

'No. I could use a break anyway.'

'Good, because I've found more files in what we laughingly called the civic archive. It's really just a corner of an attic.'

'Thanks for going to all that trouble. You shouldn't—'

'No problem. Now ... these are some of the diaries kept by my pred-ecessors. The earliest date back to just fifty years after the sinking of the pirate fleet. I believe it contains eye-witness accounts that the priest recorded.'

'Wow, I really do have enough material for a book.'

Dimitri awarded me one of his sharp glances. 'If only your publisher would commission such a volume, you would be most welcome, Thomas, to stay here and write it.'

'Why, thank you.' I was both touched and guilty, especially as I planned to betray his trust.

He moved a little to one side, eyeing me in the light filtering through the blind. I found the smile on my face becoming fixed. *He's seen the guilt in my eyes*, I told myself. *Damnit, I knew I couldn't keep anything hidden from him.*

'Thomas?'

'Yes?'

'Are you feeling all right?'

'Fine.'

'You're looking pale. And I'm sure you've lost weight since you've been here.'

'Oh, that's me, I'm afraid. Once I find something that interests me I become obsessive. I forget to eat.'

'Well, take care of yourself, Thomas. Don't overwork.'

'I won't. But thank you for your concern.' I realized I meant it. Again I was touched by the priest's considerate nature. Despite his fearsome appearance with the huge patriarchal beard and fierce eyes I realized this was a man of sensitivity.

'Come into the garden,' he told me. 'We'll have coffee and honey cake.' Then he flicked back the sleeve of his black robes. 'I need to be at the harbour at one … a boat blessing, which might be of interest to you. But after coffee, what do you say to a walk to the cliff-top? Perhaps it's time you had a closer look at the Church of St Demetrious, yes?'

'I'd love to see the church, Dimitri. Thank you.'

If those laser eyes of the priest could have seen inside my head, he wouldn't merely have been surprised by what he saw there, he would have been appalled.

'Are you sure you don't need to rest, Thomas?'

'I'm fine,' I lied. *Just one of many coming your way, Father. I will truly regret the dishonesty, too.* 'I'm out of shape, that's all … too much sedentary work.'

'Rest here against the rail.' He nodded back at the distance we'd climbed from the village. 'This is the halfway mark. Ninety-two steps.'

'Another ninety-two to go? Phew. You need a chair lift.'

'Ah, good idea. Good idea! Maybe if you write your book about St Demetrious, it will bring us enough tourist income to pay for the chair lift and an extension to the quay; then we can accommodate cruise ships. Maybe even extend the paved road as far as the beach in the north bay. There is space for a new hotel there.' His eyes gleamed at the thought of bringing prosperity to the island.

My eyes were gleaming, too, I guessed. But for altogether different reasons. Before leaving the priest's house I'd coughed more blood into tissue. My chest felt tighter, as if a solid mass vied for the limited space within my rib cage. My lymph glands were tender to the touch. Lethal signs that the tumour had come creeping back to its lair.

For a moment I leaned against the fence to catch my breath. The marble steps ran down in a gleaming curve to the village that shone a dazzling white in the mid-morning sun. Fishing boats and pleasure craft glided through the straits into the harbour. Further away on the beach were dozens of sun-toasted bodies, while in the shallows, white flecks of foam marked the position of swimmers cooling off in the ocean. A perfect day.

Discretely, I coughed more blood into my hand.

'You've picked up a cold,' Father Dimitri said. 'Are you sure you want to continue? We can visit the church another day?'

'I must have inhaled a little too much book dust. I'll be fine.' Even so, I shot a glance at the steps as they hugged the steep hillside. At the top was the white-painted church with its hundred-foot tower. Instinctively my eyes found the single window. A black recess like the orbit of a skull. Was *he* up there looking down at me, somehow divining what I intended?

I'm coming, St Demetrious, I thought. *But, in all honesty, sir, it's no longer you I want to see.*

The sun pressed with all the force of hot metal on the back of my neck. The next ninety-two steps were gruelling. The tumour was a greedy child. It merrily devoured blood sugar carried in my veins intended for muscle. My legs began to ache. Climbing each step, an act of self-inflicted torture. Lizards sitting on stones at either side of the path watched me toil past with a contemptuous flick of their tongues. And my tumour sat in my right lung, gorging on nutrients my body stupidly fed it. For a moment I could swear it laughed at me. Throaty chuckles echoing up my trachea.

The priest had the constitution of a marathon runner. Climbing 184 steps in ninety degrees, while wearing neck to ankle black robes didn't slow the man. It didn't even make him breathless enough to stop talking. Instead he outlined his vision for the island. How money earned from tourism would one day provide a hospital. At present, seriously ill people had to be transferred by ferry to a neighbouring island. 'A two-hour journey,' he told me with sudden anger. 'Two hours is too much for the sick and the old. For a heart case it can be lethal. We must have our hospital, Thomas.'

I agreed. However, only a phlegm-laden crackle escaped my lips, not articulate speech. The heat bore into my back as I stared at the tower. *Are you watching me, Saint Demetrious? Do you know my intention? Will you condemn me?*

Lizards scuttled through dry vegetation, producing a crackling sound loud enough to make you half-believe invisible men ran through it. Scents drawn from wild thyme by the sun filled my nostrils. Birds cried overhead as they circled. *Vultures waiting for the dying man to expire*, I thought with a grim smile. *Hey, not yet, guys. Give this dehydrated writer with shaky legs, wheezing lungs and sunburnt face a break, won't you?*

'Ah, there, Thomas. From here, you can see the north side of Valkidas … and there's the tip of the extinct volcano of Voros to the east.'

From here? The words followed a route deep enough into my skull to hit the understanding zone. *From here*. I'd made it. Taking a deep, *deep* chest-crackling breath I looked back down at the village and harbour, now reduced to toy-town dimensions by distance. I had been joking about the chair lift. But 184 steps in this heat? *Oh boy….*

Still perspiring and trembling from the climb, with the spiky flavour of blood on my tongue that I'd once more coughed up, I made it to a boulder enclosed by an ornate iron fence.

'The Rock of St Demetrious,' Father Dimitri announced with a wave of his hand that rustled a black sleeve.

'This is where he sat and kept watch over the island?'

'Until the church was completed and he moved into the tower.'

Wiping sweat from my upper lip, I walked round the armchair-sized stone, peering at it through the iron bars. A plaque in several languages read: THE ROCK OF ST DEMETRIOUS. HERE SAT THE SAVIOUR OF VALKIDAS FROM 1660 TO 1673. EVER VIGILANT.

And, as I ran my eyes over that lump of black rock that bulged from the cemetery, I felt the lump in my own lung beat with a dark pulse all of its own. Tumour and saint stone alike would be deeply rooted. Immovable. Perspiration dribbled down my chest. Sunlight flashed from marble gravestones, dazzling me. Even the ocean was an incandescent splash of electric blue – one so bright I could barely open my eyes. My legs spasmed so painfully I had to clench my fists. Snakes hissed through clumps of wormwood. A bird piped as shrilly as a dentist's drill. And all the time I sensed a pair of fathomless eyes staring down at me from that single window in the tower ... although beyond that opening I could discern nothing but darkness.

'Now, you'll be wishing to take photographs,' Father Dimitri said. 'Please take as many as you need, then I'll unlock the church for you. There are wall paintings of the miracle that are—'

'Father ... Father!' An unfamiliar voice cut through the cemetery.

I turned to see who was shouting. I was so dazzled by sunlight all I could make out was a shadowy figure bounding along the path.

'Dimitri?' called the priest.

That name again – *Dimitri* – had the islanders never anticipated the confusion they'd cause by naming their first-born Dimitri?

'Father.' It was a young man, worried sounding. 'It's my grandmother. She is much worse this morning.'

'I'll come straightaway, Dimitri.' The priest glanced at me. 'Are you coming back to the village, Thomas?'

'I'll stay and get these photographs.'

'Very well.'

'But perhaps you could let me have the key to the church?'

He paused and fixed me with that penetrating gaze again, even glancing back at the window in the tower. 'Of course, Thomas.' He handed me the key. 'But you will lock the door when you leave? There have been problems in the past. Some visitors haven't shown respect.'

'You can trust me, Dimitri.'

'I'll see you back at the house, perhaps. For lunch?'

With that, he joined the youth, who bobbed impatiently at the top of the steps, then together they ran down them, the priest a fabulous sight in his robes, kicking the black skirts out as he ran. A giant bat shape against white marble; sleeves transformed into darkly beating wings.

I returned my gaze to the church tower. 'OK, Saint Demetrious. You. Me. Alone.' The flippant line appropriated from some melodrama sidled from my lips. But the flippancy provided just a modicum of psychological armour plating. Now I was here, I'd have to crush my civilized inhibitions into some dark place where they couldn't dissuade me from my course of action. Again I indulged in melodrama. 'It's time to do this thing.' I gripped the key tightly and walked to the church door. *Endgame.* The pulse in the tumour grew stronger; it leeched vitamins from my bones, plundered my flesh for nutrients: all in preparation for its final – *and fatal* – assault on my body.

The interior of the church? I don't remember what it looked like – all I recall was the smell of polish, as I ran through it. The staircase was easy to find. I followed the steps upward, past a bell attached to a rope, then up, up, up. The stairs ended at a door of ancient black timbers criss-crossed by iron bands. The hinges looked as if the makers of canon had forged them. I tried the key Father Demetrious had given me in the hope it was a case of one-key-fits-all in his building. But no. It didn't budge the lock. I looked through the keyhole. Beyond a gauzy veil of spiders' webs I saw a block of light. The window, I guessed. Also, tantalizingly, a squared-off corner of carpentry that could have been the upper corner of a high-back chair, perhaps something that

resembled a throne. *But how do I break through that formidable door?*
Even as I considered the problem I sensed the tumour in my lung
stretch itself, and reach out with crab claws to sink a pincer into my
heart, and another sharp pincer into my liver. It grew at a formidable
rate. As if to set this suspicion in CAPITALS – boy, was it eager I
didn't miss the point! – a cough erupted in my chest to exit through
my lips, sending droplets of rich, pink blood from my lungs to speckle
the wall in front of me. Time's running out, whined a voice in my ear.
Time's running full-pelt for the mortuary in-door. For cancers don't
always kill through the remorseful spread of the growth. They produce
blood clots that break away to plunge into the bloodstream, where
they're carried to a lung to cause a fatal thrombosis. Or they shoot to
the brain to trigger a stroke. Or they lodge in the heart in order to
execute that *coup de grace.*

This did it – a detonation of purple-edged terror worked the magic.
I ran back down to the body of the church. I grabbed the heavy brass
crucifix from the altar then pounded back up those stone steps to the
door. I took two savage blows at the lock. It didn't even tremble. That
thing was staying put. Then what made me do it, I don't know, but I
turned my fury on the huge hinges. After the first blow one of the hinge
pins snapped. I belaboured the second hinge at the bottom of the door.
That took twenty or more full-blooded strikes, then that hinge pin, now
so brittle with age, disintegrated into tiny pieces. I rammed my shoulder
to the door. It fell inward with a roar like thunder that reverberated in
the room with ear-pounding force.

Not pausing now, I walked across the fallen door into the chamber,
my eyes taking details in ravenous glances. Bare stone walls. Bare stone
floor. A window with views of open ocean and the town far below. In
front of the window the high backed chair from where St Demetrious
had gazed for the last 400 years. I lurched forward to look closer. It took
a moment to sink in. Then I laughed out loud. Maybe God has a sense
of humour after all?

But our lookout saint wasn't important to me any more. What was
important was the pulsing, beating, growing, fulminous cancer inside

my lung. And with fearful symmetry of equal importance was that flagon of Cemetery Wine blessed by the priest four centuries ago, on the night pirate ships burned. When St Demetrious chose his destiny. Standing on a simple block of stone was a glass bell jar. Beneath that an earthenware flask. I recognized this as the priest-blessed flask of liquor from the old daguerreotype photograph. Sealed alcohol lasts forever. Archaeologists have drunk medieval brandy. Millionaires drink malt whisky a century old. This potent brew of pure alcohol, infused with aniseed and leaves of wormwood harvested from graveyards at midnight, would be as immortal as St Demetrious – the saint who'd reputedly sat in the tower for generations. Lifting the glass bell jar cover and removing the little flask of liquor, I turned back to the chair.

'I would have liked to say hello, St Demetrious. It was a pity you weren't home.' I raised the flask to the empty wooden throne, offering a mocking toast. '*Glorious in absentia.* Maybe next time, sir?'

A wild spirit came upon me. A blaze of excitement seared my veins. I pictured the red, pulsating malignancy inside of me and thought: *What the hell!* The clay seal wouldn't budge in the mouth of the bottle so I broke its neck. '*Cheers.*'

For a second I thought I was drinking water. There was no flavour – there *seemed* to be no flavour – but it had been locked inside the very molecules of the fluid itself. As I swallowed the second mouthful, its taste, its potency, exploded across my tongue to sweep down my throat with all the power and the glory of a Pentecostal wind. This Cemetery Wine was *the* elixir. I willed myself to believe that its spirit would race through my blood to the tumour and defeat it. Reduce it to dead cells. A slime of cell matter that would melt away to nothing within my body. Reeling now from the power of the drink, feeling it blaze inside of me – a fiery cosmos in my stomach; starbursts inside my head – I half fell into the empty throne of St Demetrious in his watchtower. The flask tumbled from my fingers to shatter on the floor. That's the last memory before the tide of darkness swept over me. Then nothing, until ...

*

Until … Until the voice.

'Thomas … Thomas. You're awake.' A statement rather than a question. 'Open your eyes.'

'Father Dimitri, what a terrible man you must think I am.'

'A frightened man. You were dying.'

'It showed that much?'

'You drank from the flask?'

'The Cemetery Wine. Yes. And I'm afraid I broke it.'

'Fear makes people desperate.'

My eyes were open properly now, seeing the priest standing there by the window in his black robes.

'It tasted fresh. I expected it to be stale after so many years,' I told him. 'And it knocked me out.' I chuckled, appreciating the melodrama. 'I was dead to the world.'

He smiled. 'They say there are three stages when drinking Cemetery Wine. The first stage is just drinking. The second, the drinker lapses into unconsciousness. The third stage is hallucination. You see what you *want* to see.'

'And what do I *want* to see, Father?'

'You believed so strongly in the power of the elixir you broke in here and drank it – to cure your illness, and to live forever.'

'No, Dimitri, I don't believe it is the elixir of life. Not now anyway.'

'Why not?'

'Because the room is empty. There is no St Demetrious sitting in the chair, keeping watch on the faithful. There aren't even any bones.'

Father Dimitri tilted his head to one side, watching my face. 'Thomas, who do you think I am?'

'The parish priest.' Even as I spoke my heart gave a terrific lurch, because he'd opened his hands, revealing burn scars on the palm. I looked at his foot and saw the steel leg calliper for the first time.

'I'm thirty-seven years old, Thomas. I'm not Saint Demetrious. But what do you see on my hands?'

I see burn scars that form themselves into stigmata – Holy Crosses seared into his palms. I see a crippled leg. I see a man who is four centuries old. In

his eyes I divine the memory of his blazing plunge on to the pirate ship. I
turned in the chair to see that the door hung on its frame once more;
the flagon was intact beneath its glass cover. That made perfect sense.
The power that cured me and that would make me immortal had rein-
stated the door and made the smashed flagon whole again. *Miracles –
believe me, they are real.*

The priest stepped to one side.

At that moment I knew: Father Dimitri *was* Saint Demetrious. He
worked for the island's economic prosperity as well as providing spiri-
tual guidance. His time was too valuable to sit here in the tower,
watching for pirate ships that would no longer come. Through the
window I saw it was winter. The leaves had gone from the trees. The sea
had turned grey. So I had slept here in the chair for six months while the
elixir not only restored me, killing the cancer, but elevated me to that
exalted status of a man who would live forever and ever.

Gently, the priest spoke again. 'Remember, that third stage of intox-
ication, Thomas. You will see what you *want* to see.'

'This is no hallucination, Father,' I told him, smiling. 'It's real.'

'Thomas, listen to me. It is an effect of the spirit: *you will see what
you WANT to see.*'

'You require proof, Father?' In a single movement, I stood up and
dived through the open window. One hundred feet below me I saw the
cemetery. I saw wormwood and the Rock of St Demetrious.

*While I fall, I replay in my mind the events that brought me here. From
sitting in the taverna that first evening, through to this leap from the tower.
Now I face the final test in my belief that the miraculous liquor is real. In
a few seconds I will hit the earth. If I can stand without a mark, a strong
and healthy man, I will know that the legend of Cemetery Wine is true. And
then everything will be all right. My sickness will be gone. And my life will
be longer than comprehension. The air rushing into my face grows stronger.
It roars in my ears. The graves hurtle toward me. I close my eyes. Feel a surge
of exultation. As soon as I reach the ground I will be safe. I only have to wait
one moment more …*

9

ENGINE OF VENGEANCE

I SMASH THE bottle against the factory gate. 'Ungrateful buggers! After all I've done for you lot! You're not going to get away with this. By the time I've done with you, you'll wish you were never bloodywell born!'

Beyond the wall, the guard dog barks. The night watchman is peeking out from his stinking little cabin; he daren't face me. There's bugger-all I can do to hurt him, though, or rip down the factory – the factory that is mine; my property; I built it up from a wreck to being the living, beating heart of this town: its only source of freshwater. Before that everyone was in rags. They were dying. I gave them back their lives. And this is how they thank me.

The canal runs black as hell by the glass works. Above the roof there's a red glow in the sky. There they work the nightshift. Furnaces melt glass scavenged from landfill sites. It'll make bottles, like the one I smashed against my factory gate. In the darkness, lumps the size of my fist move along the path. These are rats. They say those hairy little buggers outnumber humans a thousand to one now. No one else in their right mind would walk the canal path at night for fear of being torn apart by the rat army, but the animals sense I'm not someone to be tackled. They smell my rage. When they stick out their pink tongues they must be able to taste what boils inside of me. *Vengeance!* Sheer lust for revenge powers me. So I stomp along the path. I growl. I snarl. I catch a glimpse of my blazing eyes reflected in the canal waters. *As God is my witness, I'm going to make those traitors suffer.*

So angry, so full of rage, not to mention a gallon of Calder-Brigg bitter, I don't realize I've wandered through a break in the razor wire into the Isolation Park. Still in a mood sour enough to turn cream to vinegar, I crash through bushes, long past caring that I'm breaking the one law of my stinking town that is *never* broken by its mutton-brained population. Yes, my friend, the very ones I saved from a mucky, painful death fifteen years ago. The very ones who jeered and wore idiot smirks on their ugly faces as they chucked me out of my office.

'Hey you … yes, you up there! Stamp on me. Go on! Put your big iron boot on my head; crush me!' I laugh. Christ, it feels good to yell at one of those iron thugs. 'I'm talking to you.' I rip the grass apart at my feet to find a stone. Better still, I find a house brick. A big heavy block that would crack a man's skull. '*YOU WITH THE BRASS BOLLOCKS!*' Powered by fury, I hurl that chunk of fired clay. It clanks against a thigh of metal.

My mind's blazing. That heart of mine is going THUD-THUD-THUD! Blood roars through my head. I'm ready to let fly with my fists at a metal man a hundred feet high. I don't care anymore. I'm on fire with rage! I could roar so loudly at the town it would smash to atoms. The image of destruction excites me. Makes me laugh. Makes me dance. Round and round the legs of the robot I go. I rip a branch from a tree so I can whip its metal ankles. *Fall, you miserable little town. Houses of Calder-Brigg crumble. Collapse on your people. Brick walls crush your children. Co-op burn to the ground. Statues topple. River burst your banks. Town hall rot to your grubby foundations. As for you, Mr Mayor – you can fart yourself to death!*

Anger put muscle in my arm. I strike the robot's leg with the branch so hard it makes the whole thing chime like a bell. All of a sudden I stop this mad carousing. I stand still. I'm here in the darkness. Rats still bustle through the grass. My God. I'm here in the Isolation Park. I've just been thrashing one of the Lump Men with a branch. I'm panting, shivering, my teeth are chattering and I don't know whether to be gripped by panic or shout in triumph. I've done *everything* that nobody ever does. I've entered the Isolation Park. I've assaulted one of the steel

Lump Men. Now the earth should open. I will be sucked down into the fires of hell.

But that hasn't happened. The Lump Man hasn't even raised his ruddy great boot and kicked my rawping gob. I approach the robot. Slowly this time; very slowly. I rest my palm against the bulging curve of its heel. It's a big bugger. Very big. I look up into the darkness. I can make out the huge tank of a head that's a hundred feet up in the air. Now, this is making me think about them for the first time in years. From here, I see three more of them. The figures stand high about the town. Iron giants. They carry a metal staff in each hand. Frozen warriors. Each in their own Isolation Park – a football pitch-sized quarantine zone surrounded by razor wire. And now I've committed blasphemy against these brass-balled gods. And ... AND! ... I've not been struck down.

For the first time in hours I'm calm. Icy calm. Thought runs clearly again. 'Time to take stock, old son,' I murmur. 'Decide what you do next.'

Then, without a second thought of consequences, or danger, I sit on top of the robot's giant foot. I could have been some old boy passing a moment or two on a park bench.

Rats scurry through nettles. A spiky, cold April wind brings hailstones as fine as sand out of the darkness. Above me, the hundred foot robot stands there still as death ... that is the moment memory pulls me back to the day the world ended. Of course, a new one began. But it wasn't the same for most folk. Come to that, millions didn't survive the transition. For me though, the end of the old world wasn't so tragic. In fact, the reverse. Armageddon? The End of Days? Apocalypse? I loved it. Absolutely bloody loved it.

So I sit here and do something I never do. I reminisce.

Fifteen years ago, this was me: picture a sixteen-year-old lad in his bedroom. I've got an older brother, who's a piss-head, always in trouble with the cops. I was going the same way. The only thing I cared about was Leeds United. My dad worked for the parks department, cutting grass, planting shrubs, tending flower beds, that kind of thing. Mum

worked at Netto. My life revolved around going to see Leeds play whenever I could, or kicking a football about the yard of the old mineral
water factory. There they'd once pumped Calder Hills water out of the
ground, put it in bottles and charged the same as a pint of beer. Next
door to that, a building that housed restored steam engines. This was
the industrial stuff, not locomotives. My dad loved to hang round there
to watch the pistons go in and out, and iron wheels go round and
round, as the things merrily farted steam. Mostly, I avoided going to
school. I mooched round the bus station. Caused trouble. Got chased
by security. I loved chips and curry sauce from Al Muhrad's chippie.
Sometimes I'd treat myself to a deep-fried Mars bar. Just imagine it:
sucking at that hot chocolate as it melted into batter flavoured with fish
from the cooking oil. Paradise, bloody paradise. Other times I'd watch
my brother painting graffiti on walls along Tannery Lane.

That was my life. Then one January afternoon, a Saturday it was, I
lay on my bed watching football on telly. Outside: brutal cold; snow on
the ground. It made the world all black and white. Kids were snow-
balling. Teenagers rode motorbikes. My dad was downstairs reading
about steam engines (by heck, he had a thing about old machines). As
he did so, he dunked a Twix into his tea. Eyes glazed with ecstasy, he'd
slide the finger of chocolate in and out of his lips. Revolting. That reaction of mine bawled 'hypocrite!' considering my liking for sucking
deep-fried Mars bars. Anyway, he'd been banging on about me missing
the toilet every time I went for a piddle. It made Mum ballistic. Dad
kept snarling, 'Son, if you can't hit bull's-eye, sit down when you need a
number one.' I hated him using code names. Number one. Number
two. I ask you?

So ... with me watching a Leeds United striker magnificently
booting the ball into the back of the net, and Dad moaning about the
bathroom carpet getting peed on – that's when the Lump Men arrived
and the world went wrong for everyone ... for everyone, that is, but me.

First: the picture on the telly broke up. Missing the game annoyed me
to the point of throwing punches at my pillow. Eventually, I realized it
had gone quiet in the street, too. Then came thunder. Thunder? So

what? The weather was rubbish. But do you get thunder with snow? So, I looked out. Sometimes you see something so odd it makes you laugh. I laughed so loud that Dad called upstairs, 'What's so funny up there?'

'Dad. Guess what?'

'Don't muck me about, son. My tea's getting cold.'

'Robots.' I laughed again. 'There's all these robots coming into town.'

'That's it, play the fool. See how funny it is the day you get sent to prison. You'll be laughing through your backside then.' Before he slammed the living-room door he shouted, 'And stop getting number one on the bathroom carpet. You're mother's going to kill you if you do it again.'

Urine spots on Mum's pink bathroom rug? That would be the last thing on her mind. The Saturday the Lump Men arrived would be her last.

At that moment, however, kids in the road screamed at the sight of the robots. That made me laugh even harder. Seeing kids scared always amused me back then. I was a rotten little sod, then most would affirm I'm a rotten *big* sod now. Listen. Have you seen the Long Man of Wilmington? It's the chalk outline of a man cut from turf on a hillside. The Stone Age people did it. A giant figure walking with a staff in each hand that's as tall as him. In a fair imitation of this were hundred foot men that strode into town. Each carried a giant staff in each hand. Oh, yes, they were robots. I had no doubt. Big metal things they were, in strangely dull silver. Two arms, two legs. On top of a cylinder neck they boasted a tank of a head; well, that's what it resembled to me. Something similar to the tank of a petrol tanker, balanced horizontally. They seemed to have a pair of huge eyes. Only when I examined them more closely – when I dared – they could have been twin holes through which they sucked air to cool inner-workings. Nobody knows of course. They could have been vitally important to the robots. Then they could have been nothing much. Just two holes inserted into the face as a joke.

I watched them work. The thunder sound came from their feet crunching the ground. When they reached houses they kicked their way through, like naughty kids kicking cardboard boxes to pieces. They used the hundred-foot iron staffs as scythes to cut down pylons, telephone masts, or slice houses.

From me ligging on bed, eyeballing the telly, to utter end-of-the world chaos took all of twenty minutes. People fled into their homes for safety. When they watched from their windows, as other houses were splattered by the huge feet, they fled back out into the road again. I saw people slipping on snow-covered pavements. Some fell so heavily that they left red splashes behind.

Dad checked the commotion. When he did, he yelled something or other to me, then ran out of the house. Later, he'd find that a huge iron boot had gone through Netto to crush Mum as she scanned mushy peas, or beer, or sausages, or whatever through the checkout.

My old history teacher, who I always ignored, said something important (I realize with hindsight); it took months after the robot invasion to retrieve the memory, but now I remember him quite clearly, standing in front of a picture of a ruined Greek temple – all white pillars and statues without heads – and he said very clearly, 'Class, remember this: civilization seems to be indestructible. It is, in reality, a house of cards. It only takes one puff to bring it down. Just one small puff.'

Jarvis had put up his hand. 'Sir? Will you be that small puff, sir?'

My history teacher's prophecy was accurate. Civilization was there one day, then the next it had gone. The robots had only destroyed maybe ten per cent of the buildings in Calder-Brigg before they moved on. The town hall still stood there, lording it over the market-place. Factories looked as they always did. Most of the houses were unscathed. The robots had smashed the main bridges, railway lines and the power station, but roads, canals, lots of shops and even Al Murad's chippy were still perfectly trim. Yet society had vanished. Civilization had flown away before that puff of robot aggression. Within weeks of the invasion, Calder-Brigg could have been a petrified forest through which we survivors scrambled like rodents. We were hungry snot-smeared things. We even stopped talking.

Eventually, the robots would kill us all. That's the only reality we knew. Because every so often they would march back through the town.

One hundred foot high men, colossal shafts of iron in each hand; they would use these to swipe at people, buildings, farm animals. You name it. What a bloody mess. There'd be men and women with heads as flat as deflated balloons. The force of the blow would burst brains from skulls, like you'd squeeze yellow gunk out of that zit on your chin.

It all stopped a month or so after the invasion; however, people had stopped checking calendars by then; they were too busy finding fresh water to drink – water didn't come from taps anymore; those reduced to drinking from the canal turned scabby round the lips and died. I got by eating snow – but only from the tops of walls or roofs. Snow from the ground was as bad as canal water.

Anyway ... a month, at best guess, after the invasion, four robots returned after smashing up Leeds city centre. They marched through a snowstorm – swish, swosh went those iron rods. The KFC on Skinner Lane got trashed. A foot went through the roof of my old school, right into the classroom to crunch the desk where I'd sat when I'd bothered to turn up. Thunder, screams; half-starved people vented bowels, then desperately clawed their way through snowdrifts to escape. A few, I remember, gave up. They lay down to wait the final stamp of the metal sole. Then ...

Ffft ... Well ... not even a *ffft*. The robots stopped. They *stayed* stopped. That was fifteen years ago. They haven't moved an inch since. Statues ... just metal statues. If you examine them closely you see the surfaces aren't smooth. The metal has a bubbled, lumpy appearance. I refer to it as iron or steel but nobody can truly identify it. Little peaks rise from the surface to form uneven spikes. The appearance of stippled icing on a cake. Maybe the surface of the metal skin had been melted long ago then had cooled again to leave the random pattern of spikes, bumps and blobs.

The day the robots became statues was the day that everything electrical stopped working too – not that there was much left apart from watches, battery-operated radios, toothbrushes, cameras and a few odds and sods of other now useless devices.

My dad found me living in the back of a car. 'Did you hear, son?

147

NATO detonated nuclear bombs high up in the atmosphere; they created a huge burst of electromagnetic radiation. It worked. It killed the bloody robots. We're saved!'

'If that's true, they've also knackered all the other electrics. Nothing works anymore.'

'Don't split hairs, son. Electrical equipment will recover. It'll be back to normal in a few days.'

Fifteen years later they're not back to normal. Wire doesn't conduct electricity evenly anymore. If you can find a music player that still works it stutters the song like crazy. The best you can get out of a torch is a pointlessly brief pulse of light every now and again.

People speculated about how come the government didn't put everything right. They wondered why the army couldn't destroy the robots using missiles. Sometimes we even asked ourselves where the robots came from? Who sent them? What was the bigger purpose behind the invasion? But the answers? There were never any firm answers. Only opinions. And those opinions became myths.

And, as the weather got warmer, more people died. You see, there was no fresh water to be had. People drank out of water-butts, puddles, streams, rivers, ditches – they died by the hundred.

That's where I come on to the scene. With a rope and bucket Dad and I hoisted water from the well at the mineral water factory. Clean, sweet, pure, bug-free, it saved our lives. Using clean water as money we paid people to drag one of the old steam pumps from the museum. Fired by coal, it did not have an electrical circuit in its big old iron body. Within a year I could pump clean water back into the mains again. I'd saved the townspeople. Even if civilizations didn't exist elsewhere (and we had to deal harshly with raiding parties from Leeds, Wakefield and York) we had our own well-ordered town back on its feet. In Calder-Brigg agriculture flourished. Factories, using steam power, recycled steel and glass. Water-mills spun wool into cloth. Miners ripped coal from the ground. Breweries fermented tasty beer.

Meanwhile, the robots remained as statues. Wherever they stood frozen, we erected high fences round them to create the Isolation Parks.

Not to keep 'em in, of course, they wouldn't be contained by barbed wire, if they came back to life. No, it was to keep the people well clear of those iron totems. They still radiated an aura of evil. Townsfolk hated them, but their fear was too great to allow them to try and destroy the monsters. So, let sleeping dogs lie. That's the maxim. Gradually, over the last decade and a half, bushes and trees grew within the fenced zone; so now the robots stand knee-deep – that's around twenty feet high to you and me – in a bubble of leafy green. Someone started calling the robots the 'Lump Men'. Well, they do make a dirty great lump. The name stuck. Not that people dare approach the Lump Men. Or even look at them, if they can help it. Calder-Brigg folk have become painfully superstitious. Just have a gander at the rabbit feet dangling from belts.

All I wanted – all I deserved – was a say in how the town should be run. That, plus a few privileges.

That's why the ungrateful wretches threw me out of my own factory – the very one that pumped clear, healthy, *life-saving* water into their stinking homes.

So, here I sit on the metal foot. No home, nowhere to go.

Hailstones strike the metal skin. The huge Lump Man vibrates; it produces something akin to the soft chime of a bell struck by a padded hammer.

'You hum if it makes you happy, old friend.' I smile up at the mechanical face hiding in darkness. Particles of ice are white spits against black sky. 'You know, you gave me the best years of my life. Before you came along I was heading for jail. Afterwards, I became rich. I had real clout. I owe you a debt. I should really repay you … but what with, eh?'

A voice comes from the darkness. Not the Lump Man, no, this is familiar. 'I might have guessed that you'd try and make a deal with these things, once the town had thrown you out.'

'Dad? How did you know I'd be here?'

'I've been following you ever since you left the pub.' A man of sixty pushes through the grass. 'You know, son, throwing bottles at the factory, or talking to these things won't help you make peace with the town.'

'I never want to make peace with those bastards. They can rot in hell.' Anger runs hot again. 'Did you see how they dragged me out of my office, Dad? They pulled me out by my feet.'

'You've made them hate you, son.'

'Now I suppose you're going to tell me to come live at your house. So you can treat me like a child again.'

'Hardly. I've been warned. If I take you back in they'll evict me.'

'So you're scared of them, Dad.'

'I can't fight the whole town. Besides, why on earth should I protect you? You've become a tyrant. That's what you are. You threaten to turn off their drinking water, if they don't obey you. You're a rotten little Hitler.'

'Thanks for your support, Dad.'

'Now you'd sell out to the Lump Men, if you could.'

'These things don't work anymore. But I wish to God they did.'

'Come away from here. It's not safe to be near them.'

I pat the top of the metal foot as I sit there. 'This little beauty? They're harmless now. They just stand around making the place look pretty.'

'Don't make fun of them, son.' Dad's nervous. 'Come away from here. Look, I'll get you a meal. You can sleep in the old bus.'

'You still petrified of the Lump Men, Dad?' I laugh.

'You always were a twisted little bugger.' In the near darkness, his eyes are bright as lamps. 'They fenced them in for a reason.'

'The townsfolk just got superstitious. The robots are harmless.'

'Oh? Harmless, is it? Remember your brother? He was full of mischief like you. After they stopped moving he went back to his graffiti again. He painted his name on the legs of one of these things, then he started coughing blood.'

'He got cancer. Getting it at twenty is bad luck, but he wasn't cursed by the Lump Man because he wrote on it.'

'Don't underestimate the danger.'

'If they were toxic, it's gone now. See this one? Ivy grows right up to its bloody chin.'

My father steps closer, jacket collar round his ears. He's shivering hard, only it's not down to the cold night, it's the sheer terror of being so close to the Lump Man. He daren't come any closer, so he stands there in the long grass, and starts talking in a fast, low voice. 'Those things aren't dead, lad, they're sleeping. We didn't kill them with that electromagnetic blast fifteen years ago. All that did was knacker *our* electrics.' He blew into his hands; steam billows round his face. Yet I still see the scared glitter of his eyes. 'You know, I've had years to think about them. I'll tell you what I've worked out.' But at that moment his voice dies. In Calder-Brigg it doesn't do to talk about the Lump Men. The town's mutton-heads believe it brings ill fortune.

'Go on,' I prompt.

Dad clenches his fist, then surges on. Maybe he thinks he will be struck down for speaking his mind, but here goes: 'The Lump Men came; they attacked towns all over the world. We saw it on television before the power failed. But nobody knew where they came from. Of course, there were all kinds of stories. Like they were built by terrorists, but how could terrorists invent machines like that? Or the Russians set them on us. Only before the televisions packed up we saw Lump Men wrecking Moscow. Do you know what I believe, son?' Above him, the metal giant towers in the sky. Great God Death in all His dark majesty. 'In my heart of hearts, I know that these machines have been on this world for thousands of years. They lay at the bottom of the sea, or under the sand in deserts; there they bided their time until human beings got too clever for themselves. OK, we built cities, we cured diseases, we could fly to the moon, when we had a mind to. But do you know what we devoted ourselves to? We spent all our time hating. We hated politicians. We hated foreigners. We hated our neighbours – our employers, celebrities on telly; we turned it into a bloody art! We put more work into despising men with different accents than we did grafting in factories. That was our real industry. We produced suspicion, manufactured sneers! We built our loathing for our fellow man higher than any ruddy skyscraper!'

I've never seen Dad as furious as this, nor as eloquent.

'Don't you get it, son? We brought this on ourselves. Because we thought everyone else was rotten it brewed up hatred in the world. There was so much anger that it filled the atmosphere like smoke. The sheer, bloody rage we generated reached out to touch those machines: it brought them to life. Our anger was petrol to them. It fuelled them. So they came out of the sand, or the bottom of the sea, or wherever they were sleeping, and they wrecked our countries – they kept destroying and killing until our anger turned to fear. When the anger had gone they just ran out of fuel. So it wasn't our bombs that stopped them. We were just too terrified to hate anymore. That's when they went back to sleep. So all the blame for the world ending is ours. We did it to ourselves!'

I jump to my feet to stand on the Lump Man's giant foot like it's a stage. From there I bellow down at my father, 'Yes, you brought it all on yourselves! All the death and destruction. I'm glad it happened. I wouldn't have had a chance to make anything of my life if the world hadn't gone belly up! And don't moan that it was all society's fault that I was a useless good for nothing kid. You and Mum did nothing to encourage me to be a better person. The pair of you treated me like I was just this stupid little runt who made your lives a misery. You should have praised me and my brother. All you did was complain. As far as the pair of you were concerned your sons were nothing more than piss marks on the bathroom rug!'

Instead of arguing, he begs, 'Come down, son. We can go home. I'll make us something to eat.'

'You talk about hate fuelling these things.' I slam my hand against the robot. 'Well, my mother and father hated me!'

'Don't say these things. Come down here.'

Come down here? In that frame of mind I'm going to do the opposite to what that man, who calls himself my father, demands. 'Down?' I yell. '*I'm going up!*'

'No!'

I run to the giant's shin. There the ivy has grown thick – a regular rope ladder, it is. I begin to climb. Dad runs forward as if to grab me. Yet his fear of the Lump Man stops him dead. Now the clouds break. A bright moon shines through. The handholds made from knots of vine are plain to see. It's all so easy to climb, too. In moments I reach the bulbous knee joint. Soon I'm past that and scaling the thigh more than thirty feet from the ground. I glance down. Dad's wringing his hands. 'Don't go up there. I don't want you to die.' He's shouting stuff like that. Yeah, as if he ever cared about me in the past.

Anger at him – fury at Calder-Brigg's rabble – it all fills me with energy. It makes me as agile as a blue-arsed baboon. Up, up I go. Hooking my fingers into the tough strands of ivy, I scale the iron man's belly. What I'm trying to prove, other than my contempt for the sobbing man in the weeds below, I can't say. Maybe I'll climb its face then look the Lump Man in the eye. Or maybe I'll be throw myself off its head. Of course, those mutton-heads of Calder-Brigg would be frightened of my corpse after it had been in contact with the metal monster. They'd leave me to rot where I dropped. Parents would scare their kids with stories about me. 'If you don't brush your teeth the maniac who climbed the Lump Man will creep into your bedroom tonight and steal your eyes.'

There, seventy feet above the canal bank, I yell at the town. 'You scum! You ingrates! You should get down on your knees, thanking me for saving your lives! I'll make you pay! All of you!'

My father is fleeing alongside the canal. Its water gleams silver in the moonlight. Trees appear as dark blobs. Beyond the canal are the factories. At street junctions there is the smudgy yellow glow of oil lanterns. There's the church; the stained glass resembles jewels, gleaming all red, blue and gold out of the darkness. Across town are the huge, shadowy figures of the other three Lump Men. The stationary comrades of the one to whose torso I've fastened myself. In some houses faces appear at the window. There they are, little blobs of flesh, pushed up to the glass to hear me shouting myself hoarse.

See those men and women in their snug little homes! They'd be dead without me! Anger breaks over me as a wave. Now I'm too angry to shout. I cling to the ivy on the Lump Man's chest. Rage shakes me until my teeth bang together. Then it happens. I know this will be the outcome.

I begin to fall. For a second I imagine my plunge through cold night air to thud into the stinging nettles seventy feet below. My bones will snap like twigs. Only it's not like that. I don't fall *down*. I fall *in*. Suddenly, there's nothing solid beyond the strands of ivy. I tumble into the plant growth like I'm falling through a curtain.

I'm inside the Lump Man's chest. Where the heart would be is a cavity maybe ten feet in diameter. When I try to grab hold of the ivy to haul myself back outside, my fingers press against a smooth, transparent surface. It's resealed itself. I'm trapped inside. The walls have this soft glow that illuminates my cell. The glow, however, isn't bright enough to interrupt my view of the town through the chest wall. I see the houses, the church, my old school, still with a hole in the roof where a robot foot went through all those years ago. There's the pompous pile that's the town hall. I even see my father still lumbering along the canal path toward home. Of course, I look for a way out, but it's like standing inside a tennis ball; walls, floor and ceiling curve seamlessly round me. They aren't featureless, however: that's when I realize that people have been here before me. On sections of wall that aren't transparent someone has scratched pictures and words in letters I don't understand. There are drawings of old sailing ships, horses, antelope, men with bows hunting animals. These have been done in different hands at different times. The hunting scenes, with naked bowmen, resemble cave art. The pictures of ships with oars and sails could have been copied from Roman vases. Just for a second, I have a clear mental image of men and women from different eras finding themselves somehow in the robot's chest, then eventually killing time by scratching these representations of their life with knives or flint arrowheads.

Dazed now by the immensity of it all, I press my hands to the 'glass' chest wall of the Lump Man. My hands sink into the transparent material. There the fingers begin to melt, fingernails part from skin to float for an inch or two before it sets again, holding them there, like little pink seashells in hard resin. I scream. Fibres (my nerves?) stretch out from my partially dissolved hands into the transparent substance of the 'window' then merge with it. I howl … a howl that's as loud as a dog with a burnt tail. But with the pain there is the sweetness of release, too. The sensation of thorns being drawn from my skin. It hurts, but the relief is beautiful. My scream becomes a sigh.

Even though the glass holds my melted hands, my glare is drawn back to the town. Hatred surges through my veins. Sheer loathing of the townsfolk blazes; a furnace of loathing in my chest. The Lump Man judders. The scene tilts … and I know the robot is taking its first step in a decade and a half.

One foot lifts into the air. Foliage dangles from the toes. Then we move forward; a sensation of swaying, true, but mainly a sensation of speed and smooth motion. Its arms are raised so the iron fists are level with its shoulders. In those fists are gripped the hundred-foot long staffs. The noise coming from my mouth isn't a scream any longer; I am baying with glee; a yell of exultation. I'm hot with excitement. The thrill of seeing Calder-Brigg from this height – *from this vantage of power* – is so intense that I no longer notice that my hands have melted into the clear chest wall to bind me there. I imagine the terror of the towns-people – seeing the Lump Man walk again must drive them mad with fear. How I wish I could make this brute trample them.

One foot splashes into the canal; it sends a tidal wave racing along it. Another foot kicks through a wall. I see the church. All those sermons I sat through. The sapping cold of the place robs the life from your bones. All those wasted hours I was forced by my parents to sit on hard pews. The moment my eyes fix angrily on to the clock tower the robot swings toward it; marches to the church, then drives one of the colossal shafts through the clock face. The force of the blow sends masonry tumbling into the graveyard. A marvellous thought occurs to me. I turn my hatred on my old school. Yet another piss-pot of a place that killed children's spirits for generations. When I focus my anger on that dull brick building the robot changes course in order to advance toward it. Seconds later, it wades through classroom walls, its feet blasting solid architecture to dust. A cloud of pulverized brick forms an orange fog in the moonlight.

So that's it? I only have to direct my anger at a target for it to be destroyed by the Lump Man. This is so easy. Bang! There goes the town hall. Crash! The police station is fragments. The staffs become scythes that cut the constabulary edifice down. The force of the robot's blows hurl masonry two miles away to splash down into the park lake.

So what else do I hate? Who do I hate? There he is. A little beetle of a man; a dark speck, hobbling, exhausted, up Skinner Lane. As I might prod an insect with a stick, I prod my infuriating father with the end of the staff. His arms, legs, torso and head become a sticky smear on the pavement. Job done. I laugh with the pure joy of vengeance. Revenge is the most delicious dish of all.

But! The question … the really *big* important question is this: 'Who do I hate most in the world?' I savour the moment as I repeat the question. 'Who do I hate most in the world?' I search inside my head for the identity of the person who has caused me the most harm. Eyes closed, I look for that man. I rummage around for his image. Because it must be filed away in my mind. The hateful, spiteful, sadistic individual who hurt me the most. So I hunt for the identity of my worst enemy. My headmaster? No, he wasn't the worst. The cop who arrested me? I hate him, but I don't hate him the most.

So who do I hate?

I open my eyes. *There is his face.*

It is reflected back at me from the glass. 'Oh, yes, he's the worst of all.' Consciously, this isn't what I want at all. But unconsciously I desire that ugly, cruel human being to be hurled into darkness; to be gone forever and ever….

'No! Not me! Leave me alone!' The response of the coward.

The Lump Man plunges the staff into its chest.

And I am no more….

Is this a dream? Sometimes I don't know. But I'm sure I'm in the head of the Lump Man. Before it reached into its chest to mangle my body it yanked my mind out of my skull. My thoughts continue to exist in the structure of the robot. So: this is my existence now: day after day, I gaze out over Calder-Brigg. Rain, wind, snow, sunshine. Birds build nests in bushes. Geese migrate as leaves turn red. Tides of workers go in and out the factory gates. Boats glide along the canal. The Lump Man hasn't moved since I caused its rampage. Trees have grown as high as its waist, so I surmise as many as twenty years have gone by since my 'death'. Children no longer fear the Lump Men; they play games around the iron feet, or write rude words on their ankles.

Calder-Brigg has its revenge on me. I'm trapped in this iron skull. The captive watcher. An eternally lonely observer of others. And, yes, this is my curse: to watch the people of the town live their happy lives. Eventually, one day in the far off future, the Earth will swallow this machine. Then the machine, and I, will sleep underground. Until the time humankind learns to hate once more.

Then we will awake. And there will be vengeance.

10

THE OLD MAN AT THE GATE

'I BET YOU daren't.'

'Bet I dare.'

'Daren't. There's a ghost that lives there.'

Ivan chipped in, 'Ghosts don't live in there, anyway. Ghosts are dead people.'

'If ghosts are dead, how do they move about and moan and that?'

It was an interesting philosophical point, and the boys debated it noisily. When they couldn't agree what the difference was between a phantom and a demon, they settled the argument by seeing who was the first to be pushed off the fence. Not that they really resolved the phantom/demon dispute, but it was immensely satisfying to see Ivan tumble off the rail and on to the dusty earth.

That day in August was a great day to be eight. Blazing sunshine worked up a thirst for an ice-cream, and there were still three glorious weeks of the summer holiday left, making school seem as far away as Timbuktu. The four sat on the fence, chewing sweet clover stems, and looking at the gatehouse to the park.

'My dad said in olden times a man would stand guard at the gate-house and not let anyone into the grounds,' John told them.

'Why'd they do that? It's a park; anyone's allowed in. Even Ivan in his stinky jeans.'

John, who was regarded as the brain-box of the group, declared, 'It wasn't always a park with swings and things. There used to be a big house and the park was its garden.'

'Even the football field?'

'Nah, they didn't have a football field then. It was all private. And they had the gatehouse, and a guard to keep trespassers out of the grounds.'

Ivan scratched his head, ruffling his thick ginger hair. 'And that's where the ghost is.'

John sighed. He wanted to be a scientist when he grew up. 'Ghosts aren't scientific. That means they don't exist.'

The gatehouse still held their attention, though. It was set in the ten-foot-high brick wall that ran around the park, and resembled something like a miniature version of the Arc de Triomphe. Park visitors had to walk through the archway in order to gain entry. The gatehouse, itself, had two windows at one side of the arch – these had been bricked-up, which added to the air of mystery. And there was an ancient timber door set between the pair of windows. It hadn't been opened in years, and from what the boys could tell had been nailed shut. Each of the four boys mulled over what the rooms inside the locked up house would be like. They'd be dark, silent places. Maybe there'd still be tables and chairs in there? A dusty bed, perhaps, that had belonged to the old gatekeeper?

John thought: *There are no ghosts. They don't exist.* But, as he chewed his clover stem, he couldn't help but wonder about them. And he couldn't help but picture the interior of the gatehouse. So dark and airless. Like a tomb.

At last Ivan spoke. 'What's a trespasser?'

It was still early in the afternoon. They were reluctant to go to the park too early. Their money was limited, and the call of the ice-cream van parked by the park lake would be irresistible. The boys dared Ivan to knock on the gatehouse door and run away, which he did – and he was satisfyingly terrified when they made ghostly cries as he knocked. Then, as something of a diversion, they went down to the river to throw stones. Then they headed out to the railway line to watch the high speed electric trains tearing by.

The railway line and the river created an effective barrier at this side of the park. In fact, the only way home was either via a footbridge across the river, or through the gatehouse archway into the park. Of course there were other entrances at the other side of the park, but at this side, only the one, and it was impossible to climb the sheer brick walls, because they were so high, and were topped with jagged shards of glass. Ivan had gone on ahead; all of a sudden, he came puffing back to the others, his face as red as his hair.

'Hey! Look at what they've done to the bridge!'

The gang hurried to the bridge full of expectancy. Something dramatic had happened. Something amazing! But what?

DANGER! KEEP OFF! UNSAFE STRUCTURE!

'It was all right this morning when we crossed it,' Ivan said, poking the sign with a stick, clearly hoping that just a prod would be enough to send the entire bridge plunging into the water.

'Well, it isn't now,' John told him. 'They've closed it off. Look at all that fencing. You can't even climb up the side to get on to the steps.' He surveyed it more critically. 'Look, the bridge is dipping in the middle. If you try to cross it, it'll collapse and you'll fall in the river. And my dad says that river's twenty feet deep.'

After waiting ten minutes to see if the bridge would tumble spectacularly into the deep muddy waters of the river, they grew bored. And thirsty. The sun was hotter than ever. Ivan began to reminisce about the huge ice-creams he'd devoured on holiday in Spain. The temptation of the ice-cream van grew so intense they all agreed to return to the park. As they approached the gatehouse, Ivan pushed back his ginger fringe and declared, 'John, it's your turn to knock on the door.'

'It's not.'

'Is.'

'Nah. Can't be bothered.'

'John's afraid of ghosties!'

'Am not. Scientists say there's no such thing as a—'

'Do it then.' Ivan grinned. 'If there's no such thing as ghosts they can't get you.'

The boys eyed John expectantly. It was a challenge. If he even tried to laugh it off they might think he was a scaredy cat. They might not even bother calling for him tomorrow. He'd be out of the gang.

'Yeah,' John said, finally. 'Why not?'

The others walked in single file into the park and on to the sunlit football pitch. The allure of the ice-cream van had become so great that they started to run toward it. John decided to walk past the locked gate-house door. After all, the rest of the gang were too excited about ice-creams to bother about the dare. They'd never even notice whether John knocked on the door or not. The notion of the place being haunted was just childish anyway.

As John walked through the arch, however, he stopped in that deep pool of shadow. He reached out, and with as much coolness as he could muster, bunched his fist then knocked on the timber door. Beyond the timber door, echoes of his fist thumping the wood disturbed the silent interior of the little building. He waited to see if his friends had noticed his act of bravado; however, their eyes were locked on to the van with the big plastic ice cone on top. John shrugged; he was about to follow them when there was a tremendous squealing noise. He froze. It was the sound of ancient hinges creaking; rusty metal screeched on rusty metal. Then the gatehouse door opened so violently that the vacuum it created sucked the boy through the opening.

Gripping the door frame, to prevent himself from falling into the shadows inside, he regained his balance.

Terrified, John watched the door swing inward. Darkness. A darkness as solid as stone lay within. Then something else moved. John realized an object was rushing toward him, seemingly from an unimaginable distance, even though the room must have been small. It was as if some-thing, or someone, was running from a tunnel that led deep inside the park wall. As it ran, a distant shouting grew louder and louder and louder. Within seconds those violent shouts were so loud they battered John's ears. Their sheer ferocity made the boy freeze. He daren't even try and run away. He could only watch.

From out of the darkness came a huge red face. John did not notice a body; only a face that emerged from the doorway to fill his field of vision. It was an old man. He was nearly bald, and his jaw was shaded with stubble.

John was appalled. He couldn't think coherently. All he knew was that this angry man was shouting at him. He was so angry that his face burned a fierce red. John could not understand what the man was shouting. Yet it went on and on.

At last John found he could move his feet. He tried to bypass the frightening figure and run into the park. But the old man barred the path, and yelled out his fury. A long, long way away, John saw his friends at the ice-cream van. It seemed as if they hadn't yet noticed he was missing.

Again, he tried to dodge by the raging man, and again his way was blocked. And in the deep shadows under the archway all he could make out clearly was that huge, red face, set with blazing eyes that glared into John's own eyes – they glared with such power that the boy's legs turned weak as water.

In panic, John turned and fled from the gatehouse, back in the direction of the river. He was so frightened he couldn't even move properly; he felt as if his arms were unnaturally stiff, fingers pointing down, like he was a soldier standing to attention. All around him, the world had undergone a transformation – everything seemed too bright and too big. Trees were towering things, their leaves were green fire … or so it seemed to the frightened boy.

I want to go home, he told himself. Want Mum and Dad. Even his baby sister wouldn't annoy him now. And he no longer wanted that ice-cream. Nothing but going home. That's all that mattered now. He longed to walk up the path to the house, then close the door behind him. And be safe from the shouting man.

DANGER! KEEP OFF! UNSAFE STRUCTURE!

John stood and stared. He'd reached the high fence that sealed off the bridge. No way home. Unless you counted swimming the murky river, but John could not swim, and he remembered his father's stories of foolish boys who'd gone into that river never to come out again. The only other way home would be to somehow climb down the sheer face of the railway cutting and run across the tracks. Even if he could do that without falling, he knew he wouldn't cross the line, either. For John had faithfully promised his mother he'd never walk on the railway tracks. Express trains thundered along them at a hundred miles an hour.

The gatehouse. It had to be the gatehouse. That was the only way home. He must pass beneath the archway, and walk by the gatehouse, which was part of the structure. It would only take five seconds.

John tried again and again over the course of the afternoon. Every time he got close to the gatehouse, the door shrieked open, and there was the man with the red face. He shouted so furiously at John that the boy wanted to cry. People walked in the park, or kicked balls, or threw Frisbees. But not one noticed the shouting man, or John trying to join them in the park.

Eventually, he tried to climb the park wall, yet the brickwork was completely smooth. But if he could somehow reach the top, how could he cross the broken glass set into the concrete? His hands would be cut to pieces.

Then he waited for more people to enter the park via the gatehouse, so he could slip through with them. Surely, the red-faced man wouldn't shout at grown-ups?

None came. No one could cross the broken bridge. That was the only access to the outside world from this side of the park.

Night fell. John crept back to the river-bank and curled up beneath a tree. He must have slept a long time, for when he woke he saw Ivan and the rest of the gang riding bikes along the river-bank. He was overjoyed. He ran after them, panting out their names, but he was running so fast he didn't have the breath to shout loud enough for them to hear. Even so, he could only have been ten feet behind his friends when they cycled past the gatehouse into the park. He was certain he'd make it this time: he was running fast, so very, very fast.

John was almost through when he heard the clack of bolts, the shriek of hinges, and saw the red face looming out of the darkness. The shouting man stood between him and the park again. No way through.

John cried all the way back to the river. There, he curled up beneath the willow tree. Heartbroken, he cried for his mum, his dad, and his baby sister. Maybe if he waited long enough, the shouting man with his frightening red face would go way?

John waited. It didn't seem that long before he caught sight of a pair of grown-ups walking along the river-bank: a man in the company of a woman about the same age. The man had red hair, and resembled someone that John knew. He looked a lot like Ivan, and John wondered if Ivan had a big brother. But when he thought about it he knew that he hadn't. John sneaked through the bushes to take a closer look. The man and the woman kissed each other and laughed. It was strange. The man really did look like Ivan; he had the same colour eyes, the red hair, the same kind of freckles. He even had a white scar above his left eyebrow, exactly where Ivan had his.

Why does this man look like a grown-up version of Ivan? John didn't understand. Yet it troubled him as he tagged behind the couple who strolled happily along the path.

And he did not understand why this adult version of Ivan could walk hand-in-hand with the woman, and pass so freely through the gatehouse archway, and into the sunlit park. Because, as soon as John was within three paces of the gatehouse, bolts would clack like gunshots, the hinges would scream, the door would shriek open. And the shouting man, with the frightening red face, would block the entrance.

John backed away. He stared at the gatehouse; now he felt as much puzzled as scared. If it was so sunny in the park, why had it become so cold and gloomy out here on the path to the river? Why hadn't the footbridge been repaired? Why was Ivan grown-up? Why didn't Mum and Dad come looking for him? John's eyes pricked and a tear slid down one cheek. And why did the shouting man stop him from entering the park full of happy, smiling people? The little boy didn't know the answers. All John did know for sure was this: the shouting man, with a face the colour of spilt blood, would keep him outside the park.

Forever.

11

A DOG'S TALE

'I AM THE dog excavated from the ruins of Pompeii,' he declared without any prompting. 'You will have seen my photograph, or at least a photograph of the cast that was made from the mould of volcanic ash left after my flesh and bones had decomposed. There I am, wearing a heavy, studded collar. My legs are stretched high into the air, my back is arched, my neck contorted. You have seen it?'

'Yes, I have seen it,' she said carefully. 'And you say you are the self-same dog?'

'I am. Or, rather, was.'

'A curious claim?'

'But true. The caption makes much of the poor Roman dog's suffering as it died chained to a wall when the volcano erupted.'

'And so it must have suffered terribly. All that hot ash and fire, and the panicking of the town's people as the lava rolled toward them. The way the poor animal lies so contorted with its limbs stretching out.'

'Not so. Many owners of dogs will tell you that their pets sleep quite naturally like that.'

'With their backs arched and legs in the air?'

'Yes.'

'But it looks so ...'

'Uncomfortable?'

'I suppose so.'

'No, they are perfectly comfortable. After all, what must a dog make of a human being lying on a raised platform for a bed, covered with a sack of bird's feathers?'

'I see your point, but what we are discussing here,' she said, 'is the claim that you are actually a dog that died some two thousand years ago … when Vesuvius erupted.'

'I don't see your problem.'

'The problem,' she persisted, 'is that you are expecting me to believe that you are a reincarnation of that dog.'

'Well, it's a question of faith, isn't it?' he said. 'If you believe in reincarnation, then you would have no difficulty in accepting I might be that dog – which, I should add, had already expired quite peacefully in his sleep after a long and happy life as a faithful companion to a baker and his wife. They used to make the most delicious honey and almond cakes in—'

'Yes, yes,' she said a trifle impatiently. 'But in this day and age you have to admit your story isn't really plausible.'

'That animals might be reincarnated as human beings? Or human beings as animals? Or animals as animals?'

'Exactly.'

'Is this because of your scientific training?'

'Partly. As I have already told you, I am a qualified psychiatrist.'

'And those qualifications enable you to dismiss reincarnation out of hand?'

She sniffed. 'I am not qualified to deliberate on theological matters, but I do suggest your belief that you are a reincarnation of the dog found at Pompeii borders on the delusional.'

'But you have no personal belief in reincarnation?'

'No.'

'That the soul might vacate a dead body to return to a living one?'

'Definitely not.'

He took a deep breath. 'Will you please explain to me, then, why I, a cat, am talking to you, a dog, here at the bottom of Miss Fanshaw's garden?'

'Completely delusional,' she said. 'I am not a dog. And you are not a cat.'

'Who's delusional now?'
'I'm not.'
'You are,' he insisted.
'Liar,' she snarled, and chased the big ginger tom up into the tree.

12

OUR LORD OF QUARTERS

Constantinople. AD 1401.

THE MONK GREETED the Emperor's entourage at the steps of the palace, just as the siege-engines recommenced their bombardment of the city. His eyes flashed with fear; his right hand clenched around the Cross of the Orthodox Church. Approaching the Emperor's chamberlain, he bowed, trembling.

'S-Sire,' the monk stammered, 'I beg to convey the Emperor to the Church of Holy Wisdom.' Terror gripped him. 'It's the demon, sire … the demon has been prepared.'

The chamberlain motioned the monk to lead on. Ahead, the vast dome of the church cut a smooth, dark mound from a star-filled night. The terrified monk moved quickly, head bowed, as he muttered prayers of self-protection.

Following in the tail of the procession, the slave. This youth from rural Mistra tingled with excitement. Often he'd been beaten for staring. Yet tonight he could not escape being beguiled by this exotic sight. The imperial bodyguard flanked his Imperial Majesty, Manuel II. A tall, grey-bearded figure, clad in the gorgeous purple of kings, he glided with serene grace across the square to St Sophia. This, the greatest cathedral in the world, lay embedded in the pulsating heart of the fabulous city of Constantinople.

Metropolitan life enchanted the slave. From the life of a tanner's boy in a Greek backwater to this splendour! His mother fluttered with pride that her son had been dispatched to the capital. Before he'd left she urged him to do well. If he impressed his masters he might become a freedman. Once he attained wealth he could restore the social-standing of his once noble lineage. 'But a greater purpose may fall upon you,' his mother had told him. 'If your Emperor's life is in danger then you must sacrifice your own to preserve his. He protects Mistra from barbarians. Save him, and you save your brothers and sisters, too.'

At that moment, his senses overflowed. Beautiful palaces, the elegant homes, the great square that spawned alleyways lined with taverns, warehouses, shops, brothels, workshops. Tonight the streets were deserted of people, yet aromas still thronged the place: mouth-watering scents from the bakeries, spiced lamb roasting in ovens, sandalwood incense from shrines, the rich perfumes of the courtiers. It swamped the slave's mind.

To prevent the city's charisma from making him giddy he focused on the Emperor's fool. *Infuriating little beggar!* The clown made the slave angry. Not because of his vulgar jokes but because he was disrespectful to royalty and commoner alike. He cavorted in a comical cut-down version of the Emperor's own robes. As he pranced he brandished a stick. Attached to the end, an inflated pig's bladder and a fistful of keys that tinkled like bells. 'What a beautiful night!' trilled the clown. 'What a gorgeous night for love.' He cupped a hand to his ear. 'Hark! A delicious night for a siege.' In the distance, the *thump* of rocks being hurled into the city by Ottoman catapults. 'Ah! And what a ravishing night to meet the demon!' With his jester's bladder-wand he struck the monk on the buttocks. The weight of keys hurt the man, which only compounded his misery. Nervous laughter sprang from the lips of the courtiers. The clown sang out, 'Our friend with the tonsure fears the demon. What? Aren't Christ's prayers powerful enough for you! Don't you believe our saints can protect you from the devil locked up in that poor little hut?' He pointed at the sacred edifice with its soaring buttresses and mighty dome.

The slave gritted his teeth. *The clown is making mischief again by implying that the monk isn't pious. He wants the man to be whipped.*

'You don't fear the demon, do you, ladies?' The fool singled out a duchess in extravagant gold silks. 'Oooh, I can just see you ogling the demon. Yes – ogling! You'll caress the naked devil with your glances. Heart pounding in your breast, you will gasp, "Oh! Handsome demon, sir. Will you make me your bride? Hop on board this stately galleon of female flesh. Sail me in umpity-bumpity waters to your heart's delight!"'

The courtiers sniggered. This only angered the slave. *Why don't they cut out the imbecile's tongue? He's not amusing; he's a sadist.*

A rock hurled from a siege-engine crashed into a house nearby. Dust, pale as a ghost, rose above the rooftops.

'What a lovely night for bombardment!' The clown shrieked with laughter. 'What a beautiful night for death!'

One of the catapults dumped its missile into the square. With a slap hard enough to make the pavement tremble, a headless corpse found the earth again. Unperturbed, the Emperor regarded the cadaver: evidently, from the uniform, a captured Byzantine soldier. The courtiers were less stoic. They fluttered their hands, whimpered, backed away from the bleeding ruin.

'Fear ye not!' piped the clown. 'Dead men don't bite. Especially those without a head.' He rapped the cadaver with his bladder-stick.

The moment he did so, the chest of the decapitated corpse heaved. It seemed as if it had returned to life, and eager to draw air into its shattered torso.

'Witchcraft,' cried one of the ladies.

Even the clown sheltered behind the dignified stature of the Emperor. Guards drew their swords, ready to battle the enchanted corpse. As horrified courtiers watched the writhing of the bloody husk, pellets of fur sped from its neck.

'Rats!' squealed the clown. 'The naughty, naughty Ottoman have stitched rats inside the fellow. Then they …' He mimed carrying a body to the catapult, lying it in the scoop, kissing it fondly, then pulling a lever to fling it into the heart of the city.

The slave knew that Ottoman forces, who now besieged Constantinople, intended the rats to spread disease through its population, so weakening their resolve to hold out. Those scurrying rats unmanned the monk. Screaming in terror, he fled toward the church.

Several courtiers followed in blind panic. That sacred colossus would, they prayed, offer divine protection.

'Ah ha!' The clown applauded their flight. 'They're eager to see the demon.' Then he fixed the slave with a cruel eye. 'Or have they forgotten that he's in there? The diabolus. The evil one. The captive Satan.' He winked. 'As you, too, had forgotten. Isn't that so, my little Greek goat?'

It wasn't the slave's place to answer. Instead, he obediently followed the entourage that remained with his Imperial Majesty. The beautifully clad advisers, the secretaries, the bald eunuchs, and the bodyguard who bristled with weaponry.

'Here goes, little goat!' The clown linked arms with the slave. 'Let us lead our Emperor, so he might gaze upon the demon!' Then he called out to the entourage. 'Follow me! Remember! Don't spit in Church. No cursing. No nostril picking. And absolutely no farting!'

Silence. The cavernous interior of the church lay engulfed in quietude. With total silence came utter stillness. Even smoke from the incense burners appeared to hang motionless within the immense void of the dome: pale ghosts, neither rising nor falling. The myriad of pillars that supported the structure were still as cedars in an enchanted forest.

The courtiers froze at first sight of the demon. Every single man and woman locked their gaze on that figure. Nobody, it seemed, dare draw breath in its presence. The slave's heart pounded. He strived to absorb every detail of the creature that sat on a wooden chest in the centre of the floor.

A man strode from the gloom. His proud military bearing and arrogant thrust of his jaw proclaimed his exalted rank.

In a deep voice he boomed, 'Don't be afraid of the beast. He's uglier than sin itself, but I, myself, have bound him with straps made from elephant hide. Even Hercules couldn't break those. Besides, here in this fortress of God he will be powerless.' He bowed smartly. 'Emperor, I am your devoted servant, General Simotas, commander of your Eastern Legions. It was I who captured the demon. I humbly offer the creature

to his majesty.' There was nothing humble about this cock-sure soldier.
'May it bring you amusement.'

'The Emperor is most pleased.' The chamberlain eyed the demon
with unease. 'Perhaps you would describe its capture for the court's
edification.'

'I would be delighted, sire.' The general clearly relished the art of self-
glory. 'I led my men to scout for Ottoman forces. Whereupon in Edessa,
close to the source of the Euphrates, I encountered the town elders.
They begged me to save them from a demon that had been discovered
beneath a pagan shrine. My men were so frightened by the unnatural
darkness within the tomb that I ordered them to stand back.
Thereupon, I entered alone.'

Eyes shining, his voice growing louder, the general declaimed his
heroic deeds. Meanwhile, priests lit oil lamps that encircled the *thing*
sitting on the box. The lamps' glow clearly revealed the demon in its
most awful detail. The seated figure captured the young slave's attention. Endlessly, his eyes roved over a body that mingled beauty with
repellent monstrosity.

The demon appeared to have the dimensions of a mortal man. It sat
on the chest of reddish wood as a mortal rests upon a bench. His eyes
were closed. He did not move. Yet how could he move? Surely he must
be dead. Such a ruinous body could not possibly be alive. In the lamplight, the slave feasted on the minutiae of its blasphemous anatomy.
Perhaps three-quarters of the demon's body consisted of dried flesh that
adhered like dry mud to a stick. Part of the ribcage lay exposed. Beneath
it, could be glimpsed a fist-sized brown lump that was the heart. Along
one forearm, which rested on its lap, the bone had been entirely denuded
of muscle. Yet that limb terminated in a perfectly formed hand. Fingers
curled in slightly. Nails, a healthy pink. Short yellow hair framed a
blighted face. That countenance resembled those found on the ancient
mummies of Egypt. Fissures ran down its cheek. One shoulder was white
bone, the other was clad in the firm flesh of an athlete. Likewise, the legs
were mainly decaying sticks of shin and thigh. Yet the right leg beneath
the knee was clothed in flesh. The foot appeared entirely mortal.

What struck the slave most forcefully were the curious additions to the body. Those elephant hide restraints around the wrists were readily explicable. It was the more esoteric accessories that made the slave tremble. For, running from the heart, which showed behind the ribs, flowed a slender chain. An extraordinary chain, no thicker than a rat's tail. Its delicate links were of a blood-red metal; they shimmered with an inner radiance. The chain connected the heart to an iron loop in the timber chest. A tether of sorts? Even more striking, the sight of what had been embedded in its flesh – the good flesh, that is.

There, in the lamplight, gleamed dozens of metal disks. The slave recognized them as coins. Gold, silver, bronze. Some perfect disks, some misshapen in the manner of archaic currency. Many bore the heads of known kings; others, from distant outlands, had been impressed with mysterious hieroglyphs. By what process he didn't know, but the coins had been neatly embedded. And in rows, so that one slightly overlapped the other until it appeared the metal disks resembled the scales of a fish.

The general rested his foot on the box as he grandly pointed out features of the demon. 'Behold armour fashioned from coins. See the chain embedded in the heart?'

Emboldened, the clown approached. 'General, he who captured the demon – yet who missed seeing the Ottoman army march over our borders. Sir, don't your guts go all watery in the demon's presence? Has fear purged your colon? Brave, noble, sir. Aren't you bedevilled by nightmares?'

The general had no intention of answering, but the Emperor nodded. 'Tell him.'

'As you desire, Your Highness.' The general had no idea that the Emperor doted on the clown. 'As you might have noticed, the demon's eyes are closed. It is quite blind. Nor since its capture has the creature moved even a finger. The demon is intimidated by my presence.' He pointed at its mouth. 'It dare not even speak.'

'*Until now…*' The demon's head darted. Jaws snapped. '*…there was nobody worth talking to.*'

It spat an object at the Emperor's feet. The slave saw it was a bloody finger. The general stumbled backwards, blood pumping out over his fist.

The demon's eyelids slid back to reveal plump, white eyeballs. In each, the iris was formed from a gold coin. When he rose from the box the elephant-hide restraints around his wrists pulled tight, but they didn't trouble him. He merely looked Emperor Manuel in the eye. 'You are the ruler of this empire?'

Unflinching, the Emperor met the demon's gaze. 'I am. What's more, I have no terror of you.'

'I'm delighted to hear it.' The grotesque face tightened in a smile. 'Seeing as your grunt did such a poor job of introducing me … I am The Lord of Quarters.' The smile became pure menace. 'It is time we opened negotiations.'

'Why should I negotiate with you? I have everything. You have nothing.'

'You tell him!' The clown brandished his jester's stick. The keys jingled loudly, until their echoes in the dome above became a peal of bells. 'Ha! The Lord of Quarters? He's nothing more than a pigeon carcass. All bone and bad pennies.'

'Shush, little fool.' The demon bared his teeth – coins set edgewise into crimson gums. 'Or I'll tell the Emperor what secret doors those keys on your rod open.'

This statement worried the clown. Mouth clamped shut, he sheltered behind his master's purple robes.

Still mantled in quiet dignity the Emperor spoke. 'I have seen many a novelty brought to the city. A twin-headed lion, a counting ape, a Persian girl who could float in the air. Nothing interested me. So what do you bring that will?'

'What you *need*, of course. What you *wish* for with all your heart.'

'I am Emperor. I have everything.'

'You preside over an empire in decay. It is a withered little thing in comparison with the Byzantium of two centuries ago. The city is crumbling. Its palaces are propped up with timbers to stop them toppling into the gutter. Sir, this is what you need.' The Lord of Quarters ran his fingers over bright, gleaming coins that sheathed his flesh. 'Money. And money is power. I speak the truth, don't I?' He flashed the gold coins in his eyes. 'The treasury is empty. Your knights ride warhorses that are so old they're not fit to pull garbage carts. Army wages go unpaid. Meagre platoons fight with broken swords. Your warriors don't even have the thread to darn their socks. Am I not right?'

Instead of replying, the Emperor turned his head slightly as the thud of a rock from an Ottoman catapult echoed inside the church.

The Lord of Quarters took pleasure in that symphony of destruction. 'Constantinople is under siege. Its city walls are rotten. Children could kick holes in its gates. They won't keep out the invader for long.'

'I am promised money.'

'But when will it arrive? Those foreign kings, who once offered you finance, keep it locked away. Instead, they'll make deals with the Sultan when he is ruler of this noble slum.' The Lord of Quarters' softly spoken words painted images inside the minds of everyone present. He described the imperial treasury. That apart from dust, ankle deep in every vault, all it contained were empty boxes. He restated the Emperor's poverty. That he lacked the money to even police a fish market, never mind vanquish the sultan's army. Or confound the enemy ships that blockaded the port. Soon Byzantium, poor, impoverished, ill-nourished Byzantium would die. Constantinople, its capital, would be over-run. The once revered imperial dynasty would end. Then the demon spoke of riches that lie in the treasure houses of neighbouring realms. How vaults overflowed with coins. Foreign kings complained that the coins cluttering up their palaces were a nuisance. Accountants overseas were at their wits-end to find storage for their mountain of cash. Blast those infernal coins! Fling them into the river. Use them to repairs holes in the roads. Coins, coins, coins! Bury them. Shovel them into wells. Anything to be rid of them. The whole world outside Constantinople was awash with money. In this city, however, it would be easier for the Emperor to pull stars out of the sky than gather even a handful of change.

With his picture of the Emperor's destitution so adroitly accomplished, the Lord of Quarters hissed. 'Listen, I can invest in your empire. You will have enough good, hard cash to restore this decaying city to the glorious capital it once was. You will recapture past splendour.'

The crunch of another catapult missile lent emphasis to his statement.

The Emperor's shoulders sagged. He knew all would be lost if he didn't act on the demon's offer. 'If I agree, what do you require in return?'

'I am the Lord of Quarters.' Gloating oozed through the voice. 'Therefore, I want a quarter of everything.' He licked those cracked lips. 'A quarter of your empire. A quarter of your people. The appetites of my Cenobites masters are insatiable.'

'What will happen to that quarter of the population you demand?'

'Ah, a detail that shouldn't concern you. Your Empire will be restored to the glittering jewel it once was. For you, that's the matter of supreme importance.'

'Will the Cenobites harm my people?'

'You, sir, are hardly the one to be squeamish. Your life is a litany of execution, mass-blinding of prisoners. You've even castrated your own nephew.'

'Where is the money?'

'Lift the lid.' The Lord of Quarters stood aside from the wooden chest as far as the leather restraints would allow. The coins in his flesh chinked as he did so. As did the blood-red chain that trickled delicate links from his heart.

The Emperor raised the lid, hanging on to the hem of his cloak, the clown.

'Old chicken carcass is tricking you,' sang the clown. 'There's no gold, only paper to wipe your behind!'

The demon shot the clown a fierce glare. 'That is my contract.'

'The print is awful small.' The clown pantomimed reading the indenture's rash of miniscule lettering. 'Clause, sub-clause, penalty-clause, warranties, codicils, exclusion notices, terms of payment, terms of forfeit. A contract is a riddle dressed as a puzzle …' Crossing his eyes, he scratched his head. 'Or is it a puzzle clad as a riddle?'

The Emperor sighed, 'I need time to study it.'

'Of course.' The demon smiled. 'Your jester speaks the truth. You must read the contract and unravel the complexity of its language. Then, when you have the document all figured out, sign it.'

The Emperor frowned. 'How will you deliver the money?'

'There's no gold involved.'

'What?'

'Sign. And the invaders will go.'

'How will they be compelled?'

'My Cenobite masters have their ways,' chuckled the demon. 'Read the contract, then sign!'

The clown opened his mouth to add a vulgar comment.

'Sign in the fool's blood.' The demon toyed with the heart-chain. 'Oh … by the by, you will have a special coin struck to commemorate the breaking of the siege. When you do, add this chain to the coin's alloy. Let us agree that it will symbolically seal our deal.'

Understandably aghast at being used as an inkpot the clown scrambled under the Emperor's cloak to hide. The Lord of Quarters enjoyed his fear. 'Skewer the infuriating little piglet. Dip your pen in his vein. Sign the contract. Then pull the chain from my heart.'

The slave had been watching events closely. It had been disturbingly easy to picture the demon becoming lord of a quarter of the Byzantine Empire. True, the slave knew nothing of the Cenobites, but it wasn't difficult to imagine the demon's masters. Surely the Cenobite would be as malevolent as this creature with its scale-like adornment of coins. Then, in his mind's eye, he saw the heart-chain being dropped into a pot of molten bronze that would become newly minted coins. The bronze solidus would quickly be in circulation. Virtually everyone would carry such a coin. In exchange for goods and services, it would transit through bakery, tavern, brothel, church and tax office alike. And in that coin would be a trace of the demon's heart-chain. It would spread through the empire, just as plague spreads through a population. The slave recalled the corpses filled with live rats that were catapulted into the city. Isn't there a similarity? The rats are tiny, yet the disease they spread wreaks huge damage. Might not the Lord of Quarters be infecting the monetary system in much the same way as the Ottomans attempted to infect the populace?

Guards bellowed curses as they endeavoured to drag the clown from the Emperor's purple robes. The clown begged his master to save him. Meanwhile, the Emperor wiped away a tear. He was sorry to do this, so very sorry, but sacrifices must be made in order to restore Constantinople to its former glory.

When the Emperor had second thoughts regarding his beloved clown the demon spoke confidentially. 'You know those keys? The ones on the fool's staff? Well. They open the doors to your concubines' rooms. Need I say more?' The Lord of Quarters chuckled. The heart-chain quivered to the quick rhythm of his amusement.

Clearly, it would be calamitous if the demon's chain came to be smelted with the alloy for the coin. Just what kind of disaster, the slave didn't know, but it would be grave. Instinct told him that, for sure. Just as instinct told him this procurer for the Cenobites had been waiting entombed for centuries. There, he'd bided his time for such an opportunity as this. Yet what could the youth do? The Emperor wouldn't listen to advice offered by a slave.

The guards had the clown by the ankles. They tugged. However, for the sheer love of life he hung on to the imperial robe. The courtiers clamoured, either overcome by the turn of events, or shouting advice to the guards.

Now!

The slave darted forward. He gripped the heart-chain in both hands.

'Not you!' the demon howled. 'It's not supposed to be you!'

The chamberlain shouted, 'Stop him!'

The slave heaved at the chain. He saw the heart pulled forward through the ribs. It peaked into a cone, such as when a thorn is drawn from skin. Another heave – the heart-chain plopped out with a squirt of dark ichors.

The guards would have easily caught the slave. However, the clown's frantic struggles resulted in a maelstrom of people trying to part jester from Emperor. Men stumbled over each other, feet caught in cloaks, soldiers tripped.

So the slave ran free. In his hands, the heart-chain. The bodyguard pursued him. There was one, however, who moved faster. The demon had snapped the leather restraints.

'*Give it back!*' The hurricane force of his shout extinguished the oil lamps. Yet in the gloom of the church his daemonic form glowed bright as a hell-given flame.

The slave fled. Never before had he run so fast. His path took him across the deserted square outside St Sophia. Above him, stars shone hard on the woes of humanity. He leapt over the headless corpse that had spawned rats. Then he ducked into an alleyway. Here, sheets billowed: death-shrouds in the darkness. They were ready if once mighty Constantinople should fall. Though who would bury its dead, let alone grieve?

Boulders from siege-engines rendered houses to dust. But worse, far worse than the thunder of rocks tumbling from the sky … *the demon wants me*. The devil ran through those death-shrouds. One flapped around his face, white cotton pulling tight, then the Lord of Quarter's visage burned its impression into the fabric, leaving a permanent shadow.

The slave raced on through the labyrinth toward the city's fortress walls. Their alternating lines of cream and red masonry resembled layers of fat and bloody meat piled high on a butcher's slab. Atop the wall, the city's defenders at last deployed their creaking, worn-out, dilapidated engines of war. With a *whip-crack* the catapults hurled missiles at the sultan's warships, where they were tightly packed in the narrow straits of the Hellespont.

'My chain! Give it back!' The demon ran so fast he blundered against buildings. Then the coins embedded in his skin would spew torrents of sparks. At that instant the slave could have believed he was pursued by a fiery comet.

Panting, the young man scrambled up the steps to the battlements. Starlight revealed the enemy fleet; soon they'd land troops where defences were at their weakest. The heart-chain clinked in his fingers. At times it was cold; other times it was hot as entrails plucked from a pig's belly. Just its touch conjured images of the Lord of Quarters coercing many a king or pharaoh of a doomed realm into signing his pernicious contract. Maybe he wished his achievements would eventually earn him promotion to the rank of Cenobite. Or maybe brokering these deals were his sole source of pleasure.

Ahead, on top of the ramparts, Byzantine soldiers loaded throwing pouches with amphorae containing volatile oils. These they ignited before launch. The slave watched the weapon, known as Greek Fire arc through the sky; a blazing rain that fell on to ships; inferno upon inferno blossomed; they introduced to the invaders a searing portion of hell on earth. Screams of agony shimmered over the face of the water.

When the slave reached one such catapult, ready for launch, he stopped dead. There he waited for the Lord of Quarters. The devil roared down at him, a snarling, spitting cauldron of rage. When he clashed his jaws together blue sparks jetted from his lips. The soldiers that manned the catapult fled in terror.

'I'll take back the chain. Then I will destroy you.'

'Go on, do it!' The slave gripped that rat's tail of a chain. 'Lord of Quarters? You won't capture even a thousandth of my soul.'

'Oh, a believer?' The creature grinned. 'How innocent. How naïve.'

'Give up, demon. You've lost.'

'Oh?'

'See the invasion fleet? It's burning. The Ottoman attack has failed. The Emperor won't sign your contract.'

'True. But will that save your bonny hide from my attentions?' The demon advanced. 'Do tell me how?'

'It won't. I accept that this is my final hour.'

'Good boy. Clever boy. Now give me the chain.'

The slave didn't flinch. 'You'll have to take it back.'

'Oh, you want to play, do you?' The gold coins in the monster's eyes flashed. 'Why not? You do realize, though, this empire is moribund. Its currency is worthless. Smell the decay. Even the palace timbers are rotting.'

'Constantinople isn't dead yet.'

'Soon though; very soon. So why martyr yourself for a city that isn't worth dying for?'

'If, by thwarting you, I've given my family a few more decades then I'm content.'

'Ah, noble, altruistic fool. And I thought the clown was the one with the jingling stick. Not the man standing right – *no!*'

The slave thrust the heart-chain through his own lips into his mouth. He didn't stop there with its metal resting on his tongue. Steeling himself, he forced the chain into his throat with his middle-finger. He felt each sharp link scrape down through his gullet. Through his chest. Into his abdomen. There it glided through the snug configuration of pathways that was his gut. One second the links burned hotly, the next they were cold as a corpse inside of him.

The demon tut-tutted. 'As if that will save you.' The creature flew at the slave. But didn't attack. Instead, his body became elongated – as slender as that of an eel. It dived head-first into his mouth.

Gagging at the force of that powerful shape, driving through his gullet in pursuit of the chain, the slave stumbled backwards, a plan crystallizing in his mind. When his body slammed into the catapult, he clambered into the throwing pouch that would normally hurl the Greek Fire. He gasped with pain. The demon's body-coins rasped the delicate linings of his intestine. Cries spurted from his lips as his gut distended. Inside him, a sensation of most horrendous pressure as the Lord of Quarters swam downward, as a pearl-diver plunges down through the ocean in search of treasure.

The slave flung himself half out of the pouch so he could punch the lever of the catapult.

A moment later, the man was no longer of this earth. The huge timber arm of the weapon flung him out across the Hellespont. That throw's brutal fury snapped his spinal-chord. All pain left him as the

Lord of Quarters clawed and chewed and raged through his inner-workings. Soon the heart-chain would be in the devil's hands. Not that it mattered anymore. The slave realized that the demon's power was limited by the rules of this infernal game: rules that he and his Cenobite overlords must obey. And those rules dictated that the demon must persuade the Emperor to sign the contract of his own free will. No doubt the monster could fly back to the church in moments; however, by then the Emperor would have gleaned that the sultan's battle fleet was ablaze. Consequently, nothing would persuade him to sign away a quarter of his empire in the full knowledge that Constantinople had halted the invasion. Thereafter, the demon would be compelled to travel the world in search of another victim.

Calm now. Detached from the sufferings of this world, the young man glided with dream-like serenity through the night sky. Below him, burning ships. Above him, eternal constellations; the radiant adornment of Heaven. He knew this flight would soon end with lethal finality. And he knew the monster inside of him could not die. Moreover, Byzantium would linger for only a few more years. That didn't trouble him. He'd given his own brothers and sisters a chance of survival. With his life, he'd bought them time. Furthermore, his sacrifice had frustrated the demon's plan to contaminate Byzantium's currency with the heart-chain. That's what was important. Unlike his body, his contentment was indestructible; his death, merely the bridge between worlds.

Receding, the lights of Constantinople grew dim. Its churches and towers drowned in shadow. He knew the time had come to gaze on Byzantium no more. The man closed his eyes, and was gone.

13

FRANKENSTEIN, VICTOR

Imagine a world of What If? *Where Frankenstein failed. Where the Monster was destroyed. Now open your eyes to* What Is – *and weep.*

SHE REMEMBERED THE words as they burnt her friend down to the bone. That would take time. She was still screaming. You see, they hate so much they hadn't killed her first.

Floating up into midnight sky, strands of girl hair burned bright yellow before flickering out into dead ash. Ruth had never seen the stars glitter with such ferocity before. A hand squeezed her shoulder. She didn't react. Her mind had locked on to the scream. *This isn't time for other thoughts.*

'Ruth,' came the whisper. 'You know you can't stay here?'

'Don't ask me to go yet.'

'Ruth, you can't do anything for Gen.'

'I'm staying.'

'If we don't go now they'll find us, too.'

She was ready to fight to stay there in the wood. Just so she could listen to the scream and watch the fire blazing against the sky. *That 'staying' is a physical expression of loyalty.* Only it would be suicide to linger in such a densely populated area.

'I can smell it. It's like roast lamb, isn't it?'

'We're going, Ruth.' A pause. 'You know we need you?'

The burning woman's scream soared into a shriek then stopped with an abruptness that made Ruth flinch. Taking a deep breath, she swung the gun strap across one shoulder.

'OK,' she said. 'Collect the others. You keep at our tail. Make sure we're not followed.'

The huge fire in the town's football field lit their way as Ruth moved into the spread of trees, followed by her team. They'd started out as fifteen. Now down to seven. As Gen had warned so often on this journey, *'God doesn't love a Monster.'*

Trees, night sky, stars glinting through branches, the smell of forest in winter; frost sugar-coating grass stalks, a glow way back there over the town, where God's Children burnt Gen's bones. *Then they'll gouge a burial pit for the ashes – one so deep they'll not fear for her DNA contaminating their aquifers. The irrational unbound. Amen.*

Ruth brooded on this as they walked along the path to the river, where they'd find the boats. At least, that was the plan. 'God doesn't love a Monster.' Gen's phrase haunted her. As did the words she'd seen on a movie poster nailed to a fence here in God's Own. *Imagine a world of* What If. *Where Frankenstein failed. Where the Monster was destroyed.*

Behind her, Joseph whispered to no one in particular, 'Don't you hate frost? It makes the leaves too loud.'

Nobody commented. Gen's fate was on their minds, too. Then again Joseph wasn't joking. *Frost turns footsteps into a crunch loud enough to warn wildlife that intruders have entered their forest.* At least these God's creatures didn't attack. They scrambled into burrows, or flitted away into the night. Ruth stepped over a dead squirrel that had been ripped by a predator. *This is what happens to the hunted when they don't move fast enough. Gen. The squirrel. The end result's the same.*

Wait – something's wrong.

A flick of her hand stopped the team dead. They held their breath, so the hiss of respiration wouldn't give them away. Staring hard into the gloom directly ahead, Ruth made out a dark shape lumbering toward them. There was the same crunch of feet on frost-hardened leaves. A flare of breath turned white by the cold. Twigs rattled as a heavy body forced itself through bushes. Ruth watched the man approach along the dirt path. The winter coat bulked him. Mittens turned his hands into ungainly paws.

At her side now, April caught her eye and silently mouthed, 'Back?'

Whispering, Ruth said. 'No. He's alone.'

'These people don't patrol by themselves.'

'See how he's limping? He's hurt himself; he's going home.'

'That means the others will be close.'

Joseph moved forward to add, 'Just hope they don't find the boats.'

'What now?'

'Keep low.' Ruth nodded at the lumbering figure. 'He's heading away from the path.'

The man took ten paces into thickening undergrowth then paused. Looked right. Looked back. Even with his poor night vision he realized he'd lost the path. Muttering to himself, spurting jets of white vapour from his mouth, he made it back to the path, then started walking faster. Ruth saw he was a too-heavy man in his fifties. Carrying his rifle soon became tiring for him, so he'd slung it over his shoulder. Its long barrel swished through overhead branches. When it caught firmly enough to drag his shoulder he cursed it. *Now the outcome's inevitable.*

Moments later, he saw the team crouching beneath the trees.

'Christ!' It came as a gasp, squeezing out yet more vapour.

Ruth saw he started to fumble a mobile phone from his coat pocket then, as she moved forward, he realized calling in his discovery wouldn't save him, so he hoisted the heavy rifle from his shoulder. She knew the cumbersome weapon would slow his movements, while she could move with the grace of a panther. In near silence, she raced forward along the path. Before he could shout an alert to his friends she stretched out an arm to clamp her palm over his mouth. She felt the movement of his lips against her bare skin as he tried to shout. Beneath the soft flesh, the hardness of his teeth, which caved in under the force of her arm thrust, that sent him thudding down on to frozen ground. The man's eyes blazed up into hers. What was that emotion? Terror? Fury? She grimaced as she bore down with the heel of her hand, until his skull gave way with muffled popping sounds. When she was sure the stranger was dead she hauled his body away into the bushes. That would give them time to get away. She nodded her approval as the others picked up the man's rifle, together with a shoe that had been sloughed off as she'd hauled the body. Quickly, Joseph scattered fallen leaves over the kill spot to disguise marks caused during the swift struggle.

Almost to her surprise she found herself smell the palm of her hand that had pressed against the man's mouth. Traces of saliva still exuded rich aromas of fried bacon, coffee and tobacco. She scooped up leaves to wipe her skin clean.

Then, as the dead man's mobile chirped, she nodded to others. 'His people will know that something's happened to him. Come on. We've got to find the boats.'

What Ruth saw at the river brought her to a dead stop.

'No,' she hissed. She didn't want to believe the evidence of her own eyes. But there it was. Lit by starlight, a boat sat on the river. 'Keep down,' she told them. 'There's a problem.'

'Forget the boat,' Joseph whispered. 'We'll stay on foot.'

'No, we need it. There's no access by land.'

April inched forward, her sharp eyes scanning the mile-wide river. On the far bank, lights from a village burned a dull yellow. 'What's wrong?'

Ruth nodded at the jetty that ran out on spindly supports to the boat. 'There's a sap under the jetty. Their patrol must have found the boat.'

'And put two and two together,' Joseph added with disgust.

April slipped the rifle from her shoulder. 'I only see one. Kill him, then take the boat.'

'There'll be more near by,' Joseph warned. 'It'll be a trap.'

Ruth shrugged off her backpack. 'We need the boat. I'm going down.'

'You really think that—'

'I don't know what to think. That's why I'm going to find out. Stay here.'

Despite her snappish response, this team was the sharpest she'd ever worked with. They now obeyed without question, taking just seconds to conceal themselves in the undergrowth, where they could watch what happened next. *If I'm fortunate, we'll have the boat. If not, they'll coolly move on while I burn.*

Moving with a silent grace, she quickly passed through the bushes fringing the forest to a dirt track. No point using a weapon. It would alert the sap's companions. Whatever she did, she'd have to do with her bare hands. Only when she reached the point where the guard had been hunkering under the jetty boards, she saw that he'd gone. Senses cranking high, she scanned the banks of the river, the surrounding trees that gathered deep shadow beneath their winter branches. Then the boat itself; it stirred on a sluggish current, lines creaking faintly. She could smell the presence of man. This one had smoked tobacco recently. *But why can't I see him?*

His reappearance caught her by surprise.

'You're late. I was five minutes from leaving without you.'

Automatically, she slipped into a strike stance. Ready to attack the moment he showed.

The man's voice came again. 'Take it easy, girl.' A relaxed drawl, coloured with something she read as amusement. 'That's why I kept out of sight, because I figured you'd be so edgy you'd shoot first before asking my name.'

'What is your name? And where are you?'

'Let's say I'm called … Marshall.'

'Marshall. Where are you?'

'Promise you'll keep those monstrous tendencies locked down?'

'Come out where I can see you.'

'Move aside, unless you want me to step on your head.'

Ruth glanced up to see the man gazing down into her face. He crouched in a branch directly above her. Her surprise contained a stab of self-anger too. *Why didn't I know he was there? He's a sap. Just a damn sap!*

As she moved back quickly, he must have seen the anger in her eyes.

'Relax. Doctor Walton hired me to ship you downriver.'

'Walton?'

'You know Walton?'

'Know of him. Yes.'

'Then you won't do anything funny, like say … rip my head off?'

'What kind of person do you think I am?'

'You tell me. It's the first time I've met a real life Monster before.'

The team moved on to the boat. Ruth saw that the man who called himself Marshall was smart enough not to run the risk of switching on any lights. In the gloom, the team must have appeared as towering silhouettes as they stepped from the jetty on to the boat. He stood with one foot on the deck and one on the jetty ready to untie the line before casting off. Ruth guessed he was aged around thirty, with short dark hair that formed a spiked fringe. Despite his serious demeanour, somehow she found herself thinking that his mouth had a propensity for smiles. His eyes were an intense blue, with a directness that sometimes caused her to glance downward from them, almost in submission. Ruth didn't know why she felt submissive in his presence. She hated the impulse that was alien to her role of team leader.

Even though he was a sap, she extended the courtesy of introducing the team as they filed past. He nodded as she spoke each name.

'This is Joseph. Asia, April, Iman, Grace, Adam. I'm Ruth.'

Do I offer him my hand? The question she asked herself took her by surprise. *The first time I've met a sap socially. So?* He stood there; one foot still on the deck, one on the jetty. He watched as if he did expect a gesture from her. *Here goes.* She held out her hand. He looked at it, his face solemn. Water lapped against the side of the boat. Stars burned bright behind his head. A whisper of a breeze hissed through the trees. Tension gathered in the night air. *He's going to turn away in disgust.*

A twitch darted beneath his cheek. Slowly, it became a smile. 'Good evening, Ruth.' He reached out. Took her hand. Shook it. 'Was that a first for you, too?'

She nodded.

Skin to skin. Sap to transfigured.

'Same here.' He untied the line before stepping on to the deck.

'Uh, pardon me.' For the first time in years she was flustered. 'Everyone, this is Mr Marshall.'

'No mister, thank you. Marshall. Purely Marshall.'

The team nodded at him as they slipped off their backpacks and rifles.

He stepped into the boat's wheelhouse, started the motor. Ruth glanced over the boat. It appeared to be a pleasure craft that had been converted to carrying cargo along this length of greasy-looking river. The marine diesel had enjoyed sunnier days from the sound of its hoarse coughing. Clouds of exhaust showed as a pale fog in the starlight. The entire vessel was not much more than fifty feet in length. It lay deeper in the water than it ought.

The sap – *Marshall*, she self-corrected – must have noticed their expressions. 'Don't worry. It'll get you there.' He lit a cigar. 'And just for you I'll pump the bilges. Although I usually keep them full to piss off the rats.' She saw his eyes snap back to the shoreline. 'Flashlights. You best get below out of sight. You monsters stand out, you know?'

Asia flinched. 'Don't call us that,' she said. 'We're not monsters.'

'Just get your can below, otherwise we'll all get fried. OK?'

Ruth nodded to the hatch. 'Asia.'

Quickly, the team filed down into the cabin. Asia shot the man a glaring look. Ruth entered last. The splash of silver from flashlights out in the trees was far enough away so as not to present an immediate threat, although you couldn't be sure who was watching from the scrub-lined river-banks. Scouts could already be calling in a sighting. She climbed down the first step to the cabin, then looked up at Marshall. He pulled on the cigar, so its tip glowed white. She'd smoked in her first life. The habit appeared so strange now. To carry a little fire in your lips? For pleasure? He raised his eyebrows at her when he realized she was studying his face.

'There's food and coffee down there, if you can use it,' he told her. 'Careful of the kettle. The handle gets hot.'

'We're not monsters. You mustn't call us that.'

'No, you aren't monsters, Ruth. You're cargo. A cargo I'm paid to deliver. OK?'

He's challenging me to contradict him. For a moment she met his intensely blue-eyed stare, then she dropped her gaze and went down below.

The rest of the team sat at benches that flanked a table that was ridiculously small for them. They were already deep in conversation.

'He's a sap. That's proof enough we can't trust him.' Asia was troubled.

'And we were promised *boats*,' Iman added. 'One boat has been sent for us.'

'A wreck of a boat at that. Did you see the rust? And the state of this cabin?'

Adam sniffed. The reaction of someone in the presence of decay. 'The man is a pig.'

'Pig or no.' Asia bunched her fist. 'We should kill him and take the boat.'

'You mean get our retaliation in first?' Ruth stepped forward into light cast by a single overhead bulb.

'He will betray us. If he's dead, he can't.'

'Asia, you complained when Marshall called us monsters. Now you want to behave like one and destroy the only sap who has ever helped us.'

Asia snorted. 'Doctor Walton will have paid him well enough for this trip.'

'He's a sap,' Adam insisted. '*Ergo*, he cannot be trusted. They hate us.'

'Listen. Everyone.' Ruth softened her voice in an attempt to calm them. 'We know we can only reach our target by boat.'

'We could take it from him.'

'Yes, we could,' she agreed, 'but do any of us know the way?'

With a toss of her head, Asia flicked back her long ponytail. 'So, we're reliant on a sap?'

Still speaking softly, Ruth agreed. 'Exactly that. For the next twenty-four hours your lives are in his hands.'

This is time for rest. With the sap, Marshall, steering the vessel along this mile wide river the team made themselves comfortable. Already, Iman and Grace dozed on upholstered benches that flanked the table. Their long legs hung over the end, feet touching the floor. Adam curled into a corner of the floor on cushions, his golden hair spilling over the dull fabric. The rest used their bedrolls. Ruth sat with her back to the wall near the kitchen galley. From here she could look up through the glazed hatchway. She couldn't quite see the sap they'd entrusted their lives with, but she saw his hands on the wheel and the way he gently turned it to guide the vessel safely along deep river channels away from the reefs. Outside, it was still night. A thin crescent moon rose over the hills, transforming the leafless trees into a mixture of silver and deep, deep black.

A sap helping the likes of us, even for money, is unheard of. There must be some other reward for risking his own life. The local population'd lynch him if they knew what he'd done. So what's in this for him? She saw the man's fingers handle a small metal casing. Suddenly alert, she reached for the gun. A second later a tiny flame sprang from the metal device. *It's OK; he's only lighting another cigar.* She relaxed again, listening to the dub-dub-dub of the boat's engine pushing them downstream. Her eyes closed. All this planning. The hardship. The secretive journey across country at night. The hiding when a sap came close. The deaths of half her team. Even four years ago they could have simply flown into the target zone by helicopter. Then three years ago Ruth's world had unravelled. She remembered being a child in her first life, when her father and brother would help her build what seemed mighty sandcastles on the beach. The sandcastles appeared as if they'd stand there proudly with their towers and their battlements forever, yet at the first lick of the incoming tide the walls of sand would turn to glistening sludge. With a few gentle pushes of brine, what seemed a hulking edifice would collapse into the ocean. By the time her family were rolling up towels, ready for the walk back to the villa, the tide would have consumed the sandcastle. She'd stand at the water's edge as they called her name to join them. For a moment or two, she'd search the area of flooded beach that had boasted their heroic castle. Then she'd shake her head and turn away. Nothing left of the castle made of sand. Not a sign.

Her own heroic world had been a castle built from sand. Or as good as.

With the muffled beat of the motor running through her body, she drifted into a sleep crowded with figures from her first life, all now long dead, and somehow the face of Marshall grinned at her from a cavern that oozed nightmare shadows. In the dream, she was curious. *This is a man that's strangely compelling.* Only she was frightened of what unseen dangers might lurk in the void beyond him in the cavern. And when Marshall called to her to come closer she shivered to the core of her bones.

Stars, a crescent moon, boat running with the flow of the current. And there are monsters down below. He grimaced and reflected on the old Chinese curse: *May you live in interesting times.* Heat from the cigar tip tingling his lips told him it was all but done. Taking one hand from the boat's wheel, Marshall threw the butt into the river where it dropped into the wash.

His night vision was good enough to make out the glistening expanse of the river, with its mud banks leading to tracts of marshland. Beyond that, valley sides rose sharply. Experience guided him along deeper channels to avoid grounding the boat – his only asset in the world. Here there were no inhabited houses. When the power supply became unpredictable the water pumps that were needed to drain low-lying agricultural land had been allowed to fall into neglect. Consequently, the water table had risen creating miles of swamp. Every so often he could make out ruined houses; they now stood in shallow pools that were softening foundations until the buildings tumbled. He saw, this time round, the church steeple in what remained of a riverside town had given up the fight against the dead pull of gravity. Almost in sympathy, his craft laboured to make headway. *Monsters make boats lie deep in the water.* He needed money. The boat's engine had to be overhauled, maybe even replaced, before it shook itself to pieces.

Lucky, this well-paid job had come along. For some reason God, or whoever whipped this universe along, hadn't seen fit to make him paranoid about the monsters. Not like the rest of humanity which was hell-bent on demonizing them – when they weren't killing them.

Even so, he hadn't been sure what to expect when he'd sat there, waiting for them to come trotting out of the darkness. He'd seen them on TV, of course, but even that couldn't prepare him for the reality. When he first saw them he'd been winded by the totality of their presence. *My God. They are beautiful.* They were tall, slim, with perfect muscle formation. *Think of those Greek warrior sculptures you see in museums. Think legendary heroes.* And their skin. It possessed a glow ... a shine that he'd never seen before. In the dark it appeared almost luminous. As if each skin cell possessed a tiny light of its own. While their eyes were so *alive* with intelligence. After all they'd endured, too. He'd been expecting physical wrecks, not this pageant of beautiful people.

Now he'd got his very own monster cargo. After trafficking firearms, drugs, illegals, even a corpse or two, he wondered about this cargo. *How much are they worth?*

What he saw lying across his bows in the water triggered an instant reaction. He flipped the propeller drive-shaft into reverse, then revved his engine to stop the boat before it hit. Almost the same moment the ancient diesel motor surged, slowing the boat, yet shaking it until the superstructure rattled, the hatch slammed back to reveal Ruth emerging with the rifle grasped in her long, powerful fingers.

'Stay down below.'

'Marshall, what's wrong?'

'Keep out of sight!' he hissed.

He was grateful that she ducked down low enough to lose her distinctive silhouette amongst the frame of the hatch.

'Why have you stopped?'

He eased the throttle down. 'Someone's aiming to stop us.' He nodded forward. 'They've strung a cable across the only channel that's deep enough to take a boat this size.'

'They knew we were coming this way?'

'Looks like it.'

'Can you run through it?'

'You mean ram it?' He clicked his tongue. 'Only if we had twice the tonnage and a steel build. This is fibreglass. That cable would slice the hull from its keel.'

He saw her bright eyes scan the wooded banks. 'I don't see anyone.'

'Me neither, but that means nothing.'

She eased her head higher. 'What are you doing?'

'Pulling over to the bank.'

'What do you want me to do?'

'Say a little prayer to your Maker.' Marshall felt a grim smile reach his lips. 'File a request that we don't ground this tub. Because if we do …' He eased the boat closer. 'Whoever strung that cable can sit up there in the trees, then pick us off one by one.'

When she'd roused the team, Ruth told Marshall, 'You stay on the boat. We'll take care of the cable.'

'Need something to cut it with? Those steel hawsers are tough.'

'We've got something.'

'Best do it fast. The sun's coming up.'

'You be ready with the motor running when we get back.'

She saw him touch his eyebrow with one finger in mock salute. *Make that a* mocking *salute.* With light streaking the horizon like the sky had started to bleed, Ruth slipped over the side of the boat. Adam and Grace followed. The muddy water came up to their hips; it couldn't have been much above freezing. She flinched. *Monsters feel the cold, too.* Grace carried a backpack slung across one shoulder by its strap. All three carried rifles. Behind them, keeping a low profile on deck, but scanning the forest for danger were the rest of the team – Joseph, April, Iman, Asia. This place is depopulated, she told herself. Maybe the cable was the act of people who don't have the manpower to mount a permanent guard on this section of river? Then another reason oozed possibility. *Does Marshall already know about the cable? Is this where he betrays us?*

She glanced to where he stood in the wheelhouse; shadow hung a veil across his face. *So … what are you thinking now?*

*

'Here,' Adam whispered, then pulled back the branches of the bush so Ruth and Grace could see. The cable had been coiled round the tree trunk so it resembled a barley sugar twist running down the timber. Hammered deep into the wood, so as to secure the cable, were hefty U-shaped staples that were thicker than her thumb. The cable ran through bushes, then out over the river to low-lying rocks in the shallows.

'We're not going to be able to untie this.' Ruth breathed deeply, knowing the only solution wasn't an ideal one.

Grace shook her head. 'Are you sure the sap can't take the boat round the far side of the cable? This wire only stretches part way across the river.'

'Marshall told me that the water is too shallow across there. The boat would run aground.'

'He's a sap.' Adam made a grim face. 'He could be lying.'

'We'll soon find out if he is. OK, what do you figure, Grace? Two pounds?'

'Make it four. We need to blow the cable on the first attempt.' She grimaced. 'The noise will be enough to wake the dead for miles around.' She slipped the backpack from her shoulder. Quickly, she drew out plastic explosive in long pliant sausages that were a garish orange in colour. With well-practised fingers, she moulded the sausages into a ring around the cable where it met the tree. This explosive produced intense heat before the blast. It would weaken the resistance of the steel hawser; the concussion should then instantly sever it. And Grace would be right about the sound of the detonation: that was the door chime to all the saps in the neighbourhood to let them know who was passing through.

'I'll use a spray fuse.' Grace slipped an aerosol from the bag. 'It only gives us sixty seconds to get clear, so be ready.' She held the aerosol nozzle five inches from the orange mass encircling the cable. 'OK?'

Ruth nodded. 'We're ready.'

Grace sprayed the chemical reactant on to the explosive.

'Don't worry about your backpack. I've got it.' Adam picked it up, then straightened as Grace finished applying the spray. That's when automatic gunfire raked his chest, face, arms, legs. Each bullet made him flinch as it broke flesh. Then he fell back.

Ruth glanced from Adam lying on the ground to the explosive that had changed colour from orange to red. Vapour rose from its surface.

Grace shouted. 'We've got fifty seconds. Run!'

More bullets hissed through the air around them.

Then Adam groaned.

'Get his arm. We'll drag him.'

'Forty-five seconds!'

Grace grabbed his right arm, Ruth his left. Then they dragged him as if he was a sled, not stopping for fallen tree trunks or bushes, either going over or through. One rotted stump disintegrated with the force of Adam's shoulder striking it. Blood soaked him. *There's a dozen entry wounds.* She looked away from his face with its mutilated mouth.

'Thirty seconds!' Grace's voice rose in pitch. 'Detonation will knock down trees. Watch for falling timber.'

More bullets smacked through branches nearby. Ruth felt a tracer tug her sleeve. Beside her, Grace gave a sudden grunt. She'd been struck, too.

'Grace? You OK?'

She didn't slow down. 'I'm fine. Ten seconds … Watch for debris.'

If anything, they ran faster. Adam skimmed across the wet leaves, his long legs, trailing behind, skittered over fallen branches.

Ruth panted. 'I can see the boat. Take—' Then the explosive set their world on fire.

Marshall heard gunfire. No mistaking the explosion, too. For perhaps half-a-dozen seconds before the detonation he saw a glow brighten in the trees near where the steel cable ran into the bushes.

'Specialist thermite explosive,' said one of Ruth's team by way of explanation. Then the blast hurled tree trunks into the air, moments later shattered branches rained down on the deck.

'You should have warned me about that,' Marshall said, ducking. 'This is the one and only boat we've got. You want it wrecked?'

'They know what they're doing.'

'They know who's doing the shooting, too? Huh?'

The big guy with the blond hair snapped back the rifle bolt. 'Anyone see Ruth?'

April lowered herself into the water. 'Asia, come with me. Everyone else stay low … identify whoever's doing the shooting.'

Marshall pointed. 'Ruth's blown the cable. We can get out of here.'

April kept on wading to the bank; she held the rifle above her head to prevent it being sluiced by the river.

Marshall called in a louder voice. 'Get back on the boat. They can catch up.'

The tall woman shook her head. 'We'll bring them back.'

'Meanwhile, we're sitting ducks. Hey! Don't your big brains tell you that?'

'We'll be five minutes.'

'I'm leaving in three.'

He was ready to start the engine when he saw figures racing through the bushes. *There's something not right about them.* He heard the team around him cock their weapons. Their attention locked on to whoever was speeding toward them.

Ruth running alongside Grace, and still dragging Adam by the arm, saw her team on the boat ready to pull trigger.

'Hold your fire!' She caught sight of April and Asia wading from the water. 'Adam's hit. Help get him on board.' Then she called to the rest of the team. 'Enemy in the forest. No sight ID. Automatic weapons. Keep watch on the slopes.' Still hauling the injured man, she plunged into the river. Asia and April came forward to help. Blood from bullet wounds, Grace's as well as Adam's, swirled red clouds in the water. She saw the way Marshall stared. *That's right, monsters bleed, too.*

Ruth's eyes locked on to his. *Why does he stare at us like that?* His upper lip even curled in disgust. 'Marshall! Be ready to leave the moment we're on the boat.'

His stare turned into a glare. Even so, he thumbed the starter. The tired old motor banged into life, jetting clouds of exhaust across the river.

Grace panted, 'If they haven't seen the boat yet, they'll hear it now.'

They'd reached the vessel when she heard Iman sing out the warning, 'Strangers.'

Joseph added. 'I see three.'

A sap peered cautiously round a tree trunk on the valley slope. Iman's rifle snapped out a round. The sap's head burst into a spray of red. On deck, her team identified more targets. When they fired their single shots, they were perfectly targeted. Another sap tumbled forward from bushes on to the beach. Another fell from Grace's shot, as she fired one-handed, while helping support Adam with the other.

Marshall bellowed. 'Hurry it up!' A couple of sap rounds splashed in the water close to the boat. He revved the motor. 'We've as much armour plate as a milk carton,' he shouted. 'She'll burn like a roman candle if we take enough hits!'

The boat had started to push forward through the water by the time they'd dragged Adam onboard. When they were all on deck, Marshall opened the throttle. Despite its age the boat surged forward, racing fast with the flow of current.

'Stop firing and lie down on the deck,' Marshall ordered. 'I'll run her under the overhang of trees; they won't be able to see us there.'

Panting, soaked with stinking river water and blood, Ruth lay on her side, but with her head raised so she could see Marshall. 'You done this before.'

'Many times.' He swung the wheel. 'Only with a different cargo. Now, watch out for branches. They'll rake the deck.'

He was right. He pushed the boat hard. More than once she heard the starboard flank of the keel scrape river bottom. The forested bank was no more than a dozen paces from the side of the boat. He was hugging the shore-line so close that not only did the trees arch protectively over them, their branches scraped the vessel's superstructure. Twigs clawed their bodies. Ruth felt a hank of hair tugged from her head. *But he knows what he's doing.* The saps had stopped firing. They could hear the boat all right. Only they could no longer see it behind its barrier of vegetation.

Moments later Marshall called out. 'Your friend doesn't look so good.' He nodded to Adam, lying unconscious on the deck, while Asia protected him from the raking branches with her own body. 'Is he dead?'

Asia didn't reply to Marshall. She turned away from him to call to Ruth, 'His heart's stopped. We need to work on him!'

Marshall ignored the snub. 'We should be clear of the trigger-happy posse. I'll take the boat away from the bank.' He nodded at the massive prone figure of Adam. 'Can you guys do anything for him?'

No one spoke as the team crowded round to do whatever was in their power to save Adam.

The cabin exterior rose to hip height above the surrounding deck. If it occurred to them it resembled an operating table, no one said. Adam lay supine on the flat structure as Joseph worked on him. He'd already sealed the bullet wounds. Now he sutured the man's torn lips where the sap's big calibre bullet had smashed his mouth. Adam lay still as marble; eyes closed.

Ruth said, 'Heartbeat.'

'Strong.' Grace replied. 'Fifty beats a minute. Airways clear. Respiration good.'

With the sun climbing into a clear sky, Marshall had moored the boat in a thickly wooded estuary beneath an overhang of trees. Even without leaves the winter branches were dense enough to screen them from search aircraft ... if the saps did possess aircraft in this area, which wasn't likely. Now there was near silence, only broken by the lap of water, or low murmur of the team. Marshall sat on the wheelhouse. He smoked one of those black cigars of his.

Ruth glared at him. 'Must you watch?'

'My boat,' he replied. He continued to regard Joseph's hands as he eased the surgical needle in and out of Adam's skin to draw together torn flaps of skin.

Asia glared, too. 'You shouldn't see this.'

Marshall pulled on the cigar. 'Because I'm a sap? Not good enough, huh?'

'Your people did this to Adam.'

'My people?' Marshall grimaced. 'I don't have any people.'

'You know what I mean.' Asia turned her back on Marshall, then moved so her own body screened Adam from the man's watchful eyes.

'I do know what you mean,' Marshall said. 'When you say "my people" you really mean "my breed … my species." '

'We're all human,' Ruth added quickly.

'Oh, really?' Marshall flicked ash from the cigar. 'Is that why you call us saps?'

'It's just a name.'

'Right. Short for sap heads.'

'No.' Ruth reacted in surprise. 'It's short for *homo sapiens*.'

He threw back his head and laughed. 'Yeah, right again.'

Asia rounded on him. 'You know nothing about us. None of your kind do. All you're obsessed with is killing our people. Exterminating us for being different.'

'As a matter of fact I do know something about you.'

'All you have is propaganda. It's been shovelled into your thick heads like – like cow dung!'

Ruth noticed that Marshall flinched when he saw the rest of the team nod in agreement to Asia's statement. *That hits a nerve.* Marshall flung the cigar into the river before stomping down the deck toward them.

'Yeah, I'm a sap. I'm ignorant. But then so are you. Let me tell you, I sat behind a school desk and I got taught about you. Yes! Mary Shelley was at that party at Byron's Villa Diodati in Switzerland in 1816, with her husband and Polidori. There she met a scientist called Victor Frankenstein. He told her about his experiments to build a man from corpses. An *Ubermensch*. And that Mary Shelley wrote a novel based on what she heard. For years everyone thought it was fiction. Only there really was a Victor Frankenstein. And he worked in secret because he was afraid the government would outlaw his experiments.'

'All you heard was the horror story.'

'But it became a *real* horror story, didn't it?' Marshall's intense blue eyes flashed. 'Frankenstein came out of hiding a hundred years ago to demonstrate that he'd somehow implanted his brain into an immortal body, and then he persuaded the world's leaders that they'd be immortal, too. *Everyone would be immortal. We all would!* But so often in this life it's only the rich and the powerful who get their hands on the goodies. Then they lock those goodies away, so the rest of us don't even get a sniff of them.' Bitterness welled in the man's voice. 'Like the cure for cancer that you guys keep secret. When you got old, the great and the glorious of Frankenstein's kingdom decided you were one of the chosen. So they gave you a brand new body that'll never wear out. You'll never get a rotten tooth, or arthritis, or angina.' He slapped his chest. 'When I'm nothing but bones you'll look just like you do now. Seven feet tall. Straight backs. Perfect hair, perfect teeth. Handsome guys. Beautiful women. Who'd have thought Frankenstein's monsters could look so ... *cute?*'

'You are ignorant,' Iman told him. 'We weren't chosen to be transfigured, so we could selfishly enjoy life at humanity's expense. We accepted the second life in order to serve men and women. All of us have specialist skills that would benefit—'

'All God's children,' Marshall said, interrupting. 'Yes, we heard that story, too.'

'Then you know we, the transfigured, never intended to harm human beings.'

His smile oozed sarcasm. 'Your intentions were always full of warm, loving benevolence?'

'Yes.'

He shook his head. 'Do you people – you *transfigured* – have any idea why human beings hate you?'

Asia glared at him. 'Blind prejudice.'

Marshall stepped forward. Ruth interpreted the move as a need to get closer to argue his point. *Grace identifies it as a threat.* Without noticeable exertion on her part Grace placed her hand against the sap's chest to push him back. By the transfigured's standards it wasn't a hard shove, but it lifted the man from his feet to send him bouncing back across the deck where his head cracked against the wheelhouse wall.

For a moment, Ruth wondered if the fall had killed him. Then she saw him open his eyes. His hand found the cut inflicted in the back of his head. When he saw blood glistening on his fingertips he gritted his teeth, then stood up.

'That's a demonstration why humans hate you.' His voice was even, yet he spoke with a force that made them listen. 'Whatever we do can not match your skill or your power.'

'We do not compel saps …' Ruth self-corrected. 'We do not compel human beings to do anything against their will.'

'You don't have to.' Marshall wiped his bloody fingers against his jacket. 'You've all lived a long time. You've seen how a child of a famously successful parent winds up living in their shadow. How they never find fulfilment. Or maybe you've seen a sibling with no self-confidence, because brother or sister is the wonder child. You did that to us. A hundred years ago, when you lot came marching out of the Black Forest with Victor *bloody* Frankenstein, and he proved to the world that he did a far better job creating life than God Almighty, that's when men and women realized they would always be the inferior species. Stupid … slow … mortal. That's us. See!' He turned his head to show blood gluing his hair. 'We break too easily.' Once more he moved down the deck toward the group. This time no one stopped him when he went to stand over Adam. 'Look how many bullets hit him. You're hard to kill. Not like us.'

Hard to kill. Yes, he's right. Ruth took a step toward him. 'Let me fix that cut. It's still bleeding.'

'Oh no …' Unsteady, he backed away from her. 'Oh no, you fix yourselves.' He turned to walk back to his cabin that was behind the wheelhouse. She heard him grunt, 'I'll take care of myself.'

Asia clenched her fists as she called after him, 'We might be hard to kill, but it's your kind who are murdering us. You've destroyed our cities. We have no future now. All because you saps are hell-bent on—'

Ruth touched her arm. 'Asia, enough.'

'But we shouldn't let him lecture us. We dedicated our second lives to helping people, then they—' Shuddering, she broke off, unable to finish.

Iman shook his head. 'Starving dogs bite the hands that feed them.'

Ruth spoke in a low voice. 'Remember, we still need him.'

Asia's disgust was obvious. 'We need a sap? Once the world needed us.'

The team fell silent. In this wilderness backwater, the boat rocked gently on the current. The winter sun possessed an icy brightness that cast long, hard shadows. The anchor line creaked. In the forest that covered the valley sides, a bird gave a mournful sounding cry. One by one they turned their attention back to Adam as he lay sleeping. He breathed evenly. Even so, his skin held a deathly chill, and the wind blowing down the valley was colder than they'd ever known before.

Later. The pale, dead eye of a winter sun sagged toward the hill. Here, forest flanked the lonely strip of water on which the boat sat. Black water. Black trees. Black crows glided through a darkening sky. In the distance thunder rumbled. *There's a storm coming.* A shiver crept through her bones. Ruth glanced round the empty deck. Everyone had gone below now that Adam had woken. He said he'd dreamed of his first life after he'd been rendered unconscious by the salvo of bullets ripping into his body. In the dream he'd been able to restore to life the dog he'd loved as a boy.

Thunder rolled again in the distance. Muffled detonations from a corner of the sky that grew darker by the moment.

Like everyone of the transfigured Ruth could recite Mary Shelley's *Frankenstein* from memory. *It was on a dreary night of November that I beheld the accomplishment of my toils … by the glimmer of the half-extinguished light, I saw the dull yellow eye of the creature open; it breathed hard, and a convulsive motion agitated its limbs.* That's the true beginning of the story at Chapter Five. What lies before was added at the suggestion of Mary's poet husband. Then again nine tenths of the novel is pure fiction. Only the core of the story is true. One night, in a rain-swept Geneva villa, a scientist gripped by nervous exhaustion from over-work, some say guilt at usurping God, and fuelled on Byron's brandy, confessed everything to the dinner guests. Victor Frankenstein had made dead flesh live. '*The demoniacal corpse to which I had so miserably given life.*' Now, two centuries later, she gazed at her reflection in the water. *There it is – Frankenstein's hideous progeny.*

Unlike the fictionalized character in the novel, Frankenstein succeeded. Fifty years after his famous march out of Germany's Black Forest his 'Reanimator Engine' had created more than a million of the transfigured. As doctors take their oath to 'do no harm' and strive to heal the sick, so the transfigured accepted a second life with a vow to 'never impose their will on humanity' and to labour ceaselessly for the good of those in their first life. Only here's the rub: the very existence of the transfigured drained humankind of its vitality. What was known as the First World in the West declined into a Third World state of existence. Later, world trade collapsed. Later still, the internet crashed – stayed crashed. Once formidable infrastructures fell into disrepair. Cities became squalid ghettoes. Industrialized nations atrophied, returning to agrarian societies. When a man's car couldn't be repaired anymore he bartered his wife's jewellery for a mule.

Humankind dreamed of a world without the transfigured. She'd seen the movie poster that pitched a fictional alternate world. One where Frankenstein had failed, and saps … men and women … were still the crowning glory of evolution.

Her eyes flicked above the horizon as blue-white lightning cut a brilliant gash through the cloud. *When humans realize they can't change the past, they change the future.* So, three years ago, they began killing the transfigured. Although there was no global consensus to tear up the long-standing treaty for peaceful co-existence, it did appear to be some spontaneous – and collective – response to a pan-global malaise that threatened the saps, and what they perceived of as their civilization. A malaise engendered by the transfigured. Disorganized, yet driven by a universal hatred, they killed the transfigured. Mostly by burning them alive. Although the cities of the transfigured were tastefully concealed from common view the saps found them. The Reanimator Engine had been smashed beyond repair. With Victor Frankenstein, himself, long ago invoking voluntary self-dissolution there would never be a replacement engine.

Three years ago, Ruth lived in a comfortable apartment on campus. Now that was gone. There had been more than a million transfigured working diligently for the benefit of humanity. *Now there's less than a thousand. And we are hunted relentlessly.*

Thunder beat its own doom-laden rhythm in the sky. On the hilltop lightning struck a man-shaped tree. *The world is changing.* She must act now in a way she would never have contemplated twenty-four hours ago. And as she walked slowly along the deck a cold rain began to fall.

'Go away.'

The tap on the door was gentle. Marshall found it deeply irritating. The knock came again. When he sat up on his bunk his head wound stung like hot wires pricked it. 'Didn't you hear me the first time?'

'Marshall?'

He grunted as he touched the split in his scalp. 'Uh … Ruth?'

'May I come in?'

'A formidable woman like yourself? If you bust down the door, what can I do to stop you?'

'Marshall. I'll only enter with your permission.'

He took a deep breath, considering. A beat, then, 'You'll have to excuse the informal décor. Generally, I don't entertain visitors.'

'Then may I come in?'

'I just said so, didn't I?'

He watched the cabin door open to admit Ruth. She reminded him of one of those marble statues of Greek goddesses. *Think long limbs in cool marble. Think uncanny beauty. Think abnormal grace.* When she lowered her head, so she could enter his cabin, her coils of glossy black hair tumbled forward over her shoulder. He saw her bright eyes scan the cabin. Perhaps she expected a squalid hovel. However, it was clean, if old. But then what's new these days? Flanking a window that looked out over the river were two Van Gogh prints in frames he'd made himself in homage to the originals. A self-portrait of Vincent before his demons robbed him of part of his ear, and *The Café Terrace at Arles at Night*. Café lights are a dazzling yellow; they bathe the underside of an awning that seems to protect the drinkers at their pavement tables from the evil-eyed stars above.

She was wearing a T-shirt. When she rubbed her bare arm with her hand it looked as if she was cold … then, she couldn't be nervous about something, could she?

Ruth broke the silence. 'Have you seen an original Van Gogh?'

'No.'

'In some he applied the paint so thickly it stands from the canvas like a sculpture. My favourite is his portrait of Eugene Boch; he called it *Poet against a Starry Sky*. A portrait of the artist as dreamer. Which is your favourite?'

'You're here to kill me.' Marshall watched her eyes dart from the paintings to his face.

'No. Why should you think such a thing?'

'You're edgy.'

'I've come to make sure you're OK.'

'Fine. Never better.'

'That cut on your head is a bad one.'

Stilted responses hint at anxiety. Her sheer statuesque build seemed to fill the cabin. The top of her head brushed the ceiling. A formidable presence that made his palms sweat. *Man and monster in close proximity.* He needed a breath of cold, winter air right now. *Outside.* Across the river, lightning flashed against the hillside. It might have thundered, but he didn't notice. This creature by the name of Ruth, with the brain of a corpse behind a beautiful face, was so overwhelming it was hard to think of other things.

'Marshall?'

'Uh?'

'May I see the wound?'

He sighed. 'If it makes you happy.'

'You don't care whether I'm happy or not, do you?'

He shrugged.

She moved forward. The breath from her nostrils feathered his own hair. He shivered. *Monster.*

'Swing your legs to one side. Now lower your face so I can see the back of your head.'

He tilted his head as she asked but still raised his eyes. She was so close now. Her high breasts pressed against the cotton T-shirt, the fabric stretched tight. He saw how they rose and fell as she aspirated. Tentative, as if psyching herself to touch a mysterious substance, she raised her hands toward his face. Paused, unsure whether to take the next step. Then lightly she placed one hand on either side of his temples so she could move his head to see the wound better.

Marshall tried hard not to flinch at this creature's touch. Even so, his stomach muscles suddenly tensed. Another involuntary reaction, his hands bunched into fists. *This reaction isn't one sided. Look what's happening to her.* He watched her nipples harden behind the veil of the T-shirt. He rolled his eyes down from her erect nipples. Now he found himself gazing at long thighs clad in a tight, black material he did not recognize. He closed his eyes. Stayed still as rock as she gently examined the wound, her cool fingertips lightly touching the broken skin. It should have hurt, but the burning retreated with the same kind of relief a cool rainfall brings after a long, hot drought.

'I can seal that,' she told him. 'Then, I'll wash the blood from your hair.'

'There's no need.'

She released his head, then stood back. He opened his eyes to see her watching his face with a deep look of concern.

'Marshall, why are you so wary of us?'

'Maybe because it's the first time I've met any of your kind. Also … maybe it's because you've gained a reputation for being killers.'

'Only because we've been compelled.'

'Or maybe latent desire.'

'Listen, in the past three years nearly a million of us have been murdered by—'

'By saps?' he interrupted. 'But don't you figure we're fighting for the survival of our species, too?'

'But when were we ever a threat to you? It's not as if we can reproduce.'

'You're sterile?'

She flinched as if slapped. 'Not me. Not females.'

'Ah, I see,' he said, understanding. 'But your menfolk are? Mules are hybrids of a jackass and a mare. Generally, a buck mule is sterile, too.'

'Is that supposed to be insulting?'

'You'll take it anyway you want.' He saw she was breathing hard. Her breasts rose and fell, the nipples still hard. Anger flushed her lips red.

'Why this blind prejudice?' she growled. 'Why don't your kind accept that all we've ever done is devote our second lives to benefiting mankind. The moment that transfiguration was complete we swore an oath to that affect. Why can't you see we are – were! – trying to help you?'

'You never helped me. You never helped my parents. They died of cholera when I was ten. Where were you when I worked at the orphans' farm and watched the teamsters sharing out the girls amongst themselves, or beating the humanity out of little kids because they cried for their mothers at night?' He launched himself from the bunk to slam his hand against her jaw, holding it tight in his fist, so he could look her in the eye. 'Where were you then?'

He knew Ruth could have flicked him away like an insect. She didn't – she kept her gaze locked on his.

'Is that why you hate us, Marshall?'

He still gripped her face. His fingers felt the softness of her skin, with firm muscle beneath, overlaying a formidable jawbone. He gave a grim smile. 'Or did I just make the whole thing up?'

'You're playing a game?'

'Or am I pointing at the real reason why saps hate you? When we watch people we love die. Mothers, fathers, sons, daughters. We humans

SIMON CLARK

— we saps! — ask ourselves: Hey, why don't the transfigured – this god-
like progeny of Dr Frankenstein – deign to leave their palaces and cure
my sister, or my father, or my baby?' Almost eyeball to eyeball with her
he shook his head. 'We waited. We prayed. You never came.' He turned
away.

She spoke in a quiet voice. 'In my first life I lived long enough to see
my parents die. My son, Joshua, drowned. I'm not immune from grief.'

'Then you won life's lottery. You became immortal.'

'So I could continue my research.'

'Why are you here now?'

'We're waiting until dark.'

'No. Your expedition! What's its purpose?'

'It's part of a scientific investigation.'

'Ruth, what you really mean is you're not going to tell me.'

'You don't believe me? What can I say to convince you?'

'You haven't come all this way, sacrificed half your team, to find a
butterfly or an orchid. It must be something vital to your people's
survival. Am I right?'

She gazed out of the window. 'You're asking me to invest a greater
trust in you.'

'It works both ways. I'm going to be hanged from the nearest tree if
anyone finds out I've been carrying monsters on my boat.'

Her eyes locked on his as thunder sounded along the valley. 'We're
looking for something we believed no longer existed.'

'Oh, yeah?'

'The prototype.'

'The what?'

'The first of our kind. Victor Frankenstein's first creation.'

'After two hundred years? You think this thing's still going to be
alive?'

'We know it is.'

'But why risk your lives to find it?'

'Because Frankenstein invested attributes in its physiology that we
don't possess.'

210

'Jesus. And I'm taking you to him?'

Her eyes had a searching quality, as if she desperately tried to find some vital clue in his expression. 'Marshall, how do you open up your heart to trust?'

'Trust? Hell, I sleep with my boots on.'

That was the moment she lunged at him. He felt her arms encircle him in a grip hard enough to elicit knuckle-cracking sounds from his spine. For a second her face hung in front of his: nose-to-nose; eye-to-eye. Then she thrust her face forward. Her mouth clamped over his. The kiss knocked the breath from his lungs. He heard her own breathing race with a passion he'd never experienced before. He tried to pull back. *Think decay, think maggots, think dead men's eyes.* His flesh crawled. He pictured her body from her first life. A decaying mass of liquefying muscle, glands and internal organs in its grave. Just above those lips that pressed against his was a brain that should be dead, too. Then, worse than this knowledge of dead things; worse than the crawling sensation down his back; worse than this creature's monstrous strength that made him a man of straw in comparison, was the tingle in his body.

Ruth released him so she could tear off her T-shirt. Then she cupped his face in her hands to kiss him again. Tenderness. Passion. He wanted to scream at her to get out. Yet he glimpsed the shape of her perfect breasts with their hard nipples. His own far from perfect body felt as if it had ignited. He hated the way he responded to her assault on his senses. Part of him despised the treachery of his flesh as lust roared through veins, just as thunder bellowed across the water. He loathed his reckless drive to rip away his own clothes, then hers, then kissing her breast, then rubbing her sex with his fingers. But when he pushed himself into her hot, shining body he felt nothing but ecstasy.

With the encroachment of dusk, they left the sheltering creek for the main flow of the river. Marshall steered his craft. Experience guided them through narrow channels bounded by rocks that would tear the keel from the boat if his concentration lapsed even for a second.

Ruth watched. His silhouette curved like an archer's bow as he leaned to one side so he could see the prow slice through black river water. Lightning smote the hills in splashes of electric blue. Thunder boomed. There was no rain yet, but its presence weighed heavy in the cold air. Adam joined them on deck. His bullet wounds were already skinning over. Even so, the rest of the team stood close by, always protective of their own. Grace, Asia, Iman, April, Joseph. Their eyes were bright with anticipation, yet there was anxiety, too. *For all of us, this is a voyage into the unknown.*

After what had happened this afternoon, when Marshall had made love to her, there'd been awkward silence as they'd gone to the mess-room for something to eat. She'd told Marshall that Adam had recovered and that even a new set of teeth would eventually grow through the gums to replace those smashed by the machine-gun rounds. Marshall had merely grunted in reply.

Sex with a monster. Now he's ashamed. Bruised by his passion, her body tingled. She had to speak to him again, only she didn't know if he'd listen.

Marshall swung the wheel, taking the boat into a tributary of the river. Here, valley sides closed in to form a gorge. Hemming the water at either side, were cliffs 300 feet tall. Amid the rocks that rose like eye-teeth from the river-bed were spiralling whirlpools. The boat's motor thudded like an excited heartbeat. She smelt river water and the moss that ran a green skin over the rock. Seconds later, lightning revealed an ugly fortress of a building embedded in the cliff-face. It was as black as the night sweeping in to drown their world.

'Listen to me!' Marshall sounded as if he announced a victory. 'No one but me can bring a boat into this gorge. This is the only way in!'

Ruth stared up at the building. *This is Drancourt. More tomb than dwelling.* For a second, she thought she saw a face there that was a cold white in colour ... then it was gone.

The prototype?

'I always thought the place was a ruin,' Marshall was saying.

'What made you come here before in the past?' Iman asked.

'If you run cargoes like mine, it helps you stay alive, if you can find a secluded layover or two.'

'You've been inside?'

Laughter cracked in his throat. 'In there? That ghost house? You've got to be joking.' He pointed toward the base of the building. 'There's a mooring point on that rock; you're going to have to climb up the cliff to your buddy's front door.'

Ruth slipped on her backpack, then checked her rifle was secure. 'Team, are you ready?'

They are. They're high on adrenaline. The moment Marshall lashed the boat to the mooring ring, Ruth leapt on to a narrow stone ledge beneath the towering building. Then began to climb.

As Ruth climbed the wet stone, she glanced back at the boat. She saw April, who'd been assigned to guard it, and watch Marshall, too. After all, he was their only ticket out of here. Only no sign of Marshall. She stopped climbing, so she could look down the cliff to the ledge. Then she saw him. Along with the team, Marshall scaled the vertical face, too.

'Marshall? What do you think you're doing?'

He shot her a grim look. 'I'm under contract to deliver you to Drancourt. I'm going to make sure you walk through that door.'

Shaking her head, she continued the climb the rock. Near dark now; it was difficult to see the handholds. She was grateful for the great splashes of lightning that painted the gorge a dazzling blue. Thunder slammed hard. Still there was no rain. It was there though. Building in pregnant clouds that bulged down from the sky.

The climb took almost ten minutes to scale the fifty feet to the lip of granite that led to the building – one that possessed a great forbidding face that frowned down at them. When she reached the dozen steps carved into bedrock, she paused, waiting for the others to catch up. One by one, they hauled themselves up on to the ledge. They were barely out of breath. Marshall, however, shone with perspiration. He had to sit for a few moments to recover.

'We can't wait any longer,' Ruth told him.

'OK … OK …' He held up his hand. 'I'm coming.'

He hadn't really wanted to be helped up, but she seized his hand. Effortlessly, she lifted him to his feet.

Wiping the sweat from his eyes, he said, 'Sweet Jesus. I hope this prototype is worth the climb.'

'He will be,' she replied, as she turned to the steps. 'All the women of the transfigured are to be his brides.'

'*Brides*.' Marshall stared. 'All of them?'

She glanced back down on the man as he stood there, illuminated by lightning flashes. As he stared up at her, she could see the river below him, the boat appearing like a toy in the distance.

'Yes. All of them,' she said. 'The prototype is an alpha male.'

'Alpha male?'

'Alpha male, it's the—'

'Yes, I know. The leader of the pack. The *numero uno*. The male that impregnates all the females. But that's wolves and lions, not—'

'Monsters?'

She watched him climb the steps toward her. The team followed, watchful of the man who called himself Marshall. She saw the light of expectancy in their eyes.

'Is this to do with these guys being…?' Marshall shrugged at them. 'No disrespect, guys. But you've got no oil left in your sumps, have you?'

A twitch around the men's eyes was the only reaction to Marshall's tactless statement.

She took a deep breath. 'What few people realize, whether your kind, or even ours, is that two hundred years ago Frankenstein didn't just bolt together an ugly, shambling monster out of corpses. Frankenstein was deliberately creating an alpha male.'

'Why?'

'Why?' She longed to grab him by the shoulders so she could shout the words in his face. 'Why! Because for thirty thousand years there have been no human alpha males. They were bred out of existence when humankind developed agricultural societies. Alpha males are hunters. They don't plant corn. Civilization could not have evolved in the way that it did with an alpha male still as a tribal leader. Don't you understand? For the last thirty thousand years the development of male homo sapiens has been arrested. Emotionally, they are all juvenile males. They even shave their faces so they look like children. The only alpha males to survive exist in folklore – as gods!'

'So, you women of the transfigured are going to mate with Frankenstein's alpha male.' Marshall laughed and the skies laughed with him as thunder roared.

Asia grabbed his arm. 'Why are you laughing?'

'What if this alpha male of your creator is impotent, too?' He laughed louder. 'You'll only get egg on your face – nothing else!'

With Marshall's laughter ringing in her ears, Ruth turned, thrust open the huge timber door, and entered.

What she saw stopped her. Photographs remained clear in her memory, enabling her to identify the corpse of the man on the stone floor. He'd been shot in the chest. The team came through the doorway to stand in a semi-circle around the body.

'Marshall,' Ruth said, 'do you recognize him?'

'Doctor Walton. Damn.' He shook his head. 'There goes my money.'

Joseph glanced round the courtyard. 'Whoever killed Dr Walton is probably close by.'

Marshall added, 'And I guess we can't blame your prototype. Wherever he is.'

'He's not been dead long.' Ruth crouched beside the corpse. 'There's still body heat.' She began to search through the bloodstained clothes.

'Any money?' Marshall asked, hopeful.

'Don't you think of anything else?' She rose to her feet. In her hand, a leather-bound notebook. She flicked through it. Blood had soaked into the edges of the paper, so what she read was crimson framed. 'His diary. Last entry this morning.'

'What's so interesting about that?' Marshall asked. When she didn't reply he added, 'Can't you read it later?'

'It's important,' she told him, speed reading the pages, one after another.

Adam asked, 'Does Walton mention us?'

'No, but ...' Ruth still read the pages. 'Doctor Walton writes about Marshall here.'

'Me?' he said astonished. 'What the hell is he writing about me for?'

She didn't reply, concentrating on the dead man's rushed handwriting.

'Hey, what's he saying about me?' He reached out for the book. 'Listen, I said—'

The sound of a machine-gun firing a long burst echoed from the walls. Marshall stopped talking and looked round for the source of the shooting. Ruth slipped her rifle from her shoulder.

Marshall stayed her hand. 'They're not firing at us! It's back there.'

He means the boat. Ordering the team to take cover, she and Marshall raced back through the doorway. Fifty feet below them the boat burned as fiercely as a firework, casting out brilliant golden sparks. More gunfire sounded. Ruth watched dozens of incandescent tracer rounds strike the hull. Simultaneously, April ran along the deck. She was sheathed in flame. More tracer darted from the cliff above them into her body. Suddenly she rolled sideward over the rail into the river. The swift current carried her still body away.

'I didn't betray you!' he shouted.

'I know.'

He must have seen something in her expression that puzzled him.

'How do—?'

'Guys with guns,' she warned. Now she saw ropes hanging down from the cliff top to ledges that swarmed with dozens of saps. A man rose with a RPG. He loosed off the missile that smashed into the wall behind them. Ruth ran back into the courtyard with Marshall at her side. 'Take cover,' she yelled to her team. 'Ambush!'

Tracer spat down from the cliff to fill the courtyard with darting sparks of light. She covered Marshall with her body, taking an armour piercing round in her thigh. The pain flashed through her but she didn't let it slow her down. 'Get into the building,' she called.

The doors were locked. They were formidable constructions faced with steel. As they tried to break through into the protection of the building a rocket propelled grenade struck Joseph in the centre of his back. His whole torso vanished into a spray of blood. Ruth ordered her team to return fire. Men tumbled from their narrow ledges. If they could hit enough of their attackers, it might tip the balance. Adam went down with a grunt. This time a large calibre canon shell had struck his head, turning his brain to mush. *We're hard to kill, but even we can't take this.* Then, for some reason, the guns stopped. She noticed that the thunder had abated, too. Uncanny silence. Then came a muted clicking sound followed by rushing sounds in the air. From the clatter all round them, whatever their attackers were firing were missing their targets. Then she felt something sting the back of her shoulder. She looked back, saw the glint of silver tube.

'Tranquillizer darts.' She called out a warning to the others but saw that they'd begun to bristle with silver tubes. One struck her cheek. She felt a cold liquid spread out under the skin, numbing as it expanded. Her final thought before she struck the courtyard: *They want us alive.*

Someone's hitting me. Ruth awoke to a hand striking her face. Not slapping open handed. A full-blooded punch. Followed by another.

'This bitch is awake.'

She opened her eyes to see a heavily built sap in front of her. She was awake, but that didn't stop him punching again for good measure. This time with enough force to open a cut on her eye.

The sap who had punched her called out to another guy across the courtyard. 'They're all conscious now, Sergeant!'

'Keep them like that, Corporal,' he called back. Despite the military titles all the men wore a random mix of army combat fatigues and civilian winter clothes. Lanterns hanging from hooks in the walls revealed the courtyard to be swarming with these paramilitaries. She thought of an anthill poked with a stick.

Slowly, moving her head left then right, Ruth saw that she, along with the surviving members of her team, were manacled to the court-yard wall. The chain links were as thick as her thumbs. These saps weren't taking any chances. She straightened her legs to lock her knees, so her weight was no longer borne by her chained arms. Looking to her right again, she realized that Marshall stood beside her. His nose was bleeding. Spots of blood marked where the points of the darts had punched through flesh.

'Are you OK?' she asked.

'Me? I brought you to these bastards.' He grimaced. 'I'm sorry, Ruth.'

She noticed bundles of branches at her feet. There were cans of gasoline, too. 'They intend to burn us. When the fire starts inhale the smoke as deeply as possible. That way there's chance you will be unconscious before the flames reach you.'

He grunted. 'You think of everything, don't you?'

'I'm the team leader, Marshall. It's expected.'

The thickset man strode forward again. He struck her in the mouth. 'No talking.'

'Hey!' Marshall tried to kick him. 'You stop that!'

'Yeah, like I should take orders from one of our kind that slums with monsters.' The man smirked. 'Don't worry. You'll get the same treatment, too.'

Marshall glared. 'There's a lighter in my pocket. What are you waiting for?'

'You want to know?' He kicked a bundle of wood toward Marshall's feet. 'Well, you're not going to have to wait long. Here's your audience now. All *one* of him!' He began to laugh.

From a doorway at the side of the courtyard emerged maybe thirty men. Each held a chain that ran to a figure in the centre. Ruth saw that the shambling figure, with blue-white skin, wore a steel collar round its neck. The chains were bolted to that.

The man spat. 'This's what you came to see, isn't it? At least that's what your Dr Walton said when we squeezed his balls and he started to sing.' He nodded his head toward the limping figure. 'All this way for that thing? The prototype? It's a broken-down ruin.'

Ruth held her breath. There he was. Frankenstein's prototype. Hunks of corpse stitched together. Once a colossus, now a husk. A frail, hunched creature that could barely walk under the weight of chains the saps had fastened to his collar.

'Nice touch.' The man who'd punched her grinned. 'He's going to watch you disgusting things burn. Then he's going to burn, too.'

She looked to her right. Marshall must have thought she found the sight too painful to bear because he gave her a faint smile, 'Don't worry. They can't hurt us forever.'

'Marshall,' she hissed, 'have you seen him?'

'The prototype? What there is of him.' He shook his head. 'Ruth, your people made a mistake. He wasn't the answer to your problems.' His eyes went back to the pathetic figure now standing in the middle of the courtyard, bowed down under the weight of so many steel links. The chains, held by the guards, radiated out like the spokes of a wheel. This was symbolic. The prototype appeared too weak to even walk more than a few paces, never mind pose a threat to his human captors. What's more, a guy with a camera captured the shuffles and frightened flinches of the creature for all of humanity to enjoy.

Marshall's eyes returned to Ruth. 'He's more than half dead himself. He's finished.'

'I didn't ask that,' she said.

Marshall shook his head, puzzled.

'Look again. Look at his face. Who does he remind you of?'

'It's too late, Ruth. Don't torture yourself. It's over.'

'Look at the prototype. See his face?'

'Ruth …'

'Marshall, he's your father.'

'Ruth. Please. Not now.'

'Dr Walton was a human. But he found humankind's destruction of the transfigured repulsive. So he helped us. And just back there I had chance to read a note he'd written in his diary this morning.'

'Ruth, what's the point?'

'He'd stumbled on the prototype a long time ago. He found him living here alone with a young boy. The boy's human mother had died.'

She saw Marshall flinch. 'I'm not a monster.'

'You're no monster,' she agreed. 'You're more than a monster. You're more than human being. You are a fusion of the two.'

'Just let it be. They're going to kill us now.'

'Marshall. Dr Walton took you away to live with humans. You were four years old. That's why he was so desperate to hire you to carry us here.'

'So, what if it's true … not that I believe it. What good's it going to do us?'

'Marshall,' she spoke in even tones, 'call to your father. He will recognize you.'

'My father? Give me a break …'

'He pined for you.'

'I don't want to know, Ruth. Those hypodermics they fired at us, they're doing this. You dreamt it all.'

Coolly, she insisted, 'I haven't dreamt it. It's true. Call to him.'

Men came along the line of captives. They piled branches round their legs as high as their knees. The thickset man opened the can of gasoline.

'Please, Marshall.' Ruth locked eyes with him.

'Let it go.'

'Just one last thing for me. Remember this afternoon. Please, just one last thing.'

Marshall glanced from the man with the gas can, to the pathetic withered creature in chains in the centre of the courtyard. Above them, in the open sky, lightning flickered in the clouds. Thunder was muted now. Dying.

Taking a deep breath, he grimaced. Then as if humouring her, he called out, 'Hello? Hello!'

Their captors laughed as if Marshall had lost his mind.

He called again. 'Hello. Hey, look across here. Yes, you!'

Wearily, as if the prototype's head was too heavy for his thin neck, he struggled to look up.

'Hello, I'm Marshall. Look at me.' He turned to Ruth. 'See? Nothing. The old guy doesn't know me.'

She breathed, 'I think you're wrong.'

'Talk all you want, monster.' The man poured gas over the wood at Ruth's feet. Then he splashed more into her face. 'Talk all you want!' He chuckled.

Desperate now, Marshall cried out, 'Hey, you! Do you know me?'

Ruth saw the way the prototype's drooping eyelids flicked back, exposing bright yellow eyes that fastened on to Marshall. The transformation took Ruth by surprise. The shrunken creature suddenly straightened. His captors holding the chain leashes had been laughing and mocking; now they sang out warnings to one another to keep a tight grip on the links.

'He knows who you are,' Ruth called to Marshall. '*He knows!*'

The guy with the gas looked uneasy now. He threw the can at her feet, then fished in his jacket pocket for matches.

'I don't know what good this is going to do,' Marshall hissed, before calling out to the figure that now stood inside the circle of captors with his head raised. 'Father! It's me! Father!'

Ruth saw the prototype straighten his bowed spine, so he stood tall above the men. His yellow eyes burned beneath their hooded lids. In the flicker of lightning she glimpsed straight black lips that ran like a gash across the face, while his skull appeared as an enormous bulging, hairless dome, where stitched flaps of skin stretched tight across that formidable forehead.

The captors were agitated now. She heard them calling for guns. Thunder suddenly barked with a ferocity that made some cover their ears. Even the muscular guy fumbled the matches as he drew them from his pocket. They fell to the ground. Nervous, he dropped to his knees to scrabble through the branches for them.

In the centre of the courtyard, the prototype tugged almost gently at the chains that held him, as if only just noticing them for the first time. The thirty men who held them took the strain, stopping the creature moving toward Marshall. For a moment, it appeared as if the prototype had given up the fight. Then he raised both hands to the sky, calling out in a strange, throbbing cry of such power that it even overwhelmed the thunder. Then came the transformation. Muscle bulged from his limbs.

He lifted his head. His eyes blazed. Ruth had never seen a life-force shine so bright in a man. This alpha male of Frankenstein's. Snapping the collar from his neck, he swung it so the loose chains became a flail that tore through a dozen men who ran toward him. Another man leapt forward. The prototype swung his arm to cuff the side of his attacker's head. The fist breezed through skull and brain tissue like they weren't there. Even men jumping on the prototype's back weren't a real threat. He reached back to grab them, then flung bodies against the wall where they burst like rotten fruit.

Then the giant waded through screaming men who tried to flee, clawing at their own comrades in their desperation to escape. Those who couldn't move fast enough fell victim to the sweep of the prototype's huge arms that snapped human bones or shattered skulls.

Ruth watched the colossal figure approach. Where he'd once seemed ugly, the sheer energy pulsing through his body now invested him with a beauty she could barely look upon.

The thickset guy at last managed to strike a match. For a moment, he looked as if he'd fling it into the fuel-soaked wood. But the crunch of the heaviest feet he'd ever heard – ones that trod on the backs of fallen, screaming men who died in bloody agony – made him look back. He froze as the giant towered over him; the sap's head seemed to pulse as he tried to scream in terror. But not a sound made it through the muscle spasmed throat. Without even hurrying, the prototype reached out to cover the man's hand that held the burning match with his own; then squeezed. The force of the grip snapped tendons, ruptured skin, so the deluge of human blood extinguished the match. The giant thrust its face forward into the man's face. Then this colossus of bone, muscle and sinew let out such a roar that it made even Ruth sag in a faint against the wall. Pure shock struck their captor's heart like a bullet. His face crumpled in pain as he fell dying at her feet.

Later. The ropes the saps had used to climb down the cliff face to hidden Drancourt became the means of exit for Ruth, the surviving members of her team, Marshall, and the prototype. The prototype climbed first.

They followed. They would always follow him now, this their alpha male. And he wasn't so much leading them to the cliff top, as he was taking them into a new world. Behind them Drancourt burned. Their would-be executioners burned with it. *Now everything changes.*

Much later. Marshall held his daughter by the hand. The pair had followed the crowds to the top of the hill. On the grass crown of the mound stood a wooden tower with windows set in its top for perfect views over the park to the shining heart of the city. He smiled down at her as she tugged at his hand as if pulling a bell rope.

'Daddy?'

'Yes, hon?'

'Who lives in the tower?'

'He calls himself the last man on Earth.'

'But you're a man, Daddy.'

'Yes, of course I am, honey. But he calls himself the last man, even though he really means he's the last of his species. The last homo sapien.'

Thousands had gathered on that still July evening. They watched in silence as smoke rose from the base of the tower. A murmur rose, like the hum of bees in blossom, when they saw the flames climb up the tower's dry timbers. It was only then that the last man began to understand. Marshall saw a wild-eyed face at a tower window. He heard the sounds of screaming.

His daughter tugged his hand again. 'Why is the man crying, Daddy?'

'When you're older, I tell you all about it. Come on, Mummy's meeting us by the swings.'

Every day the last man had screamed to them that they were monsters. *Tonight, just for once, he'll be right.*